Praise for
Water Tower

A world ripped into three kingdoms… A terrifying imbalance of power… A clever young adventurer with a streak of reluctant heroism… James Morris's new novel, *WATER TOWER* is pure white-knuckle adventure at its very best.
— William H. McDonald, documentary film maker and author of *PURPLE HEARTS*, and *A SPIRITUAL WARRIOR'S JOURNEY*

Suit up, strap in, and hold on. *WATER TOWER* is dystopian Sci-Fi action at its heart-pounding, adrenaline-pumping best.
— Mike Hess, game concept designer and author of *SHATTERED EMPIRE*

Samuel Cutter and his artificially intelligent sidekick, Dac, take the reader on an adventure that will leave them hanging onto every word in sheer anticipation.
— Kerry Frey, author of *BURIED LIE*

WATER TOWER is a masterful blend of action, intrigue, and edge-of-your-seat excitement that will keep you flipping the pages long into the night. James Morris combines the world-building ingenuity of Philip K. Dick with a raw-edged creativity that I've never seen in such a young author. Remember this kid's name, because you're going to be asking for his autograph.
— Jeff Edwards, award-winning author of *THE SEVENTH ANGEL*, and *SWORD OF SHIVA*

D1112046

ALSO BY JAMES MORRIS

Three Kingdoms

Sky Bound

WATER *TOWER*

JAMES MORRIS

Edited by Christine E. Miller
Cover illustration by Eric Ninaltowski
Digital painting and design by Jonathan Nowinski

Water Tower

ISBN 978-0-9838844-3-9

Typography by James Morris
10 9 8 7 6 5 4 3 2 1

First Edition: July 2013

A big thank you to my close friends and family, for putting up with my insanity and incessant questions while writing this book. And to everyone that has helped me along the way. You're all absolutely amazing.

Prologue

Ten years. That's how long it has been since anyone has journeyed to the Sky Nation. For these ten long years life on the surface has been deteriorating with death rates increasing, tyranny strengthening, and depression blanketing the broken land. It became so bad that a boy of only fifteen years old was driven to do anything to escape this harsh reality.

About two months ago the boy escaped the surface. Boarding a transport along with his best friend and two others he successfully traveled to the Sky Nation. In spite of being separated temporarily early in their journey, the four managed to reunite later, only to learn that the Sky Nation was in the midst of a revolution. All of them were recruited to help protect the land from being taken over by evil forces.

The same young boy who had rebelled on the surface fought with uncommon valor against those threatening the Sky Nation. He is the reason it still stands. The forces trying to overtake the Sky Nation are dumbfounded and terrified by this boy's defiance and willingness to fight. And now, the battle is only getting bigger.

"How is it that one boy can thwart all our plans?" grumbles a man from his seat upon a throne.

"I'm sorry, Master," a man standing before the throne apologizes weakly, bowing so low he nearly kisses the floor. "The boy was an unforeseen obstacle. I didn't know what to do."

"Of course you didn't," snaps the man on the throne. He sounds more than slightly disgusted. His tone exudes power and demands control. "Regardless of the fact, you should have been able to outsmart a simple schoolboy."

"My deepest apologies, Master," says the man on the floor, bowing even lower. "I won't let it happen again. I will go back and dispose of the boy immediately."

"And what makes you think you can?" asks the other, pushing himself up from his seat. He walks methodically towards the bowing man, clearly in no rush. He alone decides his pace, another demonstration that all others are subordinate to him.

Steven, the bowing man, begins to feel a force which grows stronger as his master draws nearer. An aura of raw power that exudes from him, creeping along the walls and floors seeking to dominate and consume. In the dimness of the throne room, Steven can almost see black tendrils reaching out to him.

"I will repeat myself only once," says the master, now standing above Steven. "What makes you think that you can take down the surface boy, or even stand against him?" His voice mocks and antagonizes.

Steven, without looking up, starts to fabricate an answer in his mind, but the words catch in his throat making him sound as if he's choking out half-formed thoughts.

"Sir," he finally manages to say, "how could you presume that I would be incapable of being a match for a mere schoolboy?" His voice cracks.

"I have no evidence to think otherwise," retorts the other. "You have yet to answer my question, Steven."

"My deepest apologies, Master," repeats Steven. As the blanket of malevolent power creeps ever closer to him, Steven suddenly feels his skin becoming itchy. So much so that scratching it off seems the only relief. "I can handle the boy *because* he is just a boy. Because he is just a babbling little fool. Because..."

"You had legions," the master breaks in, raising his voice, "and yet, he was able to defeat you. The boy is more than just a 'babbling little fool'. If he is, then your incompetence must truly be boundless."

"My apologies, my Master," Steven utters yet again, making a motion to get down on his knees. But as he is dropping, his dominator speaks again.

"Stop your groveling. You have failed me thus far, and no amount of whimpering will change that."

Steven stands up straight. The master walks closer to him, forcefully grabs his jaw in his hand, and jerks Steven's head to look directly into his eyes. "You assured me that the Sky Nation was within your grasp, and that there was only a small, broken resistance."

"They were. There was!" Steven exclaims as best he can with his jaw in the iron grasp of his master. He starts to panic. "The boy must have revitalized them. He broke soldiers out of the rehabilitation center. That must have increased their numbers." For an instant, Steven knows he has said the right thing, and some relief crosses his face. Yet a deep scowl remains on his master's face.

"How can I forget?" his dominator spits out. Pulling Steven's face closer to his own, he hisses, "You lost nearly all our prisoners."

A realization of the magnitude of his failure shows in Steven's expression. But still, he *must* make his master understand.

"It was the boy," he says. "We had him, and he seemed to be submitting, but it turned out to be a trick."

"So a simple boy defies me and outsmarts you." The master's voice has dropped to barely a whisper, sending a shiver down Steven's spine. Steven can't even produce a syllable in response and his eyes are met with a cold glare. Dark claws are reaching out to Steven, who hopes this is just his imagination. Terrified, he feels like he is about to scratch his skin off for real. Beads of cold sweat cover his forehead.

"Master," Steven pleads, holding the claws at bay. "Please, give me another chance. I will not fail you again. I will crush those who stand in your way, and take for you what you desire."

"I have nearly all I desire already," Steven's master says, glowering at his underling. "All I want now is for you to clean up your mess and stop the boy!"

"The boy is nothing but a surface rat..."

"Which makes him all the more dangerous," the master roars as he abruptly pushes his captive away. Stumbling and falling, Steven rubs his jaw while the other continues his tirade.

"How long has the boy been unwittingly opposing me? How long has he been the thorn in my side?" Steven's master seems genuinely curious and distraught about this. It's a topic he has been thinking long and hard about.

"I don't understand," Steven says, standing up, "The boy has only just arrived." His master's face reflects that he is beyond enraged.

"Before the boy came up, we were experiencing challenges on the surface." The master's voice is tight with frustration. "Refusals to work, manufacturing delays, lags in worker efficiency, attacks on factories. One factory in particular was the focus of all the trouble. I wonder if it was the factory where the boy was registered."

There are always minor shows of insubordination at the factories, but none were as bold, rebellious, and great in number as those at this particular one. It got so bad it appeared this factory would be shut down. The ringleader of the mayhem was never identified. Oddly, though, in the past few months the disturbances have all but disappeared.

Steven wants to ask his master more about the factory problems and offer his services, but for the moment he wisely chooses to hold his tongue. The master becomes more perturbed as he talks and his face appears to deepen in color. He pauses and takes time to compose himself, though all he needs is an instant before he has regained control.

"The boy has been a nuisance like no other. His capacity to defy and irritate me is immeasurable."

"So what do you want, Master?"

As the master returns to his throne and folds his hands over his lap, it feels to Steven as though the dark, powerful aura has filled the entire room. It is a nearly palpable atmosphere, seemingly capable of suffocating everything it envelopes. Caught up in this force, Steven senses it is draining his very will... and his ability to resist the relentless itch! Though he struggles to show no signs of his discomfort, he finally can stand it no longer and scratches his arm, instinctively fighting this malevolent energy trying to claim him.

"I want you to eliminate Samuel Cutter," the master says with an evil smile and murder in his eyes.

Chapter One

"No! You monster! Get away from me!" I yell, trying to keep my tormenter at bay.

"Shut up and take this," my tormentor insists, trying to shove something down my throat. I start kicking and squirming. I don't plan on making this easy for him. "Just settle down and drink this," he says calmly, trying to get me to lower my defenses.

"Never," I bark.

"I'm trying to help you. Just drink it," my captor demands.

"How do I know you're not trying to kill me?" I ask. I'm not falling for any stupid tricks. I've seen a movie or two. I've got this down.

My tormentor sighs. He's torturing me and actually has the nerve to sigh. Sorry if my pain is boring you!

"If I was trying to kill you, you would already be dead," my potential murderer informs me, drawing back. "Besides, there are much better ways to kill you than with this." He holds up the glass of liquid. "A simple slash with a sword, or a push off a platform—less those boots of yours—would do wonders." Why does that do nothing to reassure me?

"Now stop complaining and drink this!" He again offers me the drink. I don't know what he's expecting, but my answer hasn't changed. I am not drinking that concoction. I push his hand away, which offers little in the way of real defense, but is symbolic at least.

"I hope you realize that I'm not going to drink that," I tell him again, crossing my arms stubbornly.

"Oh, for the love of..." His voice trails off in frustration. "Can somebody please hold him?" he says to some of the guys behind him. Two of them advance on me and pin me down.

"You sure I can't hurt him?" one of them asks. My tormentor shoots him an angry glare in response.

"Geez, sorry I asked," says the guy who apparently wants to injure me. "I should've just done it."

"Now Sam," says the captor-in-charge, turning his attention back to me. "You are going to drink this, or I will shove the entire thing down your throat."

"Sounds really gentle," I say sarcastically.

"Just do it, Sam," says the guy to my left. "I don't think he's willing to take 'no' for an answer."

"But I feel like I'm about to burst. That stuff could kill me." Which is true.

"You're fine," my tormentor says. "You haven't turned purple, so you'll live. Probably."

"See, the 'probably' is what worries me." I try moving my arms, even though two people already have their hands around my wrists. They're unconcerned about my feeble gestures of resistance.

"Stop being a baby and man up," says the one who wants to hurt me. "If you can lead the charge in an all-out battle, you can take this."

"Just do what you're told, and we'll leave you alone," says the guy to my left. The guy in front presses the glass of electric-blue liquid forward again. I look from the man to my left to the one on my right.

"Can't believe you guys would do this to me," I say. I take the glass of blue liquid and down the entire thing in a few large gulps. Immediately, a feeling of warmth spreads throughout my body. Some of the bodily soreness ebbs away, but in its place comes a splitting headache. I start rubbing my temples as the warmth diminishes, and put my head between my knees.

"This sucks," I say, handing back the empty glass.

"You needed it," my tormentor says, accepting the glass and walking it over to the sink. The two guys let go of me and walk over to the couch, where they plop down.

"That wasn't so hard, now was it?" asks the one that *didn't* want to hurt me. The other flips on the television.

"That stuff is fine at first, but after a while, it's not so pleasant." I look over to the guy who's now rinsing the glass. "Why did I have to take all of that, Jinn?"

Jinn finishes cleaning the goblet and sets it down. He turns to look me in the eye. Jinn is a man whom some would describe as handsome although I don't think of him that way at all. He's been my friend since I came up here to the Sky Nation over a month-and-a-half ago. At the moment, Jinn's face looks a bit stubbly, maybe because we were up all night fighting for our lives. Shaving isn't exactly the number one priority right after a big fight.

"You had to drink the entire thing because that's how much you needed," he says simply. For a select group of people – of which I am apparently one – Blue Elixir accelerates healing. Lucky me.

"I wasn't that hurt," I argue.

"You could barely walk," Jinn says sternly. I open my mouth to argue again, but think better of it. After everything that happened last night, I really couldn't walk all that well.

"Shall we review?" asks the guy who wanted to hurt me earlier. His voice sounding excited. That's Arthur, resident blacksmith and big-time ass. "Apart from normal battle wounds, you suffered the effects of being thrown against the floor a couple times, flying through the air uncontrollably, crashing a sky bike into Jinn's roof, and—my personal favorite—going down in a sinking battleship. I had high hopes that last one would kill you." Love you, too, Arthur.

Now the other guy who grabbed me speaks up. "You just can't handle the fact that you have to make Sam whatever he wants from your shop, cost-free. You made a bet with Jinn, and lost." That's Mark. I've known him since I first came up here to the Sky Nation. He's Jinn's best friend and has some of the world's most amazing, yet frightening, pajamas.

"That was my first mistake," Arthur says. "Never think that Jinn isn't planning something." I laugh at Arthur's stupid comment. Jinn made a bet with him that I could impress him. Apparently Jinn put up quite a bit of money. Glad I won.

I hear pounding on the stairs and turn my head towards the stairwell. There stands my best friend in the world, John. Figures he would make all that racket. John, whom I've known for years, is one of the only people up here that I knew on the surface.

"Sam," he calls, running over to me, "your dad's waking up."

"Great," I reply blandly. The entire reason I came up here to the Sky Nation is now awake upstairs. It was a lot of work for a lot of disappointment. I helped the man break out of prison along with maybe ninety percent of the unjustly-persecuted Ravens. The Ravens are a resistance group that banded together to fight the New Power. Last night there was a big clash between the Ravens and the New Power, which somehow I managed to be in the middle of.

"Don't you want to come see him?" John asks. He's been in prison for most of the time we've been up here. While my relationship with him has gone down the toilet, John seems to idolize my father. Blah.

"Do I have to?" I ask. John shoots me a look that I would expect from my mother, not my best friend. I get up with a sigh. John turns around and briskly walks back to the stairs. I grudgingly follow him. We go up the stairs and down the left hallway. Jinn has a huge house with more rooms than he will ever need. Lately though, it seems that more and more of these rooms are filling up.

The house is laid out roughly like a giant triangle. There is an enormous front yard and an even bigger backyard, but the house itself is triangular. It fans out as it extends from front to back. John and I head up the stairs off the entryway, then down the hall to the left. I could count doors we pass in the hallway if I cared enough to want to find my dad's room in the future. But I don't care and don't count. John stops in front of one, knocks, and pushes it open.

"How're you feeling?" he asks. I see my dad lying in bed covered head to toe in bumps and bruises. One bruise in particular, on the side of his face, catches my attention.

"Did I do that?" I ask, gesturing to his face.

"Sure did," he says. I smile. "I'll be honest," he adds, "that one hurts the most."

I smile wider. I know it's wrong to enjoy someone else's pain, but he deserved it. When I was breaking him and a bunch of Ravens out of prison, he wanted to leave most of them behind, more concerned with saving his own neck than helping the others. I had to do something to shut him up. After all, he was trying to tell me what to do.

"You deserved it," I say. Ten years ago, my dad left my mom and me on the surface to look for a better life up here. I was only five years old at the time. I found out he was captured and taken away, and I came up here to get him back. Now that I have him, though, I want a refund. Not exactly what I was expecting.

"If you had listened to me, we may not have had to fight at all!" my dad says. Nice... barely awake and already trying to lecture me.

"But aren't you glad we did?" I say semi-sarcastically. I hurt way more people than I wanted to in the fighting, but at least the New Power was scared off. Hopefully they'll stay that way.

Nathan, King of the Sky Nation, returned home after the fight—*typical*, I think a bit resentfully—and hopefully now he'll keep the peace. The New Power wanted Nathan's throne. Nathan has been missing for years, apparently taking a "short" trip to go see his dad, Gabriel. By chance he bumped into his sister, Sarah, doing exactly the same thing. The difference is that while Nathan has the Sky Nation to look after, Sarah just goes on adventures and sees the world. All three layers of it. The only slight problem with Nathan defending his throne is that he is about to take off again!

Earlier this morning—was it really just this morning?—Nathan got a call from his brother Kane, who rules the Water Nation. Apparently, something not so good is going on down there, so Nathan is going there to help out. At best, Nathan will only be up here for a few days. But at worst, he'll be gone later today.

"No, I'm not glad we fought," my dad says. "Those other guys looked like the team to join. They had the numbers and the good weapons." My dad, always the optimist... Glad I met him, now I'm ready to get rid of him. "If I was still in command," he continues, "none of this would ever have happened. We would be safe." Right.

"You 'commanded' a bunch of scared prisoners that chose your idiocy over the New Power," I argue. When I found my dad, he was in control of this whole underground area of the prison. Oh yeah, did I mention that I was arrested? Twice. It's okay. I only actually wound up in prison one time.

"And they stayed hidden. I did exactly as I had promised and kept them safe."

Suddenly I'm ready to hit him again. But instead of putting my dad on the floor again like I desperately want to do, I turn around and leave the room.

"You just can't handle the fact that I'm right!" he calls after me. I keep walking, deciding to check on some other people up here I know in another room. I knock on a door and push it open.

Charley and his friend are inside. The two of them used to be New Power, but they quit and joined us. Even though one of them was asleep during a giant fight that was literally right outside his window, they both helped tremendously with the whole getting-out-of-prison thing.

"How're you guys doing?" I ask, sticking my head in their room.

"Still alive, aren't I?" answers Charley from his bed. He can't drink any Blue Elixir, so he had to go the traditional gauze-and-cast route. I almost would've preferred that to having to drink as much as I did. And even with that amount, I'm still sore. I'm not sure it did much more than enable me to walk.

"I guess you are," I say. Charley's friend is still out. He was down yesterday, and he's still out today. "I didn't wake you up, did I?" I ask. Being considerate sometimes occurs to me a little late.

"Yes. Yes, you did," he says, digging his head into the pillow.

"Oh, sorry," I say, feeling like an idiot. "I'll let you go back to sleep."

"That'd be nice," Charley says, nuzzling deeper into his pillow. I shut the door and move on. Now that I see someone who looks that tired, I start to feel the exhaustion from last night creeping up on me. The floor looks very comfortable right about now, but I disregard the desire to pass out myself because there are a few more people I want to look in on. I go to another room where I know two of my friends from the surface, Rick and Fred, are staying. I knock softly this time, then open the door.

"Sammy!" exclaims Fred, sitting up in his bed when he sees me. "How's it going, buddy?"

"Yeah, we heard you crying like a baby from up here!" chimes in Rick.

"I wasn't crying," I say, looking at my feet.

Yes, you were! adds an annoying little voice in my head.

I was wondering when you would chime in, I think back. No, I'm not crazy. Not with regards to this voice, anyway.

I was waiting for the best possible comment. Sometimes being quiet and waiting works, the voice

17

lectures me. Figures.

"You can't sneak up on me that easily," I say aloud. My friends shoot me a strange look. They're not used to seeing me talk randomly. Rick and Fred have been in prison the entire time we have been up here in the Sky Nation. They were only recently broken out by Yours Truly.

A hulking mass of metal walks up behind me. I don't need to turn around to know he's there. I can hear him and feel him.

"Did you really think I wouldn't be able to feel you getting closer?" I ask, still without turning. "You can jump all over my brain, yet you think I can't tell when you get close? You're physical now, and I have more experience with that than you."

"My inexperience won't last long," says a voice from behind me that sounds identical to the one in my head just a moment ago. I turn around to look at my metallic friend, who is connected to me telepathically.

"And why do you think you'll suddenly be better than I am, Dac?" I ask. His real name is Digital Alternative Core Processor, but I shortened that to Dac. He wasn't too crazy about his new name in the beginning, but I don't think he really cares anymore. His body is new. He used to be just an AI trapped in the flying boots that I'm wearing, but when I put them on, he bonded with me. Must be because I'm so special. But now he is eternally in my head, which sometimes is a real pain.

You know you love me, he says in my head. Dac
can read all my thoughts and probe all my memories.
Recently, I got Arthur to make Dac this body. He'd been
asking for it since we bonded, and I promised I'd get it
for him. Apparently, bonding with an AI is rare, but the
fact that he hasn't tried to take over my body and mind
is almost unheard of.

*How do you know I haven't tried to be superior to
you?* he asks. In all honesty, I don't know, but I really
don't believe he has tried. That, or he's failing miserably.

"Anyway," I say, bringing my attention back to Rick
and Fred, "how are you two doing? I know that last night
sucked."

"No, it was loads of fun," Fred says scornfully. "I just
love getting my butt handed to me in one of the most
painful ways possible."

"We still won, didn't we?" I point out.

"Because you managed to turn into a giant bad-ass
partway through," Rick remarks. "We didn't do the big
work. That would be you, that Jinn guy, the walking
armory, and Tin Man over there." Dac flashes an
indignant look, for a robot. Somehow he can do that.

"If you cannot call me by D.A.C.P.," he interjects, "at
least call me by the name Sam insists on using—Dac."

"Fine," Rick says. "You, Dac, and the other two were
the ones who won that fight, not us."

"Everyone was important," I say, meaning it. I'm not one to say things just to fluff up a story or my own ego.

"Thanks," Rick says, collapsing onto his bed.

"I'll let you guys sleep," I say.

"'Bye, Sam," Fred says, waving. Everybody is tired, except Dac, of course. None of us slept last night, we just fought and fought and fought. Luckily, it all paid off. I would be so pissed off if we lost! Actually, I would probably be dead. I shut the door to Rick and Fred's room and head to my own, which isn't down the hall, but over on the right side of the house. It's kind of isolated, but no place here is really that separate from any other.

I push open the door and drag myself into my little home-away-from-home, followed, of course, by the hulking mass of metal. It's a normal-sized room with a few dressers for clothes, which I don't have much of anyway. The only things in here I have from the surface are a box with a couple hundred dollars that my mom collected for me, the backpacks John and I brought with us, a few shirts, and maybe one pair of jeans and two more that are all ripped up. Other than that, I have my necklace, which I'm no longer even convinced is from the surface.

Last night, or was it this morning? We were fighting so long, everything seems blended together. This morning, though, Nathan, King of the Sky Nation, came home and brought his father and sister with him. They told me that the necklace can only be worn by one of Sarah's descendants or by Sarah herself. Basically, for me it was something like *Surprise! You're a prince. Good luck getting people to not call you that.* Yup, I am the fourth child's great great great great great (I'm not sure how many "greats," to be honest) grandson.

"I feel so sorry for her," Dac remarks out loud. "She's stuck with you as her legacy." As always, an encouraging word from him.

"Hey, I'm not so bad," I counter. "After all, I did do most of the fighting last night." I turn around and look at Dac's metal body. "It's still weird seeing you this way. I'm used to thinking of you as a pair of boots and a voice in my head."

"Charming, Prince," Dac retorts. If he could wink, he would. "You wouldn't have made it if Arthur and I hadn't shown up and saved you."

"I still did more than you," I say as I plop down on my messy bed. It's crazy. Less than two months ago, I was in my room on the surface. If I were still there, another day in the factory would be over and I'd probably have a few more cuts and bruises, but I would still go back the next morning. Instead, there's now a giant robot in my room, and I'm on a floating platform in the middle of the Sky Nation. I never said my life is normal. I close my eyes and let myself sleep for a little while.

Chapter
Two

I wake up and wonder if maybe the past month has been a dream. It all seems surreal. But the soreness from yesterday instantly reminds me this is no dream. I look around and see that Dac left my room. I guess hanging around and watching me sleep isn't world's most interesting thing. And his body is less than a day old. I bet he's outside figuring out how to use it.

I swing my legs over the side of the bed. It's still the same day I fell asleep, and I passed out in my clothes. No need to change.

I get up and head downstairs. The upstairs hallway is empty. I guess everyone is out and about. I check the kitchen and there's no one there either. Where is everyone? Out back? Nope. I'm afraid to check Mark's room. I'm used to his pajamas now, but I still break out laughing most times I see them. I doubt anyone's in the front yard, but figure I might as well check.

When I open the door, I see...everyone, actually. Jinn,

Mark, Arthur, Charley, Jackson, Rose, Todd, Rick, Fred, John, my dad (for some reason), Dac, Nathan, Gabriel, and Sarah are all here. There are a lot of people in the yard. I might as well add one more.

"What's going on?" I ask anyone willing to answer, scratching my head. I'm still a little out of it from just waking up.

"Good to see the kid's still alive," Nathan says.

"Seriously, Sam," John asks. "Where were you a few minutes ago?" I shoot him a look.

"Sorry, I was just a little tired from everything that happened last night, and then being filled to bursting level with Blue Elixir," I reply.

"How much did you have?" Nathan asks. "There is an amount that will make you very sick." I look at Jinn. He refuses to make eye contact. So he must have known about the too-much mark.

"I drank a couple glasses of it," I say, still looking at Jinn.

"And you're still on two feet?" Nathan asks. I'm sure it's a rhetorical question. He can see that I'm standing. "I don't think anyone has been able to drink more than a glass and not be extremely sick."

"He just slept for a few hours," Mark says. "Probably exhausted after being up all night." There we go. At least he has a little reason. Nathan gazes off into the distance as he scratches his chin, thinking.

"It was probably just a fluke," Nathan says. "Anyway, before you arrived, Sam, I was asking if any of you would like to accompany us to the Water Nation. Our ship is plenty large enough to accommodate all of you."

Everyone's quiet.

"You're joking, right?" Jackson says. "We all just put our lives on the line for you because you were gone and couldn't handle it yourself, and you're already leaving again?" I couldn't have put it better myself.

"And you did such an excellent job that I believe the Ravens can hold the fort, so to speak, while I deal with a crisis," Nathan says defensively, maybe realizing that he is acting like a major idiot.

As I listen, I realize there are now two people in this group I really want to hit but haven't yet. There would be three, but I already hit my dad so I don't think he counts. The new target is Nathan, but punching a king doesn't seem very smart. The old one is Todd, Rose's douche-bag boyfriend. Rose is Jackson's daughter, and Jackson is ready to punch Todd, too. Maybe we can join forces and really wail on him.

I think you're just jealous that he's dating Rose.

"Hey, gramps," Todd calls Gabriel. This isn't going to end well. Gabriel is a man of stories and legends, the man who singlehandedly conquered the planet. And he doesn't look very happy about being called "gramps."

"What is this hunk of junk?" Todd continues,

pointing at Dac and hanging all over Rose.

You're right, Dac says. *Let's get him.* I smile. It's nice to know he's on my side. I've also learned that I am the only one who can insult Dac and not piss him off. *Don't push your luck.*

Don't worry, I will, I think back.

"That 'hunk of junk' is one of my greatest creations," Arthur says. Man, is Todd trying to get as many lethal enemies as possible? I would be happy to help him with that.

You're horrible, Dac says. *As much fun as it would be to watch Arthur dismember that loser piece by piece with each different weapon he has—*

And I'm sadistic? I think at him, cutting him off.

We can't do that here, Dac continues, ignoring me. *It's still wrong.* What a shame.

"Seems like a giant can opener to me," Todd says. Arthur lunges at him. I want that fist to connect, but Mark and Jinn grab him and hold him back. Todd takes a step back and laughs in Arthur's face. Arthur proceeds to drag Mark and Jinn a couple feet, still trying to get to Todd, who won't stop laughing.

"Enough," Gabriel says, unfortunately preventing Arthur from reaching his target. "In light of this demonstration from my friend," he says, glaring at Todd, "the invitation to accompany us to the Water Nation has been revoked." Arthur gives Todd a very childish I-win-you-lose face. Todd looks over at Gabriel.

"Whatever," Todd mumbles. "I didn't want to go anyway. There's too much weird wet stuff there anyway." Is this guy for real?

"That 'wet stuff' would be called water," Sarah says. I'm liking my great-great-whatever grandma more all the time. "Are you sure you want to be dating this twit?" she asks Rose.

If there was any doubt that you two are related before, it's gone now, Dac says. I smile again to myself.

Rose looks really flustered and confused, then glances at Todd as though reevaluating everything she knows.

"Come on, baby, let's go," Todd says, dragging Rose off somewhere. I'm not sure where he's going. He's kind of stuck here on Jinn's platform until Rose and Jackson leave. Gabriel watches them go, respectfully silencing everyone from speaking until they're gone.

"Anyway," Nathan says, "we were planning to head down later today. All of you, with the exception of that Todd kid, are invited to join us below." Everyone starts mumbling to one another about whether they should go or not. Jinn steps forward and gets on one knee.

"I will go anywhere you command, my king," Oh, give me a break. Jinn was in total control of his life and now this Nathan guy shows back up and he's incapable of independent thought.

"Way to grovel, buddy," I say under my breath. Somehow, my comment's heard, because Nathan speaks up.

"He's not usually like this," Nathan says apologetically, looking my way. "It'll wear off in a day or two." I shrug. Nathan seems pretty sure of this. Maybe Jinn is just trying to be respectful and it's gotten to an annoying level. Shrugging it off, I speak up.

"I'll go," I say to Nathan and Gabriel. I've already seen the other two nations. Why not break a few more rules and see them all?

"And I'll be able to get to know you," Sarah says. Whatever, a few questions usually don't hurt, now that I'm not on the surface. A few minutes later, nearly everyone says they'll go. The only ones staying behind are Charley, Jackson, Rose, and Arthur.

"I have to clean things up around here for a little bit," Arthur says. "Idiots like this brat," he gestures to me, "have a habit of destroying the place. Any chance I can come down later?"

Gabriel nods. "Of course you can. Our phones will be altered to work at the appropriate levels required by the depth of the Water Nation. You may call us as soon as you are ready." Respect Gabriel, he respects you back. Good to know. I'll remember not to piss him off... Or at least resist the urge as long as I can.

Jackson and Charley have their own reasons to stay

behind. Jackson needs to take care of Rose, and Charley wants to spend time with his family. He wasn't apart from them before, but according to him, he's not the "action hero" type.

Rose doesn't have an excuse because she isn't here, having been pulled away by Todd. Gabriel is taking that as a sign she will be staying up here with him.

The people that I'm most shocked are coming along are John, Rick, Fred, and my dad. They all got out of prison less than two days ago. I'm fine with John, Rick, and Fred, but my dad just gets me riled up.

"Would you be able to leave me on the surface?" my dad asks.

"Certainly," Gabriel says. "But may I ask why?"

"I haven't seen my wife in over ten years," my dad explains. "I want nothing more than to be able to see her right now." Oh, he's not coming with us. Good. I'm sure mom will love to see him. She can see how prison changed him.

"It is best to be with your loved ones," Gabriel agrees. "We can only drop you off at the waterside. I am sorry if this inconveniences you."

"I can find where I'm going. Unless we moved while I wasn't around, I still have the address memorized. I can take a taxi." My dad looks over at me. "Are there still taxis?"

"Yeah," I say. "Hard to pay for, but easy enough to

find." Hard for *me* to pay for, anyway. All my income was from my hours in the factory, and most of that went to the house and food. My mom did all she could to help, which made it easier, but we didn't have a whole lot of cash to use for leisurely stuff.

"Excellent," Nathan says, clapping his hands together. "It's settled. We shall leave tonight. Now, if you will excuse me, I need to check on this Gerund fellow that Jinn told me about. See if he will be okay holding the fort for a little while longer." With that, Nathan takes his leave.

"We'll see you all later this afternoon. I must go arrange for the transport," Gabriel says, following after his son.

"'Bye, Sam," Sarah says following her dad and brother, waving at me.

As soon as they're out of earshot, John elbows me in the ribs and says, "She likes you, dude."

"That's so wrong," I say. "She doesn't *like* me. She's my grandma, basically." John makes a face that tells me that fact apparently flew right over his head.

"No way," he says. "She can't be your grandma. She's hot!" I put my face in my hands and shake my head.

"I'd be careful what you say," I tell John, looking up again. "You might just end up dead."

"Why would I end up dead from that?" he asks. "It was a compliment." I shake my head again. Sometimes,

John just doesn't get things. For example, the nations leaders don't like being called "gramps". And nobody should mess with the people who rule the entire planet.

I watch as Nathan, Gabriel, and Sarah pile into their transport and take off. The transport moves through the air more seamlessly than any of the others I've seen. It's probably a new design of Nathan's.

Chapter Three

I spend the remainder of the day lounging around. Jinn got a call a while ago from Gerund. Apparently they did well at defending themselves, but suffered a lot more casualties than we did. Zero for us, oodles for them.

I also heard that Gerund is not exactly ecstatic about having to be in command any longer than he needs to. He was already starting to crack from the pressure and thought that everyone was out to get him. I wonder what he'll be like when we get back.

Lost in my thoughts, I'm only brought back to real life when I hear the sound of a transport landing in the front yard. I get up from my comfy spot on the grass in the backyard. There's an imprint of me left where I was lying, but it quickly disappears.

I walk up to the house and push the back door open, turning to glance at the backyard before I go inside. I look at the little dirt arena that Jinn trained me in, and at the sheds with all the Sky Bikes—minus the one I crashed—and Sky Riders parked inside them. It's a change of scenery from my life over the past fifteen years. A good change. The best I could have hoped for. It's dark out now, so a bit colder and windier. I like it that way.

The wind whips my shirt around and makes waves in the grass when Jinn calls for me from inside, breaking my trance. "You ready to go, Sam?"

"Almost," I yell back. I'm essentially all packed to go to the Water Nation, but I just need to shove a few last-minute things in my bag and grab it from my room. I run inside and up the stairs, passing people as they head down, already set to go. I push open the door to my bedroom and walk in.

Splayed across my bed are a duffel bag with whatever pairs of undestroyed jeans I own, a couple shirts, a jacket, a cell phone charger, and a few other things next to it. It starts to feel oddly identical to when I left the surface as I shove everything into the bag. The only difference is that I have a few more friends with me this time, no planning, and I'm with my idiot father instead of my mother.

The thought of my mother saddens me almost to the point of tears. I walk over to the dresser in the room, the same one that was there before I even considered trying to come up here to the Sky Nation. I pull open the top left drawer. Inside is the hand-carved, wooden box my mother gave me before I left home. I take it out of the drawer and examine it more closely than I ever have before.

The design carved into it looks like leaves encircled with twisted, curly lines. I start to put it in my bag, as a memory that I plan to bring with me and keep forever, when I'm interrupted by someone knocking on my door.

"You know you can leave that here, my prince," Jinn says. He walks inside and stands next to me, looking at the box.

"Don't call me that," I ask him. Again. "And I don't want to leave anything here. I thought I was going to take it all."

"This is your room," Jinn replies. "It'll always be yours, and you can come back at any time." I look at him instead of at the box. I'm sure it's a standard offer he gives to everyone who stays here, but it makes me feel good nonetheless.

"Thanks," I say, putting the box back in its drawer. I slide the drawer closed again and bring my hand up to touch my necklace. It's amazing that this one little piece of jewelry has done so much, and made such a big impact on my life. It confirmed that I'm a prince, for crying out loud!

I drop my hand and zip up my duffel bag. The backpacks John and I had from when we first came up here are hidden under my bed, but this time I have a few more things to bring. My duffel is just a bit bigger than my backpack, but that's all the space I need. Everyone thinks it's weird that I'm only taking the bare minimum with me, but if they were from the surface, they'd get it. I notice later that John, Rick, and Fred also have bags only big enough for the essentials.

I sling the bag over my shoulder and across my back. I look at Jinn. "Ready to go," I say. He nods and walks out of the room. I follow behind him.

It's okay to miss your mom, Dac says in my head while I'm following Jinn down the stairs. I don't see him anywhere, but he is linked to my head, so I'm not surprised.

It's not so much missing her, which I do, but more being worried about her, I explain. I've been helping her with money and everything for almost as long as I can remember. John and I both put in even more time than usual – and that was already a tremendous amount – at the factories, to make sure there would be some cash reserves for our families. I don't know how long that'll last or how much it'll help, though.

I'm sure she's fine, Dac reassures me. *You can send a message with your dad.* Whoopee. I'm sure that'll work great.

We walk outside and see Nathan, Sarah, and Gabriel's transport. Everyone is loading into it, and

Jackson is helping out.

"Hey, Jackson," I say as I walk up.

"Hi Sam," he replies. "Is that the only bag you have?"

"Yup."

He looks at me skeptically, but shrugs and offers to help me aboard. I'm guessing that John, Rick, and Fred must all be onboard already, because they have even less than me.

"Sam!" Rose yells, running up to me before I step inside the transport. Jinn, makes idle chitchat with Jackson and steps aboard, leaving Rose and me by ourselves outside. She pauses, rubbing her arm and looking at her feet before saying anything.

"So you're really going to go, huh?" she asks, looking up at me.

"Yeah." I shrug to adjust the strap of my duffel bag. "I'm sorry you can't come."

Do I even need to tell you how awkward you are? Dac says.

No, I think I have a general idea, I tell him.

"It's no problem," Rose says. "The King talked to me and said I could come, but not initially."

"Oh, that's cool," I say. I had no issues with this girl when we were in prison, but now I can't even talk to her. I'm such a loser.

You said it, not me, Dac interjects. I wish I could throw something at him right now.

"By 'king,' do you mean Nathan?" I ask, trying to figure out how to mentally hurt Dac.

"No, not Nathan," Rose answers, unaware that I'm involved in two conversations at once. "Gabriel offered it. I don't like calling him by his name because he's so powerful. It just seems wrong to bring him down to the same level as someone like me."

It takes just a couple moments of intense concentration, but I find a way to mentally kick Dac. It's much less satisfying than it would be to physically kick him, but considering that he's made of metal and isn't here, it'll have to suffice.

"Then what about Nathan?" I ask, no longer distracted by trying to hurt Dac. "You called him by name a moment ago."

"He asked us to. Nathan isn't a fan of titles, apparently. At least his own titles."

"Oh," I say. I've been calling all of them by name the whole time. Sure, when I met them, they said to call them by name, but I'd been doing that before then anyway.

You've never bothered with recognizing authority before. Neither when you were on the surface, nor when you came up here, Dac says. *And stop talking about other people already, it's getting boring. Get to something good.*

Other than being able to read my thoughts and communicate telepathically, Dac is capable of sifting through my memories. It can be annoying at times, but I guess it makes sense that he can. He bonded with me. To be in my head, he needs to know me. Still, it gets creepy.

"Yeah," Rose goes on. "There's some stuff I need to take care of up here before I leave."

Jackson climbs off the transport. "Time to go, Sam," he tells me.

Rose gives me a hug. "See you later," she says before releasing me. That was way too short of a hug.

"'Bye," I say, waving stupidly while stepping onto the transport.

I weave my way through a few super short steel hallways before I come to a large room. The transports I've been in have nothing on this one. The main room has rows of swivel chairs that look extremely comfortable, lined up in pairs. It looks and feels more exquisite than the inside of any other transport I've been on before. There are plenty of seats open, and I choose to sit next to an empty chair. Dac is sitting right in front of me. I can honestly say I never thought I'd be sitting behind a hulking mass of metal that I'm as close to as anyone I care about.

Gabriel flashes me a knowing half-grin as I walk to my seat. I throw my bag onto the vacant chair next to mine. I glance around and catch multiple pairs of eyes staring at me, but they quickly turn away when I notice them. I sigh and kick the back of Dac's chair. I know it won't do me much good, but it's symbolic.

"So what'd you tell them?" I say out loud to Dac.

"What? Me? Tell them something? Whatever could you be referring to?" I can hear the sarcasm dripping off Dac's words. I just look at the back of his head, waiting for him to crack. "Okay, I told them everything," he says.

Everyone snickers at me.

"Yeah, yeah, yeah," I say, "Let's all make fun of Sam. It's the funnest sport in the world." Not really, but I don't have any good lines for right now. I'll get them soon, though. Oh yes, I will.

I look out the window at Jinn's platform. Gabriel quietly gets up and walks to what must be the cockpit while everybody else must be replaying my conversation with Rose. Gabriel returns a minute later and sits down.

Let it go, I tell myself as I look back out the window. I notice that we're starting to move up. But that's not possible. I didn't hear the engine or feel us move or anything. But still, we're moving.

"Did we take off?" I ask no one in particular, tired of trying to work it out in my head.

"Yes," Gabriel replies as the others are just starting to settle down from getting on my case. "This is one of my son's newest designs. The vessel itself runs spectacularly, but the services I added make it nearly flawless."

Services? As if on cue, a lady walks in from the front of the ship, "Welcome aboard, everybody. My name is Linda. I will be your server this evening." Server? "Our trip should take roughly one hour to reach the first drop point for Mr. Cutter. One half hour after that, we will reach our final destination. We are not flying at maximum velocity so that you may enjoy maximum comfort."

Nathan shrugs at her mention of our velocity. "I'm still working on that part," he says innocently. Linda smiles at him.

"If there is anything at all you need during our flight, please inform me. Thank you." With that, she begins to take drink orders from people.

Because I am sitting in the back, I'm one of the last people that Linda gets to. "Can I get you anything to drink, sir?" It's an innocent question, but I'm taken aback by it. I've never been called "sir" before without it being turned into a joke or insult. Where I come from – in the position that I and others were in – being called "sir" is not a good thing at all.

I squirm uncomfortably before answering. "Do you have any soda?" It feels like forever since I've had a soda. It's stupid, but I really want one right now.

"Of course," Linda says with a smile. "Right away, sir." I squirm again when she says "sir". Linda moves on to the next person, evidently unaware of my discomfort.

She finishes up her rounds and ducks behind a wall. A short while later, she comes back with drinks in hand. It's going to take her multiple trips to serve everyone. By the time she comes out for the third time, I'm uneasy watching her do all the work.

"Do you need help?" I offer.

"Oh, that's kind of you, sugar, but I'm okay." Even though she doesn't want any help, I'm glad that I offered.

I watch as Linda takes John and my dad's drinks over to them. When she calls John "sir" like she did me, I see that he also doesn't like it so much. My dad, on the other hand, looks happy to have someone showing they are subordinate to him. Rick and Fred seem indifferent.

When Linda returns, she hands me my bubbling, brown drink.

"Here you go, sir," she says, and I wince slightly.

Apparently she notices this time and asks, "Is something wrong?" She sounds genuinely concerned.

"Could you just not call me 'sir', please?" I ask.

"No problem, sugar," she answers. I notice an unmistakable southern twang to her voice.

It's a stupid question but I ask her, "Thank you, and if I may ask, where are you from?"

But Linda smiles like she enjoys answering. "My family is originally from the Surface," she replies. "We lived in a southern area of the states, but my great grandparents moved us up here before me or my parents were even born. The accent just hasn't left our family."

"Oh, that's really interesting," I say. I consider telling her that I'm from the Surface, but I've been guarding that secret for so long that I don't tell her. Linda nods politely and walks away to serve the rest of the drinks.

It doesn't take long for everyone to get settled and begin chatting with whoever is sitting nearby. After a brief period of small talk, joking around, and Dac and me throwing playful insults back and forth both verbally and mentally, Gabriel stands up again. I watch him as he walks over to me. He scoots past my legs, throws my bag on the floor, and takes the seat next to me with a sigh.

Dac and I stop making jokes and insults, outside of each other's heads anyway, while we wait for Gabriel to say something. He doesn't speak. He just sits there, sipping on his fancy drink and alternating between watching the people in the transport and looking outside.

"Do you want to know something interesting?" he finally asks me.

"Sure," I say. "What is it?"

Gabriel turns and looks at me with a smile. ""Meeting you was almost as spectacular as it was meeting my daughter for the first time." His words surprise me. I try to say something, but find that my voice suddenly isn't working.

"Of course, you were more beaten up, cocky, and assertive than she was," Gabriel continues. "When she first saw me, I was still living my natural life. Everybody knew who I was. Sarah practically hid in a corner and did everything I said. Only after getting to know me for a while did she change and lighten up."

I don't want to interrupt him, but there's something he's said that I've been wondering about.

"What's it like," I ask, "living so long?" Gabriel looks me in the eye, sighs deeply, and takes another sip of his drink before answering.

"It is both my greatest gift and my greatest curse," he says seriously. "I have seen many that I care about wither and die around me. I have endured as I turned into a mere fairytale. And I have witnessed failure and hate many times over." He pauses for a moment. "But also, I have seen the world many times over, done and created many great things, and been with my children for centuries, watching them grow, and watching their kingdoms rise from the ground."

I take in everything he's saying. A lot of it sounds fantastic, but also much of it seems terrible and heartbreaking.

"Meeting you feels like starting all over again," Gabriel says, draining his beverage. "Linda," he calls. She walks right over. "Could I trouble you for a refill?"

Linda takes the wineglass with a smile, "It's no

trouble at all, sir."

"Thank you, my dear," Gabriel breathes, relaxing into his chair. Linda walks off with Gabriel's empty glass.

"I am glad to see that you and my youngest son's original prototype have become one so seamlessly," Gabriel remarks. Original what? Noticing the confusion on my face, he gazes over at Dac.

"Dac is the prototype?" I ask in surprise. I can't believe that he's the prototype. The boots work effortlessly, and Dac himself is so, well, smart. By the vibes coming out of Dac, I can tell that he had no idea he's the original either.

"I believe so," Gabriel says. "Nathan," he calls to his son. Nathan, who is conversing with Jinn, Mark, Davis, and Sarah, excuses himself before walking over.

"Yes, Dad?" he asks. It's so weird to hear him call someone "dad," something so human-sounding from a king who has lived as long as Nathan has.

"Is this not your original prototype for your Digital Alternative Core Processor?" Gabriel asks, pointing to Dac. I'm amazing that he knows Dac's full name. Normally with age, the mind and memory start to fail, but Gabriel seems sharper than ever.

Nathan studies Dac's metal body for about two seconds before responding, "Can't tell from the body. I'd need to see the shoes." Because I'm wearing the boots, it's easy enough for me to take one off and hand it to

Nathan. After he looks it over for a bit, he comes to a conclusion.

"Well, what do you know," Nathan says. "The only surviving pair is the original. Who would've thought?" He hands me my shoe and I put it back on. "You take good care of those," he tells me before returning to his seat. Gabriel leans back in his chair and sips his drink. I hope he doesn't have a massive hangover in the morning.

"You hear that, buddy?" I say to Dac while patting him on the shoulder. "First, best, and stuck with me."

"Lucky me," Dac says sarcastically. We both laugh over the stupidity of this concept.

Gabriel, Dac, and I talk for a while. Gabriel asks about my life, and I ask about his. I can see on his face that even he thinks my life has been less than great until recently. His stories are all spectacular. He has lived an incredible, not-so-natural life.

It what seems like no time at all, Linda announces that we're descending to drop my dad off. I look outside the window to see that none of our exterior lights are on, and that we seem to be in the middle of nowhere.

"Mr. Cutter," Linda says to my dad, "it's time to go." My dad halts his conversation, stands up, and checks his wallet. Good to know he has his priorities in order.

"It was a pleasure meeting all of you," he says as a farewell. He bows to Gabriel, who raises his wine glass, which has now been refilled about five times. Since when has he ever bowed? "Sam," my dad continues, "would you walk me out?" With a sigh, I force myself to walk my idiot father outside.

Once we're out of the transport and the others can't hear us, my dad says, "I'm sorry that I've been such a bad father." I almost think he's being genuine, but then he finishes his sentence. "But if you ever dare to contradict me, or embarrass me in front of your superiors, or disobey me again, I swear it will be the end of you." He punches me in the gut for good measure when he's done with his threat. I double over as the hit takes me by surprise and knocks the wind out of me. My father starts to walk away before I can straighten myself.

He's still close enough, though, and I yell after him, "If I ever see you again, I'll kill you." It's not a threat. It's a promise. My dad doesn't even flinch as he keeps walking. Without sparing a thought, I climb back onto the ship without another glance at my father. I briskly march back to my seat, and plop myself into it. I don't try very hard to hide that I'm fuming.

"Are you okay?" John asks me. I look over at him, venom for my father still coating my eyes. John seems to recoil a little.

"Don't ever talk to me about that man again," I say sharply. Apparently, everyone gets the memo because they're all staring at me in silence. Good. They should all know exactly how I feel about this. I throw my head back into my chair and take deep breaths to calm myself down. I don't hear or feel it, but I know that we've taken off. After about ten minutes, my breathing is even again and I am calmer.

"I know this isn't the best time to ask," Gabriel says to me, "but what do you think of my eldest son?"

Logan? King of the Surface?

"Honestly?" I ask to make sure that Gabriel really wants the truth. Right now, I'm ready to take brutally honest to the next level.

"Honestly," he confirms.

"I hate him with every fiber of my being." For what he is, what he's done, and how he treats everyone.

"I thought as much," Gabriel says, looking at the ceiling and downing the remaining contents in his wine glass.

Chapter Four

We make the rest of the trip without any other big discussions. I never do get an explanation from Gabriel about why he asked my opinion of Logan. After a while, Linda informs us that we're landing. The ship lowers vertically without the aid of exterior lights, as it did before. We must have either an extremely skilled pilot, or one that's really familiar with landing sites like this.

We touch down without a problem. Linda helps usher us out of the transport. She offers to help me with my bag, but it's only one duffel bag and I'd feel awkward, so I respectfully decline. Apparently, anyone from the Sky Nation or are royalty has brought at least a suitcase or two bags. I don't know what they could need beyond a pairs of clothes, but maybe it's just what's expected of them and how they're used to living.

With my bag slung across my back, I follow Dac, who has nothing – he's a robot, for crying out loud! – off of the transport. Before I can go far, though, Gabriel stops me, grabbing my shoulder. He has a strong grip, but I can tell he isn't squeezing as hard as he can. "Thank you for your honesty," he says. He takes his hand off my shoulder and returns to gathering his things.

Not knowing what else to do, I walk forward and exit the transport. I just told this man that I despise his son. Does that make me a horrible person? I probably really hurt the guy.

No, Dac disagrees, *it makes you honest. I've never personally experienced what this Logan guy is capable of, but just from your memories, I can safely say that I am not a fan.* Dac's words comfort me a bit and help me feel a little less guilty and terrible about what I said. I shouldn't be feeling guilty to begin with.

The scene outside isn't anything special. Everyone is standing with their belongings, split up into small groups of people they know. John is standing awkwardly with Rick and Fred. Even though John is friends with Rick and Fred, he has never really been close to them. I know them a lot better than he does. All three of them have brought just a backpack. The only reason my bag is slightly larger is because I grabbed an extra pair of pants and a shirt.

Jinn, Mark, and Davis are also standing together, waiting quietly. Mark and Jinn each have a large bag with them, but Davis has two really big ones. Why would he need two? Nathan and Sarah are standing off to the side, each with a bag at their feet. They look tense, not like they're just waiting for their dad to come out, but more like they're expecting someone or something to jump out at them. Maybe something will. We *are* on the surface right now.

Gabriel steps off the transport a minute later, thanks Linda, and bids her farewell. She steps back into the transport and a moment later, it takes off, rising back into the sky almost soundlessly, with the massive door on its side closing as it goes. Nathan has really been working on the sound thing. The others are nowhere near this quiet.

"Let's go," Gabriel says to all of us as the ship departs. He starts walking toward the coast, passing where the transport was just moments ago. Needless to say, we all follow him. After being inside the bright transport, my eyes aren't quite adjusted to the dark yet. I go off of what's close to me and what's illuminated by the moon's dim light. The moon seems so much smaller and darker down here than it was in the Sky Nation. After a minute or two, I can roughly make out what's around me and see well enough to not trip over my own feet.

Somewhere ahead of me, I see something that reminds me of a beached whale, but it's not quite big enough for it to be that. The dirt and gravel change to sand beneath my feet. The sand instantly finds its way into my shoes. Right now, I'm not loving the beach. I've only been to it once before, and that wasn't under the world's best circumstances.

As we get closer to the whatever-it-is, I can clearly tell that my beached whale guess is way off. It does somewhat resemble a whale, though. It looks large from here, but now I'm thinking most of it's still underwater.

How could John think that it's a whale? That's ridiculous! I look around and see that Dac is glaring at me.

What? I mouth to him, raising my arms like I don't know why he's looking at me.

Really? he asks me in my head. *I can hear your thoughts and you're trying to play the innocent card on me?*

It could've worked, I think back.

Not really, he says, dropping the subject. At least he isn't going to make a scene about it.

When we get closer, I can see that what I've been looking at is a giant, hulking mass of steel, about a story-and-a-half tall. Whatever it is, there are glass panels covering the front of it, giving us a view inside. I look inside, but I can't see a definite floor or bottom to this structure. Long walkways both thick and narrow run along its entire length, and towers of electronic panels are randomly placed throughout.

Next to the front dome-shaped window are two

massive lights, one on either side. I hear the sound of movement in the water other than the waves lapping the shore. I pull my eyes away from the glass, resisting the urge to put a giant handprint on it, and shift my attention to the water. I was going to look for the source of the noise, but the shifting reflection of the moon on the water captures my attention. It is something to see. Nathan, Sarah, and Gabriel are acting as if it's nothing special, but I've never experienced this before. It's incredible. The way nothing seems certain and even the moon can be moved.

"Nathan?" calls a voice from the shadows. I look toward where the voice came from. It's the same direction as the splashing I heard earlier. The splashing stops and is replaced by the sound of someone's feet. A moment later, a man steps out from the shadow of the steel structure. Soaked to right above his knees, he wears a worn-looking, dark blue jacket, patched in a couple places. On his hands are gloves with the fingers cut off. Straggly locks of hair dangle loosely over his face.

"It *is* you!" the man says to Nathan. "And you got some friends with you. Good. The more the merrier, I say." Uh?

"Of course," Nathan says with a laugh. I wonder if Nathan thinks this guy is a bit off, like I do. "Is there any chance you could pick up the others in a dinghy? I'm sure they're not going to want to get very wet."

"'Course, 'course. You going to come help me get one?" the potentially crazy guy asks Nathan.

"Yes, I'll come," he says.

"I'll go, too," I offer before they leave. They both shrug.

"Alright, come along," the strange guy says, waving his arm for me to follow him.

Nathan takes a minute to pull his shoes off. I do the same, throwing my boots and socks in my bag. I don't bother trying to roll my pants up because neither of the others is. I don't think I could get my pants up high enough anyway.

The strange, short man walks back into the water and plows forward with seeming ease, but I freeze up as soon as I get just one foot wet. The water is a lot colder than I expected. I skip out of the water for a second, making weird noises, but when I see that it's only slowing Nathan down, not stopping him, I man up and head back in. A chill runs up my spine, and my teeth begin to involuntarily chatter. I start muttering to myself something that sounds like "hachi" over and over like a mantra. Because I'm taller than Nathan's friend, the water doesn't reach above my knees, like it does on him.

I squish the underwater sand between my toes, feeling how it's both rough and soft at the same time. Each time I step on a sharp rock, I quickly lift my foot and take another step forward. By the time we reach the entrance to the metal beast, I still have not been in the water long enough to get used to its freezing temperature. I'm still shivering. The opening in the side of the structure is about the size of a small transport. The crazy guy keeps walking, not at all concerned that it looks like he will have to climb a couple feet to get up to the opening.

Paying no attention, he strolls right up a ramp to the inside. It seems like I'm having a poor track record with noticing things today. The obvious, two. Me, zero. Not a happy scoreboard... not for me, anyway.

I walk up the ramp, my pants dripping wet below the knees, the sand now washed off my feet. I follow Nathan and his friend to a small boat tied down inside the structure.

"What is this huge thing?" I ask, gesturing widely to the entire ship, I'm standing in.

"It's called a submarine," Nathan's friend says. "How is it you don't know that?" Honestly, it's because I've never seen one. I've never even heard rumors or stories about such a thing. "Now help me push this," he says after untying the dinghy. "You walked over here, might as well do some work."

I throw my bag against a wall, walk over toward the crazy guy, and start pushing the dinghy towards the ramp. It drags across the floor, and I am worried that we're going to rip it. I ease up on the pushing, but the guy yells at me to put my back into it, and I start pushing with full force again. I'm on the far right of the thing. Crazy guy is in the middle, and Nathan is on the left.

Nathan's friend jumps into the boat as we reach the edge of the ramp. "Keep pushing!" he yells. Nathan and I push until he and the dinghy are back in the water, and then we give it one more shove. He lowers the motor, which was sitting in the back of the boat, into the water and drives it ashore. Nathan and I walk back into the submarine while he picks up the others.

"Is he always like that?" I ask Nathan, wondering if I should try to wring out my pants.

"Nah," Nathan says. "He's usually worse. I bet my brother told him to be on his best behavior."

"Right, best behavior. I'd hate to see him at his worst," I remark.

"Usually someone ends up in a hospital when he gets cranky," Nathan says, like this is nothing out of the ordinary.

"Then why is he the welcoming committee?" I ask, now concerned that people usually get hurt because of this guy.

"He's entertaining," Nathan says. "And it's only my dad, sister, or me that ever comes and goes between the nations." Nathan pauses for a second, "Rodger grows on you." It seems like that's how it is with everyone in the

Sky and Water nations. Rodger doesn't seem like a very crazy name. Oh well, I guess not everyone has a name that reflects their insanity.

A couple minutes pass and Rodger comes back with everyone piled into the dinghy. How they all fit I'm not quite sure, but they do. Rodger runs the boat up onto the ramp, high enough so that nobody gets their feet wet stepping off of it. Impressive driving skills. I have no idea how to use one of those things.

"Come on, come on, let's go. Everybody off," Rodger says, hoisting the motor up and stepping out of the boat himself. Sure enough, everybody gets off, some more shakily and awkwardly than others. Still, they all still manage to get off with no face plants. So far so good. While everybody walks up to where Nathan and I are standing, Rodger shoves the dinghy the rest of the way up the ramp, back to where it was originally.

"Alright, are we ready to go?" he asks, wiping his hands on his wet, already dirty pants.

"It seems so," Gabriel says after looking around and doing a quick head count. Hopefully that means everyone is here, and that there isn't somebody he doesn't like still outside. I count for myself to be sure.

"I'ma go tell the captain we're ready to go," Rodger says, turning and leaving. I watch him as he goes, not paying much attention to what is going on around me. By the time he's out of my sight, everyone is milling around looking for a place to sit. I'm the only one still standing in the middle of the room.

"You coming, Sam?" John says to me as he starts following the rest of the group.

"Yeah," I say, joining the others. Nathan and Gabriel are leading the rest of us toward the front of the sub. Clearly, it's not their first time onboard this submarine. After we exit the main room that houses the dinghy, the space around us suddenly gets very tight. The passage narrows to a walkway that forces us to walk single-file. Although the submarine is wide, the walkway for passengers is drastically smaller and surrounded by electronics and reinforced steel plates.

Gabriel leads us like he doesn't have a doubt in his mind where we're going. He acts like he owns the place... which he probably does.

Looking around, I see a couple people running around, turning knobs and working on other parts of the sub. I fall behind the group a few steps because I'm paying more attention to what's around me than where I'm going. Before long, Gabriel reaches a passageway door. I see him spinning some mechanism in the center of it before swinging it open. The door itself looks to be about three feet thick.

After the heavy door creaks open, Gabriel passes through, and the others follow. Everyone before me walks through the opening seamlessly, so I think nothing of it. I'm preoccupied with examining the door. I've never seen anything like it before. Why would anyone ever need a door this thick? We're not walking into a bank! Are we?

When it comes time for me to pass through the door, I fail to notice that there is a slight step upward. My foot catches on the lip and I fall forward, fortunately catching myself with my hands and preventing anything more than just a few scratches on my palms. I turn my head around without standing up, casting an evil glare at the random rise in the floor. When I look back ahead, I see everyone that I came with, plus a few people I've never seen before, staring at me.

Smooth, Dac says to me.

"What!" I say defensively. "The floor tripped me." I stand up and resituate my bag on my back from where it slipped to on my side. I look at everyone around me, and it's obvious they're not buying my bogus story. I brush some imaginary dust off my jeans, hoping to appear less awkward. I notice that we're now in the room with the giant glass dome.

"Don't worry, lad," someone says. I can't see who it is, and the voice isn't familiar. "Plenty of people fall their first time onboard. Even your own Sky Lord here fell."

"Hey!" Nathan says indignantly. "You said you wouldn't tell anyone about that."

For some reason, the thought of Nathan falling like

I did doesn't surprise me. Although if someone tried to tell me that Gabriel was anything less than graceful, I wouldn't believe it. That man seems to have infinite patience and poise.

"Oh, don't you worry," the voice answers. "It's a secret the lot of us will be taking six feet under."

"Something tells me that you mean that literally, not 'to the grave,'" I chime in.

"You betcha," the man confirms.

Nathan sighs. "Geoffrey, sometimes you drive me crazy," he says.

"Is that a good thing?" quips the voice now identified as belonging to Geoffrey.

"No," Nathan says plainly. "I'm the one who drives people insane, not the other way around." Figures. I really am related to these guys, aren't I? It's becoming clearer and clearer as we go.

Out of curiosity, I start to look for this Geoffrey character.

"Don't you worry about that," Geoffrey continues. "You make me plenty mad."

As he finishes this last sentence, I finally see him. He's an average-sized man wearing dark pants and a white jacket. Topping off his attire is a thick, tangled black beard which covers part of his chest.

His eyes appear like they were glazed over, not to the extent that he looks only semi-conscious, but noticeably unnatural-looking. There's this different texture to them than I've seen before. I can't quite put my finger on it.

"We're ready to shove off, captain!" It's Rodger, who has barged into the room. He seems to be a little unstable at times, from what I can tell so far, but he gets things done.

"Excellent," Geoffrey says. He grabs a microphone that looks like it should be attached to a trucker's short-range radio, and pushes a button on the side of it. "Attention, everyone," he says, his voice amplified through the submarine's overhead intercom. "Brace yourselves for initial movement. We're partially beached, so it'll be rougher than usual." He releases the button and puts the microphone back into its holder. After he pulls a couple levers and twists a few knobs, a loud siren reverberates through the submarine.

"What's going on?" John asks in a panic. "Are we going to die?"

"Not necessarily," Geoffrey says in a serious tone. "If we're below and these sirens start wailing, let's just say that it wouldn't be good. Their song might be the last you'll hear." This does absolutely nothing to calm John, who still looks terrified. I think he's actually more scared now than he was before. He was never exactly brave, but right now he seems to be more cowardly than usual. Maybe some of my dad rubbed off on him. That'd be the worst.

Before the sirens shut off, the entire ship lurches backwards. I need to take a few steps and bend over so I don't lose my balance. Gabriel, Sarah, Nathan, and everyone from the Water Nation barely react, it looks like they just stand there normally. On the other hand, Mark, John, Davis, Rick, and Fred all fall. I normally would laugh at them, but considering that I came close to doing the same, I'm not going to say anything. Somehow, Dac manages to maintain his balance almost as well as the people from the Water Nation.

"How did you do that?" I ask him.

"Do what?"

"Not even come close to falling. Your body isn't even three days old, and you apparently have better balance than I do." It's still weird thinking that he hasn't been inside a body for even three days. He used to be just a voice in my flying shoes, but now he's standing right in front of me.

"Robot, remember? I have an unfair advantage," he says to me like I'm an idiot, which I very well may be. I'm only dumb half the time, okay!

"Oh. Right," I reply. Everyone who fell slowly gets back on their feet. I'm not going to bother asking Gabriel and his family how they stay standing. I'm just going to guess that they're used to this.

The submarine moves back on the water, skimming

over the surface. I've heard that boats do this, but I've never actually seen any before.

"You're going to like this," Geoffrey says to everyone, reaching for his microphone again. "Prepare to dive," he announces.

The submarine begins to sink beneath the water line. It's something else I never imagined I would get to see. Before long, the entire submarine is underwater.

Chapter
Five

At first, we see nothing. Greenish murk envelopes the entire window, and the darkness steadily grows. We dive for another few minutes before the sub's lights jump to life. Where there was darkness a second ago is now flooded with light. There's still nothing exciting to see at the moment. It's just the water. But as we descend further, sea life appears. A number of creatures swim with and around the submarine like they're used to seeing it, their now-familiar friend. We pass what I'm told are sharks and whales, and all sorts of other large animals. I half expect to see Atlantis at any moment.

We dive deeper and deeper, the sea life becoming more spectacular as we go. We also pass some floating waste that was no doubt dropped from the surface, but I try to ignore it. We quickly get to a point where the only visible light is coming from our headlights. They're powerful little suckers. Maybe "little" isn't exactly the right word. When I was outside, they looked enormous.

After about ten minutes of diving, something massive swims by at the edge of the area illuminated by our headlights.

"What was that?" I ask nobody in particular.

"You must mean Billy," Geoffrey says.

"What's a Billy?" I ask.

"*He* is one of Kane's pets. The Sea King loves using his brain and making creatures like that," Geoffrey tells me.

"What do you mean by 'creature'?" I ask. Geoffrey smiles.

"You'll see if Billy decides to come closer." I shrug. Even though I let the topic drop, it remains in the back of my mind.

"Are we there yet?" Mark asks.

"Hold your horses, will you?" Geoffrey responds with a sigh. "You'll see in a couple of seconds." True to Geoffrey's words, moments later I see the Water Kingdom. Piercing the darkness of the sea, the kingdom lights up the bottom nearly as bright as day. I make out buildings similar to those on the surface, but they're manufactured differently. These buildings look much more sturdy. The tallest ones are colossal.

Other than the buildings, there are giant domes littering the area, and tunnels connecting everything cover most of the space remaining. Parts of this place look like somebody took a city from the surface and sank it.

"Is this Atlantis?" I ask.

"No," Geoffrey laughs. "But we did name a town that." Of course they did.

While scanning the landscape, seascape, whatever, my eyes settle on a gigantic building that towers above the others. I can't help but stare. It has no rival in the height department. I don't think I've even seen anything as tall as it on the Surface. I haven't seen a whole lot of the Surface though so I may be surprised.

"Yup," Nathan says, walking up next to me. "Kane loves his towers. It seems like every time I'm down here, he has plans for another one." Apparently my staring was really obvious.

"What's in that one?" I ask, pointing at the tallest one I can see.

"Don't know," Nathan says. "He's been working on that one for a while now. First time I've seen it finished." I look back at the tower. Regardless of what's inside, I still want to see it. I look around the cabin of the submarine and notice that Gabriel is looking out at his son's creations with pride written on his face. I can't help but smile myself, seeing the joy and pride in his eyes.

Geoffrey must have taken up his microphone because the overhead speakers pop, signaling that he is about to say something. "Attention crew," he begins.

"Prepare to dock. We will arrive in approximately sixty seconds. Thank you." He takes his finger off the talk button on the microphone and puts it back on its stand.

We dive even deeper until we are level with the underwater metropolis. I see people walking about inside the glass-and-metal tubes. None of them act surprised or excited by the submarine. I guess when you see it everyday you get a little jaded. All of this is still pretty awesome to me.

A large door ahead of us, that I assume is the docking bay, opens up like a garage door would, and tucks away overhead as we approach. We enter the underwater dock, and the huge bay door closes behind us.

The ship comes to rest in a sling. As the sling tightens while Geoffrey lowers the submarine, the water around us begins to drain away. How this is happening at the bottom of the ocean, I don't know. As the water drains, I can clearly see the well-lit room where we've docked. I watch as the waterline moves down the front glass dome and stop at the bottom of the sub so that it's still partially in the water. The giant door we used to enter the sub now flips open, creating a perfect ramp to a wet walkway.

"Here we are," Geoffrey says, stepping away from the wheel. He crosses the room to a row of lockers and pulls one open. He throws a jacket on straight out of the locker. Next he flips a hat onto the top his head. The hat looks like one I've seen in old pictures of sailors.

Rodger comes into the room. "Are we ready to go now?" he asks Geoffrey impatiently.

"I will be in just a moment," Geoffrey replies, slamming the locker closed. Turning to us, he says, "Will you fellows be needing a tour? An escort to wherever it is you're going?"

"No, thank you," Gabriel answers. "I remember my way around, and I can show our guests all they need to know."

"Well, alright then, sir," Geoffrey says. "If you need me, you know where to find me." He looks at Rodger. "Come on, cuz. Let's head home." They walk out of the forward cabin and, I assume, exit the ship.

It seems weird that the captain of a ship would leave before his passengers and crew, but maybe the fact that three of us—

Four, Dac corrects me.

Fine! Four of us are "royalty" has something to do with it.

It still counts as three this time! I argue to Dac. *He doesn't know I'm related to Sarah!* I've gotten so used to Dac in my head that I can tell he's rolling his eyes without even looking at him. I wonder if he really did, now that he has a body. I turn around to check, but see that everyone is gathering their belongings to leave. My curiosity about Dac being able to roll his eyes forgotten,

I grab my duffel bag and follow Gabriel and the others out.

It takes minimal effort not to slip on the walkway, but fortunately we soon pass through a thick, airtight door, leaving the wet floors behind. We don't bother shutting the door behind us because there are still some people unloading and working on the sub.

I catch up to Mark and Jinn. "Have either of you ever been down here before?" I ask them.

"Never," Jinn answers for both of them. "It's extremely rare to see more than one of the nations. It's unheard of to have seen all three."

I know he's talking about me. Personally, I wish I'd only seen two of them. I could do without the Surface.

"Yeah, kid," Mark says. "You have to show us your hometown after this."

"I don't think that's such a good idea," I reply. "Where I'm from isn't exactly a desired tourist location." Mark shrugs like he doesn't care, but I know he still wants to see it.

A short while later, we come to another giant door that Gabriel pushes open. As soon as I pass through it, I find myself inside one of the tubes I saw from the sub window. Glass surrounds me on all sides, allowing me look around. If I didn't know better, I would never guess this is the bottom of the ocean. There is so much light that everything's illuminated.

I look at the city surrounding me. There are buildings that look like surface homes, skyscrapers, and abnormally large domes all around. This place appears to be its own unique city but not one that you could only find in fairy tales. It doesn't look like a city from my nightmares either so that's a positive.

We follow the twists and turns of these seemingly endless tunnels down here, somehow never passing through a building or dome. We don't stop moving until we reach the entrance of one of the large towers. It's not the biggest, but it's still pretty impressive.

Gabriel pushes a button on a call box. "Who is it?" some guy asks from the other side of the box.

"Hello, Bean," Gabriel speaks into the box. "Would you tell Kane that his father is here to see him for me?"

Chapter Six

"Who would name their kid 'Bean'?"

"That's not really his name," Nathan answers anyway. "His name is actually Benson, but none of us like calling him that. He doesn't complain about being called Bean. He actually even told us that he prefers it."

I shrug like I don't care, but I'm still curious about where the name "Bean" came from. A short while later, the door that's the entrance to Kane's building opens up. A normal-sized man is standing in the entryway. He doesn't look like anything special, certainly not tall and thin enough to remind anyone of a string bean.

"Hello, sirs and ma'ams," he says, "Mister Kane is upstairs in his workshop, awaiting your arrival. Shall I take you to him?" Do all wealthy people have a bunch of servants? Jinn doesn't, but it sure seems like the royals are incapable of doing anything on their own.

Careful, you're insulting yourself now too, remember? Dac tells me. Sadly, he's right.

What if I said royals who seem to be living forever?
Dac pauses. *That could work.*

"That would be excellent, Bean," Gabriel says. So this is Bean. Eh, his parents could've done a better naming job. We follow him into the building, where he leads us up two flights of stairs and down a bland, unembellished hallway. There is literally nothing on the walls. The only ornamentations are signs labeling what's inside closed doors along the left side of the hallway. I'm guessing most of them identify types of inventions. There are so many of them, it's incredible.

"Is this entire floor Kane's workshop?" I ask Bean.

"Sure is," Bean says. "Mister Kane is always here working on new devices and tinkering with old ones." So Kane does a lot with his hands. I guess Nathan did say that Kane made everything down here.

We reach a large opening in one of the walls. It looks like the wall itself is tucked away up against the ceiling, waiting to be called down to block access to what lays inside. That's one heck of a door.

Bean steers us into a massive room.

I thought it would only be as wide as the large entrance, but no. The room – or industrial factory, I'm not quite sure – takes up half this entire floor of the building. Parts are scattered all over the place, some almost like they're for decoration. Blueprints, sketches, and schematics are plastered over every inch of the walls. Some of the design sketches are pinned over older ones, so that the newest designs are visible. Benches, tables, clamps, and small stands supporting half-built machines of one kind or another are everywhere creating makeshift pathways. I don't see any people in all this mess, but according to Bean, Kane's in here.

Also, there are giant contraptions that I can't even begin to describe hanging from the ceiling and lying all over the floor, reminding me of a car repair shop. Some of the things hanging from the ceiling look like they are still being worked on, while others seem to be on display, simply there to look cool and be marveled at. I stare. The stuff in this room is mind-blowing. As my eyes dart about the room, I spot a elegant metal arm supported in a strange harness, wires sticking out in places, two fingers missing altogether, and a thumb sitting off to the side, linked to the arm by wires but not yet attached.

"Mister Kane," Bean calls into the room. In response, I hear the echo of a wrench clattering to the floor and muttered curses coming from within the workshop.

"What is it, Bean?" yells back an annoyed Kane.

"You have visitors."

"Tell them to go away and that I'm sick." Bean looks like he's about to say something back, but Gabriel puts a hand on his shoulder to stop him.

"That didn't work when you were twelve, and it

won't work now," Gabriel calls out.

"Dad?" the voice obviously belonging to Kane says, annoyance now replaced with traces of vulnerability. Seconds later, a man about the same height as Gabriel, Nathan, and me walks into view. Nathan and Gabriel both have muscles, as do I, but I'm noticeably smaller. My six-pack is just shy, that's all. But Kane puts them both to shame. It's not as though his arms are bigger than his waist, but he does look like he could break a person in half if he really put his mind to it. His most amazing feature, though, are his eyes. They're steel grey, but cloudy-looking in the same way as Geoffrey's.

Hanging around his neck is a chain similar those worn by Sarah, Nathan, and me. But his is different in that it has a brilliant blue gem in a round metal cage. The color of the blue gem is unlike any I've seen before. It's as if I've never seen a perfect blue until now. Come to think of it, all the necklaces have been like that with each of their unique gems.

As soon as Kane sees his father and siblings, he rushes forward and embraces Gabriel. "It's been a while," Kane says, overjoyed.

"Far too long," Gabriel responds, hugging his son tighter.

I feel awkward standing here, watching this. I didn't expect to be stuck in the middle of a family reunion. With a quick glance around, I can see that the others feel the same way.

"When I called Nate up, I never thought that you'd be coming too." Kane lets go of Gabriel and moves on to his sister. "I didn't expect to see you either."

"Good to see you, too, big guy," Sarah replies, obviously being nearly crushed by Kane's hug, but keeping quiet about it.

Lastly, Kane moves on to Nathan and hugs him. Nathan looks the most natural next to Kane, apparently having the *second* most muscle mass in the family.

"Thank you for coming, Nate. I really need your help," Kane says into his brother's shoulder.

"Of course, Kane," Nathan says quietly. "Just tell me how we can help."

"Thank you."

"You already said that."

"I know."

Kane lets go of his brother and looks around, apparently seeing the rest of us for the first time.

"Who are these people?" he asks the members of his family.

"These are the heroes of the Sky Nation," Nathan says, sweeping his hand over us.

"Heroes of the Sky Nation?" Kane asks.

"Well, they kinda stopped an evil dictator from taking over while I was away," Nathan says. "It's not that big of a deal." A couple chuckles escape from the group of us. I love how Nathan is down-playing the entire story, but doesn't even seem to be aware he's doing this.

I wonder if I should tell them that Steven wasn't the ringleader behind this whole thing, I think to myself. But because I'm so special and lucky, my thoughts aren't my own.

I've been wondering why you didn't want me to tell them about that, Dac says to me, *but seeing as I can look into your mind at will, I just found out why, and I know you're still not going to tell them.*

"You know what I think?" I say out loud to Dac, accidentally interrupting the introductions Nathan has started making between the others and Kane. "I don't think any of the others died from the connection. I think they *off'd* themselves because it's so damn annoying to have someone inside your head all the time!"

I know you don't mean that. I'm still here on the inside. Remember? Dac says in my head.

"Gah!" I groan and throw up my arms. Dac laughs audibly.

You know you love me, he says in my head.

I pause for a moment and glare at him. *You're still annoying sometimes,* I say back to him, even as I admit to myself that I actually do like the guy. *And that's cheating!*

"Who's the crazy one?" Kane asks Nathan, giving me a stink eye.

"He's talking about me, isn't he?" I say. Figures.

"Kane," Sarah says, walking over to me and putting her hands on my shoulders, "this is Sam. He's my some-number-of-greats grandson."

At that, not only does Kane give me a double take, but he starts sizing me up.

"He doesn't look anything like you," Kane comments.

"Of course he doesn't," Sarah exclaims somewhat indignantly, moving her hands to her hips. "There's more than a hundred generations difference between us. I'd be worried if he *did* look like me."

"Then how do you know he's related to you?" Kane asks, still skeptical.

"He's wearing the necklace dad made me," Sarah points out. "Only one of us can wear our own, and he has mine on. The necklace is his now."

"What if the blood is so diluted that the necklace just thinks he's yours? What if he's really mine?" Kane asks.

Sarah sighs. "The necklaces detect DNA, and besides that, I'm the only one who had kids. You guys never did."

"Oh yeah, that's right," Kane says, seeming to have forgotten that little detail. You know, just something minor.

After a moment of awkward silence, I stick my hand out towards Kane.

"It's nice to meet you," I say. I'm not quite sure what else to say to him. Sarah already told him that we're related... Wait, I know! "I'm not crazy," I add when he takes my hand. "I was talking to Dac in my head and forgot for a moment that you guys can't hear it when we do that, so I spoke out loud. That never usually happens." Great, now I *really* sound like a nut case. As expected, Kane gives me a funny look.

"Are you sure you're not crazy?" he asks me, releasing my hand. He doesn't believe me about Dac. Awesome.

"He's telling the truth," Nathan interjects. "I developed an AI that bonded with Sam, and a blacksmith up in the Sky Nation built the AI a body. That's him right there." Nathan points to Dac.

Dac decides to be his charming self and says, "What're you looking at?" Pointless line, but it might very well get Dac in trouble. I've gotten a few bruises from saying things like that on the Surface.

"Interesting," Kane says. "I've never seen an AI that's both a learning program and has a fully-developed personality." He strokes his beard stubble. "How'd you make it, Nate?"

"In all honesty, I don't remember," Nathan replies. "It was a failed experiment. I didn't commit it to memory."

"Stop calling Dac an 'it'. He doesn't really like it," I say. Even if Dac wasn't mentally grumbling about how he wants to spring at Kane and Nathan for calling him an 'it,' I'd know from past experience that he hates being called that.

"Do you at least know why the boy—"

"Sam," I cut Kane off.

"—can hear him in his head?" At least Kane seems to get the part about not calling Dac an "it".

Nathan shrugs at Kane. "I designed the jump boots with an AI that was supposed to be a copilot. It didn't work. In every case but Sam's, the AI would try to either kill their host or take over their host's body. It wasn't pretty."

"I wonder why it worked with him, then?" Kane says, pointing at me, "Would anyone be against a dissection?"

"*YES!*" Jinn, Mark, Rick, Fred, Gabriel, Sarah, John, Dac, and I all yell in unison.

"Eh, I don't particularly care," Davis says.

Thanks, Davis. I think venomously. When he was Mr. Friendly two months ago, I had mixed feelings about him. I mean, he did save my life, but he also worked with the New Power and almost got me killed a couple times. I mean, sure it was supposed to work out that was so that John and I could escape before going to prison, but still! It's about the principle! And that was mostly Mark's doing anyway. So when I found out who he was two days ago, I didn't hate him. But now I don't like him so much again.

He made it pretty clear he doesn't like you, Dac points out. He's right.

"Weren't you the one who told me it was time to

blow my cover just to get two kids?" Mark asks.

"That could've been anyone," Davis replies.

"No, it was you," Jinn offers. "I distinctly remember you calling me and waking me up from my nap, telling me to come personally." Was that why he had been so grouchy when he first picked me up? I would be scared if I woke Jinn up from a nap.

"Okay, so it was me," Davis admits, as if this is some big secret. "The kid served his purpose already. He stopped the leader of the New Power. Now we can take a look at his head." I *really* don't like him now. I'm officially changing his name from Mr. Friendly. I don't know what it's going to be, but it won't be Mr. Friendly or even Mr. Remotely Nice.

"You touch him and I'll cut your hand off," Jinn says in a monotone voice, crossing his arms. Davis walks over and reaches out to touch me. He stops his hand inches away from my arm and looks over at Jinn. Jinn's face is blank.

"Have you ever known Jinn to bluff?" Mark asks Davis. I keep standing here as if some guy's hand isn't at risk of being chopped off if he touches me.

"Only when we play cards," Davis answers. Mark raises his eyebrows at Davis' answer as if to say, "So what do you think you should do?" It takes Davis only another second before he lowers his hand.

"Good choice," Jinn says. He hasn't lost his calm this

whole stupid conversation.

"Now that *that's* out of the way," Sarah wheels on her brother and hollers, "What is wrong with you? You don't go around asking people if you can dissect them!" Kane looks genuinely shocked, like he has no idea that that's totally weird, creepy, and wrong to ask someone.

"I just wanted to know what makes him different," Kane says unapologetically. "Maybe the difference isn't in the boy, but the AI. Can I—"

"Don't even think about it," Dac cuts in. What is with Kane and putting people up on the chopping block?

I think we should put him up there, Dac says to me mentally.

No. Bad Dac, bad.

Why not? Dac whines. *He wanted to cut us both up, and he called me an 'it'!*

Hmmm. That second part is what really has you up in arms, isn't it?

Yes. I knew it.

"You need to get out of the workshop more," Sarah says to Kane. "How long have you been in there?"

"Not long enough," Kane says, sounding tense. "I have so many projects to finish, so many questions to answer."

"How many weeks have you been in there?"

"Months. I've only come out to address the nation."

"You mean, you haven't talked to anyone for

months?" she asks.

"No, except for Bean," Kane says. Bean starts looking proud of his specialness. "And anyone else I need to help keep the place running smoothly," Wow, he's really antisocial.

"That's not good, Kane," Sarah says, concerned.

"It's irrelevant. I like the quiet," Kane says dismissively. He pauses for a moment, then says, "Were you even given Pressure Pills?"

"We three have had them," Gabriel says, gesturing to Nathan, Sarah, and himself. "The others have not."

"Alright," Kane says. "Bean, would you please go grab six pressure pills? It won't matter for the robot."

Dac gets even angrier with Kane. There was really nothing wrong with the statement, but he's still fuming about the whole "it" thing. And to him, robot is generally worse. Admitting he's an AI is going to the danger zone.

Bean scurries off, back down the long hallway we came from.

"What are Pressure Pills?" I ask Kane once Bean is gone, simultaneously trying to calm Dac down.

"They keep you alive," he says. I like them already. "The water pressure down here is so intense that if you get caught outside the tunnels, you'll be instantly crushed to something resembling a marble." That doesn't sound like fun. "I designed the pills to stabilize your internal pressure," Kane continues, "so you'll be

80

able to go out there and not be crushed. Breathing, though, is an entirely different issue."

"Got it," I say before he can get into that discussion. "The pills keep you people-sized."

Bean comes back a minute later with a small bag in his hand. He opens it and shakes out the contents into his hand before passing out the Pressure Pills. They're round and a little bit smaller than a marble. For a moment I hesitate, but recall that I might become the same size as the pill if I don't take it.

"Do we have any water to chase it down with?" John asks. Expecting this, Bean brings out several bottles of water.

Wordlessly, I pop the pill into my mouth, take a sip of water, and swallow. I grimace and a twitch travels through my whole body.

"God, that's awful. It tastes like crap," I say, grimacing. Sadly, I would know.

"They're designed for functionality, not enjoyment," Kane points out. Everyone else also makes a face because it's just that bad. Jinn sounds like he's choking, and Nathan pats him on the back.

"I know, I know," he says. "Just get it down. It'll be better in no time." Once everybody has taken a pill without choking to death, Kane addresses Nathan.

"So about my problem," he begins.

"Your antisocialness or something else?" Nathan

jokes.

"Everyone is going crazy," Kane continues seriously, not amused by his brother's joke. "If it were only a few people and happening slowly, I would say it was isolated cases of claustrophobia, which are virtually nonexistent to begin with. Unfortunately, this is different. It appears that all at once, nearly every person in the nation started acting crazy. They're attacking people, destroying areas, and worshipping some cult group. It doesn't make any sense."

"Cult group?" Nathan asks for clarification. He sounds like he doesn't quite believe it.

"Yes. I have no idea who they are, or what their goals and beliefs are, but judging by what they call themselves, they could be a dangerous bunch of fanatics."

"Who are they?" Nathan asks. "What is their name?"

Kane takes a breath. "They call themselves the New Power."

Chapter Seven

"What?" I ask. If I was drinking any water, that would've been a spit-take.

"I know. Weird name, right?" Kane says. Geez. Even if he did build this entire place himself, he has no idea how to talk to people.

"This isn't good," Mark says.

"What? What's wrong?" Nathan asks.

"They must've come down here when their first attack failed," Jinn speculates, dragging a hand down his face.

"What are you guys talking about?" Sarah asks.

"I thought you killed Steven," Davis says accusingly, pointing a finger at me.

"How am I supposed to know?" I say. "I was a little preoccupied at the time with *staying alive*! You were on the ship, too. You ran ahead and left me behind for dead."

"Because I'm still important," Davis yells back. I

83

yell at him. I've had it with people acting like my life is worthless.

"You're the worthless one, you jerk," John yells at Davis, as if reading my feelings.

"Who are you?" Davis hollers. "You've been locked away for months, not doing anything."

"Watch it there," Rick says, pushing Davis' chest.

"Yeah, you don't want to hurt yourself now," Fred adds. They're both taller than Davis.

Really quickly, the room erupts into loud arguments. I don't pay much attention to what the others are saying, because I'm too busy yelling and arguing myself. The only ones not caught up in fighting are the royals and Bean.

"Hey!" Nathan yells forcefully, in an attempt to quiet all of us. It doesn't work. He tries again, still nothing. Gabriel gets tired of being patient.

"Silence!" he thunders, and all "discussions" abruptly come to a halt. In the silence, I look at Gabriel and punch Davis, who's off to my side, in the arm without looking.

"Ow," he says. Wimp.

Good one, Dac compliments me.

Gabriel gazes at us. The present royals are looking at us like we should all be locked away in the loony bin.

"Explain to me, calmly, who the New Power are," Gabriel says evenly. "It sounds like you all have some prior experience with them." Just a bit.

Even though just moments ago, we were all shouting at each other about the New Power, none of us wants to say anything now. After a few empty seconds of the "responsible adults" saying nothing, I decide to speak up.

"Bad news," I say. Brilliantly spoken. A true masterpiece if I do say so myself.

"And?" Kane presses.

"And, they're the ones who've been trying to take over the Sky Nation. Obviously that didn't work, but apparently they want the Water Nation now, too."

"Sam blew up their ship," John adds.

"I didn't blow it up," I clarify. "I just crashed it and wrecked the controls. Sadly, there was no big boom."

"Thank God for that," Davis says, then turns to Kane. "That's actually why I'm down here. I came to ask for your permission and assistance in retrieving the ship and returning it to the Sky Nation."

"Yes, of course," Kane says after the moment it takes for Davis' words to register. "There was a report somewhere around here saying the ship caused some of our tunnels to collapse." He glares at me accusingly.

Wow! He's known you for less than an hour, and already he's figured out that when something breaks, it's usually your fault, Dac says in the security of my head.

You don't need to rub it in.

"Bean," Kane says, turning to his helper. "Would you

85

be so kind as to assist this man?"

"With pleasure, sir," Bean replies, happy to do work. "Right this way, please," he says to Davis, and the two of them leave together.

I have never met someone so happy to do someone else's work for them as Bean.

"If you would continue," Gabriel says to me. I've been looking at Davis and Bean walking away. I hate Davis, yet I owe him a lot. He's the one that decided to save me from the New Power, after all.

"I don't know what they're doing down here," I say, "but in the Sky Nation they tried mind control on at least one person."

"They did?" Jinn asks.

"Yeah," I say. "They were trying to control that Armando guy. I probably should've said something before."

"That would've been smart," Jinn says. He pulls out his phone. "Damn, no signal."

"Here," Kane says, taking out his. "I rigged mine up to be able to communicate with anywhere in the world." Jinn accepts the phone and starts dialing.

"Can you do that with all of our phones?" Mark asks Kane.

"If I had a couple of hours to spare," Kane says. "It would be easier to teach one of you how to do it and let you take care of it yourself." Oh boy. Mark, always the tech fanatic, immediately gets excited.

"I'll do it!" he volunteers without hesitation.

"Good," Kane says. "We'll get right on that as soon as we're done here." Mark grins in response.

"Arthur?" Jinn says into the phone. "It's me, Jinn." He pauses to listen to what Arthur says. "How fast can you get to where they're keeping Armando?" He pauses again.

I wonder if we can listen in, I say to Dac.

That's a good question. You should get right on that.

Why me? I ask. *You're the one that can do it.*

I don't feel like it right now, Dac says, bored.

Please! I beg.

He doesn't respond for a moment. Then, *It sucks that you can't do anything special on your own.* Typical.

So is that a yes? I ask.

Give me a minute. I win.

"Apparently Sam knows something about it that he forgot to mention," Jinn says on the phone.

I don't feel anything as Dac supposedly tries to hack into the call. I'm not sure he's even doing anything.

"I'm going to kill that little idiot!" Oh, we're connected. Fancy that. "The doctors are talking about putting him under and frying his brain in hopes that it might do *something*. What does the kid know?"

"Why don't you ask him yourself?" Jinn says.

"Pass him the phone," Arthur growls.

"He wants to talk to you," Jinn tells me, handing over the phone. I pretend to have no idea what Arthur just said.

You're keeping a lot of secrets from them, Dac says.

I've been keeping secrets my whole life. It's not an easy habit to break.

"Hello?" I say innocently, playing stupid.

You don't need to play!

You've been waiting for that, haven't you?

Yes. Yes I have.

"Start talking," Arthur rumbles, leaving no room for formalities.

"Mind control," I say, as though it's a normal, everyday procedure. "It's strong, but he's fighting it, so don't lose hope."

"And how is this mind control being done?"

"Steven tried implanting an AI directly into him," I explain to Arthur. "My guess is that if you can remove it and destroy it, he'll go back to being himself."

That hurts, Dac cuts in. *I don't know any others like me, but I feel bad for the poor sap.*

No you don't, I say, just to let him know he's full of crap.

Maybe a little, Dac corrects himself. I believe that.

"How do you know all of this?" Arthur asks me.

"Armando told me," I reply. "I saw him in prison and we may have bumped elbows in the arena... Twice." It is the truth, just not all of it. I did see Armando in jail, but I was the only one inside of it. I saw him through the AI connection dream thing. It's hard to explain.

"Did you put him into that comatose state we found him in?" Arthur asks me, sounding a bit calmer.

Busted! Dac teases.

"Yes, but only because I had to in order to make sure the escape worked."

"I still can't believe you orchestrated that whole thing," Arthur says. I'll take that as a compliment. "I'm going to go get him fixed up then. I'll come down and meet you guys when he's better."

"Alright," I say. "Call Jinn when you're ready to come down. Our phones should be working by then."

"Sounds good," replies Arthur, who's back to his normal level of rage and sounds as though he'll only kick a couple puppies instead of ripping everybody's heads off. "Keep in touch." With that, he hangs up.

"He's doing well," I say, handing the phone back to Jinn. He pockets it. "Now, where was I?" I say to the group.

"Mind control," Sarah says.

"Right, uh, yeah," I say, in a lame attempt to finish my explanation.

"Well, that was informative," Dac says out loud.

"They're control freaks," Jinn speaks up. "For some reason, their leader, Steven," not their leader, "wants nothing more than power."

"He's insane," Mark says. "The man thinks he can control everyone. This mind control is just further proof."

"What does this Steven character look like?" Kane asks.

"I don't know," Mark says. "Only Sam's seen him."

Everyone looks at me.

"Really?" I ask. I thought these guys had at least *seen* the dude, or a picture of him or something. Jinn and Mark nod their heads... Wow. "Okay. Well, he looks like any other guy, but the dude oozes evil overlord. I remember his face, but I can't really describe it. Other than that, he wore a suit both times I saw him. He was dressed up in a suit when he was trying to kill us in a giant freakin' warship!" I just realized that the only ones still here in the room are Dac, Jinn, Mark, John, the royals, and me.

Really? You notice that now? Dac says, sounding amused.

It's not my fault that I notice things at odd times, I reply.

"Is he okay?" Sarah asks.

"He's fine," Jinn tells her. "This is normal."

"That's not normal," she argues, pointing at me as I stare ahead blankly while I talk to Dac.

"He's just talking to Dac," Jinn explains.

"The robot?" Kane asks, pointing at Dac.

"First they call me an AI, now a robot. Can't a guy get a break?" Dac shouts out loud.

"Just don't do that," I say to Kane. "He doesn't like it."

"Fascinating! The A—, I mean Dac," Kane says, and Dac nods approvingly, "has a fully-developed personality. It doesn't even sound like it's programmed. The personality sounds *self*-developed." Kane starts moving forward as if to touch Dac. This guy's hopeless. STOP EXAMINING DAC!

"Back. Off," Dac enunciates. Kane freezes for a moment before backing away. Dac's mostly mad that he was almost called an AI.

"Are we done talking about the New Power now?" Mark asks. "I'd like to learn how to alter the phones."

"For now," Gabriel says. "We should go. Kane, I believe you are going to teach Mark here how to alter the phones."

"Of course," Kane says. "I want to show you how it's done, then get back to my projects."

"Okay," Mark says, positively giddy. "Here, give me your phones so I can start working on them." He reaches out to collect the devices. I fish in my pocket, pull out my phone. Jinn and I hand over our phones to him.

"I don't have one," John says. Neither does Dac.

"Alright, see you guys soon. Would you take my bag for me?" Mark asks, happily following Kane into his lab.

"Sure," Jinn says, grabbing his bag and Mark's.

"Call me when he's done," Gabriel says to Kane before turning to leave. Gabriel, Nathan, and Sarah grab their bags. Jinn and I already have bags on us, and John and Dac don't have any.

We follow Gabriel out of Kane's skyscraper-type shop and head back into the tunnels. Gabriel must know all the back routes, because I still don't see a single person as we walk.

Liar. There are all the people we've been walking with, Dac points out, just to argue about something. I don't even honor that with a response.

We end up in front of what appears to be an apartment complex, and I start getting jittery. Two months, or even two weeks ago, I would've been fine with apartments, but when I was thrown into prison—or some perversion thereof—they stuck me in an apartment and tried to "rehabilitate" me. The apartment is just a little creepy to me right now. I'm sure the feeling will pass quickly.

"Welcome home, everybody," Nathan says jovially. "I call dibs on the best room."

"Not fair!" Sarah complains. "I'll race you to it."

"What? No way," Nathan says, seemingly letting his guard down.

"Scared you'll lose?" Sarah teases.

"No way, I'm not—GO!" Nathan yells the "go" out of

nowhere and takes off running.

"Cheater!" Sarah yells as she races after him into the building. The rest of us calmly walk in after Nathan and Sarah have disappeared inside.

We enter what appears to be a common room, similar to a living room. From here I can see a kitchen and several other doorways.

There are multiple sets of stairs leading up to other floors. Gabriel starts walking up one, and because he actually knows where he's going, we follow him. He climbs three flights of stairs, telling us that there are bedrooms on the middle two floors. There are no bedrooms on the first floor, and Gabriel always occupies the giant penthouse on the fourth. Jinn leaves to pick a room, while I'm stuck in the middle of a really awkward debate on the third floor.

"I'm bunking with Sam," John yells in Dac's face.

"No, I am," Dac argues back. "It'll be like we're stuck together anyway. I can hear all the guy's thoughts."

"Really?" John asks.

"Yeah, so there! I'm stuck with him," Dac says, not so lovingly.

"What does Sam think?" John asks. They both turn to me, glaring and waiting for me to choose one of them over the other.

"I just want to go to sleep," I say, tired of this argument. "Why doesn't everyone get their own room?"

They look at me as if they hadn't thought of that. Probably didn't.

"Fine," John and Dac say, and they go off to find rooms.

Geez, is it too much to hope that people aren't total idiots like I am?

Do you even sleep? I ask Dac.

I have no idea, he replies. *I'll tell you tomorrow.*

I hear footsteps coming down the stairs, and I turn to see Nathan coming down with his stuff.

"My dad kicked me out," he says without my asking. He stops in front of me and asks, "So have you found a room yet?"

"I was just about to do that," I say. I wait and see if he's going to walk away, but he doesn't.

"How was the Sky Nation?" he asks me. It seems like a pretty random question right about now.

"It was fine," I say awkwardly. "You rule the place. Why are you asking me?"

"I haven't been there for years," he tells me slowly. "I was just wondering if a lot has changed."

"I was only there for a few months. I don't know how it was before the New Power or before I arrived." I tell him, "But I'll tell you this, your name was more like a legend. Everyone held onto hope that you'd come back and fix things."

"Really?" Nathan asks in disbelief.

"Yeah," I say, yawning. "Now if you'll excuse me, I need to go find a room." With that, I leave him with his thoughts to go find somewhere I can sleep.

Chapter Eight

For the first time in a while, my sleep isn't haunted by dreams of people talking. Up in the Sky Nation, I'd be visited every night by uninvited men in conference, supposedly a result of the AI's inferior to Dac being used by others. It's not nearly as weird as it sounds.

Maybe we're out of range, Dac suggests.

Curious, I ask him, *So do you sleep?*

In a way, he replies. *The body slows down and I can choose to power it off so it recharges, but I'm always up.*

Don't push yourself then, I suggest. *It sounds like Arthur made your body more human than you bargained for.*

Maybe, but I don't mind it.

Alright, time to get up. I find my way to a shower and get myself cleaned off. Because I'm an early riser, even down here apparently, I'm up and moving before most of the others are even stirring. Dac's body isn't moving around yet so he must still be recharging. After sitting around for an hour with no one else awake to keep me company, except for Dac, which is not the same, I get bored and restless. I pace the first floor of the building for another ten minutes before I decide I need a change of scenery.

I'm going for a walk, I tell Dac so he can let the others know when they wake up.

Want me to go with you? he offers.

Nah, I tell him. *It's better you go down and get a full recharge.*

Be careful, he tells me.

I'm afraid I can't do that, I answer. *I might die in the process.*

Knowing you, I don't doubt it. I deserve that one.

Not having my phone or money that would do me any good down here, I don't bother shoving anything in my pockets before I leave. I instinctively feel for my Sky Iron sword. It's there, as always.

I try to memorize the path I'm taking so I can find my way back, but there are so many twists and turns, I get lost really quickly. Lucky for me, Dac has nothing better to do and records my route for me. He's like a personal GPS.

For the majority of my walk, I don't see anyone. It's like nobody from around here wakes up early. Or maybe it's the middle of the night still. Without the sun, it's hard to tell. If I could've chosen to sleep instead of going to work in the factory, I would've ... I think I would've chosen nearly anything over the factory.

I stop and look out at the maze of tunnels surrounding me. Other than the Hubs, where the tunnels enlarge into huge, bubble-like compartments, all the buildings project directly into the water. The tunnel lights cast an eerie aura into the vast expanse of the surrounding ocean. The illumination reminds me of the glow from my sword. It's kind of like light piercing through thick fog on the surface. It penetrates only so far before it is swallowed up by blackness. It's a little unnerving.

After a while of looking outside, I get back to randomly wandering around and find my way into yet another of the endless corridors, where I find something I don't expect. There's a person here! Well, he's banging his head against the side of the tunnel and mumbling something to himself that I can't make out, but it's still a person, no matter how weird he is... I hope this guy isn't an example of the mental health and behavior of everybody down here.

"Hey, are you alright?" I shout to the guy as I walk closer. He doesn't hear me, or doesn't react, anyway. How do I know this? He continues banging his head against the wall like he's dead set on punching a hole through it. "Hey!" I yell to get his attention, waving my hand. I keep walking forward.

Maybe he's deaf, Dac suggests.

Oh yeah, that's a good point. I stop yelling, and approach him so I can tap him on the shoulder. When I'm roughly ten feet away, the guy stops banging his head. Without taking his head off the wall, he turns and looks at me. Instantly I notice he has the same cool, gray eyes as everyone else I've met from down here. I'm going to guess they all have them. It probably has to do with the lack of sunlight. But even though his eyes have that natural cloudy look everyone down here has, there's something different about his. He keeps staring at me expectantly, like he said something and is waiting for me to respond. After looking at him for a bit longer, I figure out why his eyes don't look right.

"Nobody's home," I say.

He suddenly lets out a shrill, very primal-sounding scream and charges toward me. Automatically, I reach into my pocket for my sword. I have my hand around it, but let it go. For some reason, I don't think this guy's a bad person. I don't necessarily *want* to hurt him. I'd feel bad if I cut him to ribbons. Even though I've been training with a sword, and only a sword, for a while now, I've been street fighting all my life. This poor sucker just walked into my house.

The guy lowers his head like a bull preparing to charge. I sidestep and as he passes, I stiff-arm him. Stopped short, he falls backward onto the floor. But he still reaches out to try and sweep my legs out from under me. He catches me by surprise and I fall. I wasn't expecting him to actually know how to fight. Now I know better.

As he gets to his feet, I follow suit. He comes at me with a hook aimed for my head. I block him and send a jab to his gut. I hear him lose his breath, but without stopping for even a second, he keeps trying to wail on me.

As much as I want to end this, I still don't want to hurt this guy. If I were back home and this was like the fights I had there, one of us would probably be on the floor, down-for-the-count by now. Instead of doing what I normally would, I keep sending jabs to this guy's stomach and light hits everywhere. This guy isn't fighting like anyone on the surface, so why treat him like he is?

"Hey, wake up!" I yell in his face. No response. How rude.

"I said, WAKE UP!" I deliver a strong right hook to his temple. The guy crumples to the ground. "Oh, that is so not good," I say to myself. "Please don't be dead, please don't be dead." I start to shake the guy in hope that he'll wake up. By the time I move on to slapping him across the face, three more people turn the corner into the hall. It's bad enough that I'm standing over some guy who looks like he's dead, but I'm not from around here, and to top it all off, I'm still beating the guy!

The three new people start walking towards me. Best case, they're doctors who'll tell me the guy I just stopped slapping is still alive, then fix whatever's wrong with his head. Worst case, they're cops, muggers, New Power, evil space ninjas, or some combination thereof.

"Hey, are you guys evil space ninjas?" I shout over to them. They say something I can't hear, and seem to be intensely conferring with each other as they walk closer. That's usually not a good sign. I strain my ears trying to hear what they're saying, but it doesn't do me any good. When they get within earshot, they become silent, stopping in their tracks a couple dozen feet away from me. They're probably scared because of what they're seeing. I open my mouth to say something, but the three newbies speak up first.

"Get him!" one of them yells. The three run at me.

"Oh crap!" I yell, getting up off the floor and taking off.

I hope you're paying attention to where I'm going because I have no idea! I think to Dac.

On it, he says. Believing that I'll be able to follow Dac's directions to get back, I don't hold back as I sprint at top speed, taking several random turns hoping to lose them. But no matter what I do, my three stalkers don't seem to be going anywhere anytime soon.

Out of my peripheral vision, I see a Hub coming

up, illuminated by the lights of the Water Nation. Why not? I take the next turn towards the giant bubble, and continue in a straight shot to the Hub. I enter the Hub, which looks like a surface city meeting a sky city, contained inside a huge bubble. I don't take the time to soak in any more details than that. I am still running after all.

Need a place to hide. Need a place to hide. Looking around, I take a quick turn and see a perfect wall to hide behind. I vault over it, my foot catching the edge and fall to the ground. At least I got down here quickly. Lying flat on the ground I hear the three run past, taking heaving breaths. They come to a stop way too close for comfort. It sounds like they walk to the side of the road opposite the wall I'm hiding behind. Damn. If I kept running, they'd be out of my hair, but now they're right across the street from me! If they at least really were bad guys I could fight them seriously!

"Fast little sucker, isn't he?" one of the guy says between sucking in deep breaths.

"Scum know how to run," another of the three says. True.

Don't sound so proud of that.

"I know," replies the first one, "but he was moving faster than anyone I've ever seen. Did you look at him? He wasn't even *half* as tired as we are." False. I feel dead right now.

"It doesn't matter," the third puts in. "Whoever that guy was, he's long gone. Let's report this to Lynch."

The first man remarks, "Man, that's the one thing that sucks about this. Why do we have to report back to Lynch or a commander all the time?"

"Because we all joined the New Power and that's the way it is," answers the second. I catch my already held breath, if that's even possible.

Did you just hear that? I ask Dac.

Yup.

Volunteers?

Yup.

This isn't good.

Nope.

"Whatever. Let's go," I hear the first voice say, after which it sounds like they're walking off.

Who do you think Lynch is? I ask Dac, not getting up until I'm sure the three officially confirmed goons are gone.

Steven's master?

Maybe. That's actually exactly what I was thinking. If it is him, I plan to end this whole thing soon.

When I haven't heard the goons for a while, I get up and climb back over the wall. Now that I'm not being chased anymore, I can take a minute to look around and see what's inside the Hub.

It resembles a small city. There aren't many tall

buildings in here, maybe four or five stories is the tallest, even though the ceiling goes much higher. All the really tall ones are elsewhere and extend right into the water. The road looks like it's only for people, not cars or any other types of vehicles. This particular Hub looks to be a residential area, as it's lined with houses. This doesn't look like the most expensive place down here, but I'm sure it's better than the others. It's better than most places on the surface.

Most of the houses are dark, without a single light on. I avoid the few that are lit up. I would ask Dac to lead me right back to where we're staying, but I'm pretty sure the goons headed back that way to collect their friend. I start walking around the Hub, checking things out and looking for a possible alternate route to get back to the others.

I come across a tunnel that looks darker than the others. If I look out into the water, I don't see many lights at all in the direction this tunnel is going. There weren't many buildings near where I was staying. Maybe this'll be a way back. I start walking down the tunnel. I have no idea if I'm going the right way or not, but I'm walking. I take fewer turns than before. I keep hoping that I'll randomly stumble upon my destination, but no such luck. There aren't any useful landmarks I can use down here, either. It's not like someone's going to come up and say, "Turn left at the air bubbles, moron."

Well, maybe they would, but it wouldn't do much good. It's like when people tried to tell me to use a cloud as a reference point in the Sky Nation.

After walking a bit further, I see something.

"Finally," I say to myself. I keep walking towards what I see, happy that I've finally found my way back. When I get closer to the building, my elation fades. The building I saw is not where I'm staying. "Great. Just great." It's another Hub. I throw my arms in the air in frustration. Whatever. I've come this far, might as well see what's there. I shove my hands in my pockets and continue on towards the strangely dark Hub.

It's going to take you forever to get back here, Dac says out of nowhere. *The New Power recruits are probably long gone by now anyway.*

I might as well see what's over there.

You're an idiot, Dac says unwaveringly.

So I've been told.

I'm slapping you with a hammer – or John – when you get back.

You'll forget, I try to convince him.

No, I won't. Now go be a moron. I'm hitting you no matter what at this point.

Lovely.

It doesn't take me long to get to the Hub. The lighting inside is so dim that it's comparable to the light a full moon provides during a blackout on the surface. In comparison to everywhere else that I've seen down here, it might as well be pitch black. Being my impatient self, I don't bother waiting for my eyes to adjust.

You're gonna get stabbed, Dac informs me. He doesn't say it like there's someone behind me with a knife, but more like a definite prediction. I pause for a moment, flick my shoes, and keep walking.

I can't feel that, Dac informs me.

I know, but it makes me feel better.

The buildings in this Hub are more dilapidated and less taken care of than the ones in the first Hub. There are even some buildings that have crumbled to the ground. A good amount are missing specific chunks of them or have serious damage, but are still standing. A small number of the collapsed buildings look like an explosion is what put them down. Maybe this place was for weapons testing. Nah, there aren't any bullet holes or sword marks or anything like that, and there are shops and houses everywhere.

While I'm busy looking around, I trip over something. Actually, I should say some*one*. There's some guy sleeping in the middle of the road. That's weird. Now that my eyes are better adjusted to the darkness, I can see more of my surroundings. The place is so quiet I'm starting to hear a humming in my ears. I'm used to constant deafening noise, thanks to the factories, and my ears have had this annoying hum in ever since. I rarely hear it though.

This place is weird. As I walk along, I hear some people talking. I walk towards the voices, hoping that it's someone sane.

"Let go of me!" I hear a girl scream. Her voice comes from the direction of the voices. "Help! Help!"

Do you think she's faking it? Dac asks me. I start running toward the sound of the struggle, any lingering fatigue from my merry chase forgotten. *Why do you always have to put yourself in the worst situations?*

It just works out that way, I reply. I race toward the screaming girl. Her cries are suddenly cut off. I charge toward where I think the voice was coming from. It's a little harder now that I don't have a guide. I turn a corner and stop. Standing before me but facing the opposite direction, are three fully-armored New Power creeps, dragging a gagged girl along.

"Hey ugly!" I yell at them. All three turn around. "Man, I'm sorry. You guys aren't ugly, you're hideous!" I can see the anger rising in their faces. They look like they want to come over and hit me. Good.

Even though your insults are getting better, you really have to move past the 'ugly' comments, Dac interjects.

"Did you get your looks from your mother?" I continue.

In this case, it's okay continuing with the appearance of their moms. It's not usually a good idea, none of the looks based stuff is, but this time it looks like it worked.

"Why don't you shut your trap before you get hurt," the brave guy on the left says to me.

"Look, I can tell you're upset," I say. "You don't like me, and I don't like you. Let the girl go and come over here so we can settle our differences here and now."

"Sounds good to me," says the only one who seems capable of thought. He pulls out one of the electrically-charged batons that all New Power apparently carry. "Come on," the speaker says to his friends, gesturing at me with his head. "We'll bring the boss another one."

The two quiet ones look at each other for a moment. The one holding the girl throws her off to the side before the both of them draw their batons and head toward me.

"Oh come on guys, that's not fair," I say, backing away from their advance. I stick my hand in my pocket and grab my Sky Iron sword. I place my hands above my head, the shrunken down sword concealed in my fist. The goons laugh as they come right up on me.

I smile. "For you," I bring my arm down in an arc, elongating my blade as I go. I cut through the armor of the one who did all the talking, slicing down through skin and muscle. I stop myself before I hit bone. These guys are definitely goons. Violence is okay.

I take a step back as the guy screams and falls to his knees. My sword is emitting its usual brilliant white light, illuminating the scene. I note how much more radiant the sword is here, compared to its glow in the Sky Nation. It's ridiculously bright down here.

I see blood drip out of the armor of the guy I cut. Gross. I feel bad for goading him to attack me, then surprising him like that, but he was coming at me with murder in his eyes, and they were trying to kidnap the girl.

"I'm going to get you for that!" the guy yells at me when he's done screaming in pain. He gets up off the floor and swings at me with his baton. I deflect it. "You're going to pay! Get him!" he yells to his friends. Is it a requirement for joining the New Power to have anger issues?

One of the other goons comes to assist, but the third doesn't move. Apparently he either wasn't expecting any resistance, or this is his first fight. I can't worry about him right now. I've already got two people trying to beat the crap out of me.

I dance between my two attackers, avoiding having them on either side of me. They swing like they want to hack off my head, but that'll be hard without anything sharp. They're not the most skilled fighters I've ever gone up against, but they're not bad. One swings, I duck. The other comes at me, and I deflect him with my sword. I take a step back, hoping for a second to breathe, but not even a blink later, they're right back on me. One runs at me with his baton over his head. I ram my shoulder into him and push hard, making him fall back onto the floor. The one I injured already is still standing, and he brings his baton down at a diagonal. I lean out of the way of his baton, hearing the electricity crackle from how close it was to my ear. I knock his arm out of the way and cut across his chest. My sword again penetrates his armor and slashes him around his ribs. The blade hits the hardness of bone, but without enough force to cut it.

His armor clatters as he falls to the floor. His friend, who has gotten up by now, grabs his arm and starts dragging him away. The third New Power who didn't fight rushes up to help. I could go after them, but it doesn't feel right. Instead, I leave them with a warning.

"You better get out of the New Power before you end up like him, or worse," I shout.

They start moving away faster, dragging their unconscious friend behind them. I watch them until they turn a corner and I lose them.

"That was easy," I say to myself. I shrink my sword and put it back into my pocket. Without the light from the Sky Iron, the area is once again dim, bathed only in dim light like that from the moon. Not like the moon will reach down here, but that's what it feels like.

I walk over to where the goons tossed the girl. I'm almost positive she isn't there anymore, but if she is, I want to make sure she's okay.

When I get to the spot, all I find is a piece of cloth on the ground. It's probably what they used to gag her.

"Figures," I say to myself, bending to pick up the cloth. As I straighten up, I feel something cold on my throat, and someone grabbing me around the waist.

"Don't. Move," a girl's voice says from behind me.

Chapter Nine

"Who are you? What do you want?" demands the girl who grabbed me, pressing harder with the knife blade she's holding to my throat.

"Um, my same is Sam Cutter and I want to not get killed please."

"We'll see about that," the girl says. "Come on, I'm taking you to the others."

"I guess I don't really have a choice, do I?" I say. She starts walking. With the knife still at my throat I have to go where she's directing. I could stab her and get out of this easily, but the New Power had something against her. She can't be all bad, can she? The girl takes me through the Hub, leading me to I don't know where.

Seemingly picking a building at random, the girl looks around cautiously before we enter. The doors look like they used to be glass sliding doors, but they're stuck in the open position now, and the glass looks like it's been long gone. The structure in its entirety looks like a bomb was set off inside it, but one not powerful enough to completely implode it, just to take off chunks here and there and wreak havoc inside.

The buildings a couple story's tall, but it looks like the majority of the floors have been demolished, making the place look more like a grunge amphitheater than anything. Tons of people are sitting around talking to each other, adding to the amphitheater look. Maybe this is some sort of meeting hall. I don't think there's anywhere in here that a body isn't occupying. I notice a giant "XIV" burnt into the ground, probably with a welding torch or something more powerful. All the chatting and noise fades to silence as everyone catches sight of the girl and me.

"Who's this wet-head?" asks some guy who looks like he's in a position of power.

"He said his name's Sam Cutter," the girl replies.

"What kind of a name is 'Cutter'?" he asks.

"Mine," I reply, annoyed.

"Shut up, wet-head. I wasn't talking to you." What's a wet-head? "Where'd you find 'im?" the guy continues.

"Couple blocks from here."

"What was he up to?"

"He saved me. Fought off some New Power Snatchers," she explains. It feels like everyone in the room leans forward to hear better.

"So why do you have him at knifepoint?" An excellent

question. All eyes, except for mine, shift to the girl.

"He's got a magic sword," the girl says. Oh, you have *got* to be kidding me. "He makes it appear out of nowhere and it glows. Even if he didn't have the sword, he still beat three Snatchers like they were nothing." All eyes back on me.

"I was bored," I say. Maybe not the smartest thing to say, but when has that ever stopped me? Everyone starts talking, wondering if I'm dangerous. The guy that looks like the leader shushes everyone. He leans forward, his chair creaking.

"So are you with us, or against us?" he asks.

"I don't even know who you are," I say.

"We are the lost, the forgotten. We are those who have lost their place in society and can't afford to live out there with the others." So they're just a bunch of people with no money who've made this their home. I can relate.

"Look, I just got lost," I say. "I don't want to cause any trouble. I'll be on my way if you let me go."

"Can't," the guy says. "Snatchers are still out. You can go in an hour, when they're gone." Fair enough. They don't want me accidentally giving away the location of their hideout.

"Britney," the leader says. The girl that grabbed me looks up. So that's her name. "Take him with you. Make sure he doesn't try to leave until it's good and safe."

"Why me?" Britney protests.

"You brought him here. He's your problem." The guy leans back in his chair. "Now go!" He dismisses us with a wave of his hand.

"This sucks," Britney mumbles under her breath. "Follow me, please," she says to me, finally putting her knife away. She starts walking, making sure that I'm following her. We go out a different door than the one we came in. It looks like an exit to the back streets. I turn around once we're outside and memorize what the hideout looks like, just in case I ever need to find it again. There isn't anything very distinguishing about the building from the outside, but I think I can recognize it again.

"Look, thanks for saving me," Britney says, her voice softening.

"Your knife really hit that home," I say, rubbing my neck.

"I didn't know if I could trust you. I thought you were going to hurt me," she replies, avoiding my eyes.

"Right, because I totally would've risk my neck to help you, just so I can come after you myself." We walk in silence for a moment. "How do I know that I can trust *you*?" I ask.

"I saved your life in there."

"Right," I say sarcastically. "Sure." She doesn't say anything in response.

Britney leads me down side street after side street until she stops in front of another building. We're at a door in a narrow hall that seems more like a hole in a wall. "Try not to break anything," she tells me as she steps through it. Is she kidding?

It's a small place. The entry opens into the largest of the rooms, which is pretty barren. There's a decrepit old couch, and blankets tossed here and there. The walls literally have holes in them. There's only a single light illuminating the entire place, and it's flickering like it's on its way out. I can also see a bathroom, bedroom, and small kitchen.

"Reminds me of home," I say to myself. My mom and I had a little more than this in our two-story house, although neither of us was ever there much. Mom would come home at night, but more often than not, I would have to stay at the factory.

Britney sits on the couch. "You can leave in an hour or so," she says to me. "Snatchers'll be gone by then."

"Okay," I say and sit down next to her. She turns her head to look away.

For a moment, I think of the others. *Is everyone awake back there?* I ask Dac.

Yeah, and Mark's back with all your phones. He pauses, then adds, *Jinn's up in arms, ready to look for you.*

Tell him I'm fine. I'll be out of here soon.

I know, I told all of them. But that didn't calm them down much, if at all.

They must think I'm really fragile.

No, Dac says. *They just know you and think you'll get into trouble... which you did.*

Details. Back in reality, I hear a squeaking sound.

I am reality you jerk! Dac makes sure I know.

I sigh, then look over and see a kid half-hiding behind the doorframe of the bedroom.

"Aw, Gus," Britney says. She goes over and hugs the kid. She leads him out and sits back on the couch. He curls up into her, never taking his eyes off me. He can't be more than about ten years old.

Gus looks like he's probably underfed and his eyes show that he has had a hard life, but still somehow hold the innocence of childhood. He has the same color hair as Britney, and nearly the same skin color. His eyes are, of course, the cloudy grey everything that is characteristic of the Water Nation.

"Gus, this is Sam," Britney says, pointing to me. "He saved me from some Snatchers. Sam, this is Gus, my little brother." That makes sense.

Now that Gus knows I fought some of these "Snatchers," he's looking at me like I'm one of the most amazing things on the planet. I'm guessing not many people fight the New Power down here. Not a whole lot did in the Sky Nation, either.

"Nice to meet you," I say to the kid. His mouth drops open, and he just stares at me for a moment.

"Want to see my cannon?" he asks me excitedly, out of nowhere.

"Gus, not now," Britney says.

"Uh, sure," I say. Gus grins and runs into the bedroom as though pounds and pounds of sugar and caffeine were directly injected into his bloodstream. He reappears seconds later dragging a foot tall miniature cannon. He pushes it to the center of the room and takes aim at the wall. Gus sits back, tightly holding a string in his hand. He looks at Britney and me before looking back to where he's aiming.

"FIRE!" he yells, violently jerking the string back. There's a loud boom as the cannon fires. It recoils, and flames shoot out the front as a solid ball of metal flies out and lodges itself in the wall. The only noise is Gus shrieking with delight as I sit in stunned silence. I realize that I brought my hands up to shield my face and quickly put them in my lap. I look from Britney, who looks like she's used to this, to the wall with yet another hole in it, to the lethal, giggling kid.

I like your new friend.

You would.

Britney sighs. "Someday your little cannon is going to blow up the entire Hub."

"You think?" Gus asks enthusiastically. Britney rolls

her eyes and shakes her head in disapproval.

"His dream is to make a big one," she explains, "I think he might've even started building it already." For some reason or another, that's genuinely terrifying.

That's awesome!

Nobody asked you.

Hey, it's my right to drive you insane and bother you at all hours. In fact, I think I'll sing. He breaks out into song. I'm really going to hurt him when I get back.

No you can't, Dac sings, flawlessly adding the lyrics to his annoying song. I growl at him.

Gus is in the process of reloading when the front door is slammed open to reveal a man standing in the doorway.

"What were you thinking?" he says, scowling when he sees me. "You brought him back here?"

"Where else was I supposed to take him?" she answers in an innocent tone.

"Raaa!" Gus roars, jumping onto the mystery man and grabbing him tightly.

"Hey, Gussy," he says, holding onto Gus so he won't fall down.

"Sam, meet my other brother, Connor," Britney says.

"Hey, wet-head," he says to me.

"Er...nice to meet you," I reply. It looks like Connor is the oldest in the family.

Connor turns back to his sister, ignoring me. "You

have no idea what kind of commotion you caused by bringing him here, Brit."

"I had to do something with him," she says. "He would've gotten himself in trouble out there." Probably true.

"If he could take on the Snatchers, he'll be fine," Connor counters, not believing his sister.

"Would *you* have left him there?" Britney asks Connor.

"For the safety of everybody here, yes." Harsh. "You did something really stupid, Brit." He adds condescendingly. Britney glares at her brother, looking defeated and on the verge of tears.

"Maybe I'll just go," I say, not wanting to be an issue for this family.

"Maybe you should," Connor says.

"No, Connor, he was told to stay. What if someone gets him?" Britney objects, stepping towards her brother.

"Not my problem," Connor says. I've overstayed my welcome. I stand up and push past Connor to leave. He follows me with his eyes as I go.

"Sam," Britney starts, but I cut her off.

"I'll be fine," I say. "I'll see you guys around, I guess." With that, I leave.

Where do I go? I ask Dac. He starts giving me directions and I follow them. I pass through city streets.

Even though they were talking about how the New Power is supposed to be all over the place there isn't another soul out here. It's just as barren as it was when I first came in until I heard Britney scream. Maybe all the losers heard about how someone actually fought back and got scared.

Don't get overconfident, Dac says.

Yeah, yeah, yeah. Whatever. Really, I'm not worried.

Don't forget that you were running away from some New Power not too long ago.

That was before I fought three off, I remind him.

One of them didn't even fight.

He was probably a newbie, I speculate.

Who knows? Dac says, unwilling to give me a victory.

While I'm walking, I see largely printed on the wall of the glass dome is "Hub 14." At least I know where I am.

I keep walking, having to follow the exact route I took to get here because that's what Dac has memorized. I stop paying attention to what's around me at some point and just start turning whenever I'm told to. I ignore Dac when he tells me to transform into a seal and crawl the rest of the way back. I don't humor him with that one.

Before I make it out of Hub 14, I hear voices. And it sounds like they're coming closer. I hide behind the nearest building, pressing my back up against the wall.

I peer around the corner, revealing as little of me as possible. Out of the corner of my eye, I catch some New Power guys walking around.

"Is it almost time to go?" one of them is asking the other.

"Yeah, pretty much," the other says. "We've got four of them already. Lynch'll be happy."

"Sounds good. I'm beat." They continue to talk as they keep walking, so I don't really hear much more of their conversation. I slide around the building to a different vantage point, not wanting to lose sight of them. Finally they round a corner far enough away, and I continue on. But I keep an eye out for any others who might be lurking around.

I pass through the tunnels, reaching the spot where the crazy guy was smashing his head against the wall. How do I know it's the right spot? There's blood on the wall and on the floor, but no body. I guess the guys that chased after me must've come back for him. Either that, or he woke up.

I glance in the direction it looks like the crazy guy came from, debating whether or not to check it out. Eh, maybe now's not the best time. I don't want to keep the others waiting.

Still. I turn around to keep walking towards the complex I'm staying in, but I twist my head so that I can look down the mysterious path. I'm going to find out what's over there, but not now. Soon, but not now.

With that, I walk the rest of the way back to the complex.

Chapter Ten

"Where were you?" Jinn demands the instant he sees me.

"I went for a walk," I say. "It's no big deal."

"You could've gotten hurt," he continues.

"But I didn't. Geez, you're starting to sound worse than my mom."

"Well excuse me if I don't want my prince to get killed."

"Don't call me that," I reply angrily. I *hate* that. I hate royalty. Hate the fact that I am one technically. I've tried asking nicely not to call me *that*, but it seems Jinn isn't listening. "You personally beat the crap out of me day in and day out. Why is it such a big deal now if anything happens?"

"Because Jinn has a sense of duty," Nathan interjects as he comes down the stairs. Even though he's fully dressed in his normal clothes, he's stretching, yawning, and rubbing his eyes, like he just woke up and would really rather still be in bed. "Jinn has always been protective of us," Nathan continues. "Now that he knows you're related to my sister, he'll be just as protective of you."

"Is it so wrong that I want to protect the royal lineage?" Jinn asks. I say "yes" at the same time Nathan says "no."

"It hasn't even been a week," I say, "and it's driving me nuts."

"You get used to people acting like that," Nathan says, imparting his wisdom.

"I don't want to get used to it," I argue. Actually, more like yell at Nathan. He looks at me as if nobody has ever reprimanded him before. Well tough luck, buddy. There's a first time for everything.

"Sam," Jinn says, "I may be more protective now, but I'll try to be as close as I was before."

"No, don't try," I say. "Do." He looks at me like I'm asking a lot of him. "I don't want to be treated any differently than I was before. I was fine with that."

"Okay," Jinn says. It looks like I got my point across, although I'm not sure if he fully accepts it. "Stop insulting Nathan, though," he adds. There he goes again, protecting Nathan! Man, he is so whipped!

"You're not getting it," I say. "Why does 'royalty' need someone to protect them from the world?"

"Because we're above it," Nathan says. Before I know

what I'm doing, I whirl around to punch him, but Jinn and Mark grab me before I can connect.

"Let go of me!" I yell at them, still trying to get at Nathan.

"What's your problem?" Mark hollers at me, straining to keep me away from Nathan, who looks like he's taking all this in stride.

"Someone needs to teach him something," I say. I jerk forward, but they don't let me move.

"Sam, calm down! Stop!" Jinn says. "Dac, a little help here." I'm surprised he has Dac's nickname memorized. It's probably because he's always been good at remembering names.

Dac stands in the corner, arms crossed, unmoving.

"You haven't seen what Sam's been through," Dac says. "You haven't lived it... I'm with him." Jinn lets go of me, leaving Mark alone to do all the work, and stares at Dac in shock. The lights that serve as Dac's "eyes" give nothing away. They look cold and hard.

Wait! I have an idea. I stop struggling against Mark, who slowly lets go of me. Hanging my head, standing next to Jinn, but facing the opposite direction, I say two words to him.

"Fight me."

"What?" he asks.

"Fight. Me," I say again.

"No way," Jinn exclaims, turning me around to face

him. "I'm not going to fight you. That wouldn't make sense anymore."

"It makes perfect sense," I say, looking up at him through my eyelashes. "I'm going to show you that I can protect myself just fine."

"No," he says firmly.

"What?" I ask. "Scared I'll beat you?"

"Sam, don't," Mark says, warning me off from challenging Jinn.

"We don't need real swords," I say. "Just the equivalent." Jinn looks around, obviously trying to figure a way out of this.

"Fight him," Gabriel says, now coming down the stairs himself. "The boy wants to prove something. Give him a chance."

"But –" Jinn starts.

"But nothing," Gabriel cuts him off. "Sam wants you to back off and knows that won't happen unless he proves to you that he can take care of himself. I see no problem here." I knew there was a reason I liked Gabriel. "I'll call Kane to get you something to use as weapons, so we don't end up with bloody messes on our hands." He heads outside while pulling out his phone to ring Kane.

As soon as Gabriel is out the front door, Jinn looks at me again and lets out a huff of air.

"What are you thinking?" he asks me. "You know I'm the best fighter in all of the Sky Nation."

"I'm thinking that you need to stop acting like I'm something to protect. Nothing bad has even happened since you've been treating me like this. You need to calm down."

"Or maybe you need to stop acting like such a child," Jinn says.

"I'm fifteen! What do you expect, that I'm going to act like I'm fifty?"

"He's got you there," Mark says. Since I'm acting like a kid anyway, I sulk off to my room without another word, slamming the door behind me.

I pace my room in frustration. Who does Jinn think he is? Just because he's older than me doesn't mean he's any better. And what is with Nathan? Acting like it's alright that Jinn jumps at his every beck and call... it's not! What the hell is he thinking? Maybe he's been alive so long there's nothing but dust and cobwebs in his head. People like him make me so mad, sometimes I think killing them is the best option! I hate people like Nathan and his brother. I thought he'd be different, but so far it seems like Nathan is growing up to be just like his brother Logan.

I punch the wall in frustration, sending my fist right through it. If I wasn't so angry right now, I'd probably be excited I could do that.

Fight Jinn? I should've got Nathan to fight me. The most that'll come out of this is that Jinn will treat me like normal again. I'd get so much more satisfaction out of kicking Nathan's ass.

True, but you wouldn't be as happy, Dac says in my head.

Why are you talking in my head right now, man? I ask him. *You have a body. You can come and talk to me in person.*

As much as I love the body, it's much better talking to you this way, Dac starts. *Everything I need to say can be much more easily conveyed. Have you forgotten I can access your emotions, too?* Actually, I forgot. Now I feel stupid. *Would you prefer that I come up there?*

No. No, that's fine, I sigh. I lay down on the bed, covering my face with my hands and letting out a sigh. What the hell is with these people, anyway? Why can't there be a single good king out there? I mean, come on! All three of them suck! Well, at least the Sky Nation and Water Nation aren't ruled by tyranny. And I suppose their entire populations don't hate the world like us on the Surface.

"Holy crap!" I hear someone yell. I sit up and see an eye looking through the hole I punched in the wall. "Remind me never to piss you off again," John says, still looking at me.

"Would you go away?" I ask him. "Not in a good mood."

"I know," he says. "I was there. Let me know when

you want to talk." With that, the eye disappears.

I lie around for a while longer, feeling moody. I think about how similar Nathan is to Logan, yet also so different from him. Finally I hear someone calling me from downstairs. I walk out into the hall so I can hear them more clearly.

"What?" I yell down the stairs.

"Kane's here. Are you ready?" Mark yells up.

"Ready as I'll ever be," I yell back. I head downstairs, ready to get this fight over with. It'll be easy. I'll just beat Jinn, and everything will go back to normal. Right?

What is normal for you? Dac asks. *Really, you've traveled to all three of the nations, your apparently the first person to do that, your dad hates you, the girl you have a major crush on has a boyfriend—*

Boyfriends aren't forever! I argue.

And you have me. I can speak with you telepathically. That's not normal for most people. He has a point.

Okay, so maybe I don't know what "normal" is for me, I admit, *but I know that Jinn has never kneeled before me or offered to do everything or been overprotective before.* Dac doesn't respond.

Everyone is gathered downstairs, and Jinn is standing there holding an arc-sword, one of the electrical weapons from the arena in the Sky Nation. My guess is that Nathan and Kane worked together on creating those. Kane extends another sword to me. I

130

take it and flick it on. It'll work.

"So where are we going to do this?" I ask. Suddenly, everyone looks confused.

"I have no idea," Kane says. "We don't have many large, open spaces. I suppose you can fight right in front of this building, although there are bigger areas farther away."

"Just outside will be fine," Jinn says. "Sam says he can best me, let's see him prove it. He won't always have the best conditions anyway."

"Isn't that the truth," I say, thinking about some of the fights I've had over the past year. Getting caught on a conveyer belt in a factory is not a good thing. I walk out the door, knowing the others will follow. Really, it only matters if Jinn comes out or not, but nobody's going to want to miss this show. I turn around when I'm about fifty feet or so from the building.

Jinn is standing opposite me, finally looking like he's going to be serious. Everybody else is still filing out of the building and lining up against the wall. I really hope this'll be worth it. Honestly, I'm not dying to fight him, but I just want him to back off.

"Let's just get this over with," I say with a shrug. Jinn turns his arc-sword on, and instantaneously a column of electricity forming a sword shoots out. I do the same. We stand, unmoving, for a while, waiting for the other to act. In the blink of an eye, I start running at Jinn. He takes a few steps to help close the distance.

Our swords meet, creating the familiar whine of two arc blades connecting. I can smell ozone as it permeates throughout the air.

We push against each other to try and gain the upper hand. I quickly disengage, knowing that standing there pushing all day won't get me anywhere.

Jinn takes a step back with the disconnect, then leans into his next hit, putting his full weight behind the attack. He aims for my chest from the side, but I brush him off with a slight deflection and a few quick steps back. He hit so hard that I nearly lose my sword. I'm not given any breathing room as Jinn comes back across, lunging forward, not losing any momentum. I twist to the side so that my body is perpendicular to his. I'm just in time as his sword harmlessly passes through the spot where I was just standing.

I try to bring my sword down on his arm, but he pulls it away before I can connect. I bring the sword back up, ready to defend myself. I know that if I show him a second of weakness, it'll mean my defeat.

Are you planning on hitting him any time soon? Dac asks me out of nowhere.

WORKING ON IT!

I can't decide what's better to be on right now, offence or defense. Luckily, I know how to do both. I duck under another of Jinn's attacks, but he keeps getting closer and closer with each attempt. He's going to connect soon enough.

I kick Jinn back, knocking him flat on the floor. I go to slice at him and hopefully end this, but before I can hit him, he flips me.

He grabs my arms and plants his foot at the center of my stomach and guides me over him. I don't hit the ground like I expect. I smack against a wall instead. How did we wind up this close to the side of the tunnel? I slide down the wall, hitting the ground head first. Surprised and hurting, I let go of my sword. I'd love to take a moment to breath and then work on standing up, but I wont give Jinn the opportunity to get me. Using the wall for support, I push myself up, ignoring the pounding in my head. I scan the ground for my sword and pick it up once I find it. I feel like throwing up when I move my head. Probably best not to let Jinn know that. Luckily for me, Jinn dropped his sword as well when he grabbed me.

He is standing before I am, but his sword flew farther away. He must've thrown it when he fell instead of just dropping it. We both have our arc blades ready and in hand at about the same time. Difference? Jinn isn't swallowing his own vomit right now. Yeah, that'll be a problem. I raise my sword, feigning that I'm ready to fight, and Jinn raises his an instant later.

Even though we haven't been fighting long at all,

I'm already starting to sweat. It looks like Jinn is, too. But at the moment, I'm a little more concerned with the crackling beam of electricity in his hand than if he'll need a shower when we're done. I roll my sore shoulders and feel pain shooting up through my neck. Letting myself focus on that would be stupid, so I try to block out the pain.

Suddenly Jinn straightens, lowering his sword. What is he doing? "Okay, we're done," he says.

"No, we're not," I say. "A while back you told me never to trust you as long as you're holding something to hit me with and we're training, or sparring, or whatever." Jinn smiles, a gesture that could be good... or really, really bad. I'm guessing the latter.

He turns the arc blade off and puts it on the floor. "Happy?" he says. "Now come over here. I'll stop trying to protect you like I do the kings, you snot-nosed brat." He sticks his hand out to shake mine. I turn my arc blade off, but I don't drop it.

I walk over to shake Jinn's hand, fully expecting him to try something. I reach out to grab his hand, my eyes never leaving his. As soon as I make contact, the trap is sprung.

Jinn holds on tight and grabs my forearm with his free hand. He jerks me forward, trying to knock me to the ground so he can pin me. Knowing that he was going to try something, I'm somewhat prepared.

I grab onto his shirt, balling it into my fist, and jerk him around so that his weight isn't directed how he wanted it. I drag him down with me and because I over balance him, instead of falling down on top of me like he wanted, Jinn and I end up next to each other.

"Gotcha," I say through gritted teeth as I immediately roll onto him, never letting go of his shirt. I raise my free hand up in a fist.

"I win," I say triumphantly. "No more tricks. I beat you. Game over." I notice that my words are muffled by the sound of blood rushing through my ears, but I pay it no mind. I keep Jinn pinned, with his chest heaving as he gasps for breath, waiting for him to say something.

"Alright," he says at last, letting his muscles relax. "You can take care of yourself, and then some." Finally. It took him long enough. "Now get off me. I want to get something to eat."

I slowly get to my feet, and reach my hand out to help him up. When he's standing, before we can even take a step, I start to fall over. Jinn catches me and lets me hurl. There's all sorts of pretty colors in what comes out of me.

"Hit your head pretty hard?" he asks me.

"Oh yeah," I respond, trying to hold my head together with one hand. Jinn helps me hobble back inside. As we walk by the others, still lined up and leaning against the wall of the complex itself, I hear Nathan say something.

"Looks like you're getting old, eh Jinn?"

"Look who's talking," I say without stopping, pushing the door open. That shuts him up. When we get inside, I want to go to my room, but the prospect of walking up a flight of stairs right now is daunting. Instead, I see a couch and claim it as my own. I would make a flag and stab it into the couch, claiming this as Sam-pia, but there are a couple problems with that.

One, I don't have a flag.

Two, I don't think Gabriel would like that I stabbed his furniture.

I gingerly lower myself onto the couch. My head is still swimming, but I have a feeling lying down is going to help. Jinn comes over.

"Sit up," he says. I think about protesting, but then I see the electric-blue beverage in his hand.

"I didn't know you brought any of that down here," I say, straining to sit up.

"Very little," he says. "Only take a sip or two. I don't want to waste any." Fine. I gratefully accept it and take my two sips. The throbbing in my head instantly starts to dull. Now, instead of wanting to blow my brains out, I only want to smash every light and stop people from talking. The nausea is gone as well. All in all, it's a major improvement.

The volume level dramatically increases when the others come back into the house. I grab onto my head, trying to keep it from splitting apart, and fantasize about slapping a piece of duct tape over each of their mouths.

Well, aren't you Mister Sunshine-and-Rainbows? Dac says. Thankfully, hearing it in my head isn't nearly as painful as hearing actual talking.

Look through my memory, I say. *Go to when Jinn flipped me.* Dac is silent for a moment before I hear him say one word.

Ouch.

Yeah.

I turn my head, still cradled in my hands, and see Jinn and Nathan. It looks like they're arguing. Good. Jinn is actually standing up to the royals. Well, it's less like an argument and more like a heated conversation, but whatever.

"So why have you never let me fight you before?" Nathan asks Jinn.

"Let's not get into this, your majesty," Jinn is saying. Your majesty? Blah. Stupid. "*Your majesty*" Bah humbug.

"Well, why not?" Nathan persists.

"I don't want to answer," Jinn says.

"Why not?" Nathan's starting to sound like a little kid.

"Because I know you won't like it."

"I've been duly warned. Now tell me." Geez, calm down.

137

"I know you can't beat me," Jinn says after a pause. Oh, that's awesome.

Shhhhh, I'm listening. Shh? It's really hard to quiet your own thoughts.

Do you have popcorn?

What?

Never mind. He doesn't know the joys of popcorn.

"What?" Nathan asks, taken aback.

"You can't beat me," Jinn repeats in a monotone, taking a sip of water from a cup he's holding. When did he get that?

"Prove it," Nathan demands.

"I don't think that's really necessary," Jinn says.

"Jinn, I order you to fight me!" Oh great, now we're in the world of ordering people around. With how loyal he is, and how much he likes the royals, Jinn'll do it.

Jinn turns to me. "Sam, give Nathan the arc blade."

I knew that was coming. I take the weapon lying next to me, and weakly toss it over to Nathan. He goes to catch it with one hand, but it bounces out. He quickly reaches out with both hands to grab hold of it. Luckily, he gets it and pulls it to his chest. He may have looked lame, but at least he didn't drop it.

"Did anybody pick up mine from outside?" Jinn asks.

"Here," Kane says, handing it to Jinn. "Try not to hurt my baby brother too bad." Suddenly I like Kane a little bit more.

"I can't hold back if we want this to be a real fight," Jinn cautions.

"Alright," Kane says. He turns to his brother. "You're going to lose."

"We'll see about that!" Nathan pouts as he heads out the door. The crowd follows him more reluctantly than they did when it was Jinn and me. I'm glued to Sam-pia and don't plan on getting up anytime soon.

"You coming, Sam?" John asks me. I shake my head. He continues on his way out.

I look up and see that Dac and, oddly enough, Gabriel, remain inside.

"Why didn't you guys head out?" I ask.

I already know how this is going to end, Dac replies.

"I have no need to see my son humiliated," Gabriel says, taking a sip of something doubtlessly alcoholic. "May I?" he asks, gesturing to a seat next to the couch. Good, he doesn't want to invade Sam-pia. If he did, that would mean war.

I would probably lose.

"Go for it," I say, putting my head back in my hands. Then something occurs to me.

Chapter Eleven

"Do you really think Nathan's going to lose out there?" I ask Gabriel.

"I have no doubt in my mind," he says, taking another sip of his drink.

"But, why?"

"He's never been a fighter," Gabriel explains. "He's always been one for playing around and learning how to use things, but in all my years, I've never seen him show much interest in fighting."

"Do any of them fight?"

"Kane can hold his own," Gabriel says. "Sarah is good, but not as good as you and Jinn are." That's weird to think I'm a better fighter than two of the kings, and the queen. "Logan is the one that had a gift for violence." My stomach drops when I hear his name.

"Oh," I say in a monotone, trying to hide my hatred for Logan, even though I told Gabriel how much I despise his eldest son, the King of the Surface.

"I used to be quite the fighter myself," Gabriel continues either ignoring any spite I let slip or not noticing any. I'm guessing the former.

"Used to?" I ask.

"Yes," he says, "but I haven't had much cause for belligerence over the past few hundred years." I move my hand under my jaw to prevent it from dropping.

Holy crap, how old is he? Dac practically shouts in my head, somewhat voicing the same question I have.

What does that word mean? I ask back.

Violence. It means violence. Dac says, sorting through the dictionary that seems to be installed in his brain.

Why didn't he just say that then!? Seriously! Big words hurt.

"Isn't it kinda like riding a bike, though?" I ask. "Like something you don't forget. You just need to do it again, and you pick it right back up."

"I've yet to pick it back up again, though,'" Gabriel says.

"Maybe you should," I comment. "It's always a useful thing to be able to do."

"In all honesty, I haven't fought since all those years ago, when I first reigned the world in."

"What do you mean by that?"

"By what?"

"'Reigned the world in,'" I say, clarifying where I'm confused. "I've always wanted to believe that you did what you did for a good reason, but all the stories make you seem like a conqueror who did everything for power."

"I had my reasons," Gabriel says. He pauses and coughs. It's an ugly wet one that makes your chest rattle.

"You okay?" I ask.

"Fine, fine," he reassures me, waving it off. "Now, my story..."

"Clear the couch!" we hear Mark yell as he walks inside, kicking the door open. The fight must be over already. That was fast.

Gabriel stands up, but before he walks away, he turns to me and says, "We will finish our discussion later. Come find me tonight before you retire for the evening." Gabriel wanders to the kitchen, and it sounds like he's refilling his drink. I also get up from the couch, but instead of leaving, I just move to the closest soft-looking chair.

Kane and Jinn carefully carry in Nathan's limp body. Kane is holding him under his arms, and Jinn has his feet.

They lay him on the couch and take a step back. John, Rick, and Fred trail in a moment later. "I can't believe one of the great kings could lose like that," John says. "Makes me wonder if they all suck like that."

"Hey," Kane says sharply, glaring daggers at John. "Watch it! We can still kick your ass." I don't doubt that.

142

Well, in all fairness, John fought when the New Power attacked Jinn's house. He and my dad managed to hold their own then.

I sit there for a moment, blankly staring. Then something clicks in my mind.

"Kane," I say and he looks over at me, "what do you know about Hub Fourteen?"

He thinks for a moment before saying, "It was one of my original prototypes. The first twenty were early attempts at habitable communities. Not my greatest successes. Why?"

"Did you know there are still people living there?"

"No, I did not. I did not think my prototypes could sustain life for any period of time. Most of them collapsed. The last I knew, prototype Hubs Nineteen and Twenty were the only ones still standing."

"Well, Fourteen is still up as well," I tell him. "And here's the kicker, the people living there don't belong in the loony bin."

"You mean to say that their aggression levels are normal?" Kane asks. I forgot he likes technical terms.

"Uh, yeah," I say.

"Interesting," he remarks, lines creasing his forehead. "I must look into this."

"I'd be careful if you're planning on heading over there," I tell him seriously.

"Why?" Kane asks.

"The place is a mess. Buildings are crumbling, and the New Power likes to run around down there."

"Fascinating," he says.

"Just watch yourself."

"I'll bring Bean with me."

"Your butler?" I ask. "No offense, but he didn't strike me as much of a fighting type."

"Bean is very talented," Kane says without hesitation.

"If you say so," Kane starts to leave, but before he's out the door, I remember something else. "Oh," I say, stopping him.

"Was there something else?" he asks.

"Yeah. Do you know a guy named Lynch?" I ask.

"Why?"

"These guys that were chasing me—"

"I knew you were lying," Jinn cuts in. "It's never 'just a walk' with you." I don't care about his comment because it doesn't sound like he's reprimanding me. He sounds more like my friend again.

"Did you expect anything less?" I ask.

"I suppose not," Jinn says with a sigh, crossing his arms.

"Anyway," I say, getting back on track, "these guys that were chasing me said they had to report to this Lynch guy."

"You think he's the one in charge?" Jinn asks me. I nod.

"Yeah, I do. It makes sense. The people who've lost it and turned into soldiers are supposed to report back to this guy."

"This is something to consider," Kane says, "but right now I must gather supplies. When you are feeling better, Sam, contact me and we shall go investigate."

"Will I get a Scooby snack?" I ask.

"A what?" he asks me.

"Surface joke," I say. I look over at John, Rick, and Fred and see that they all get it. "Yeah, I'll let you know."

"Excellent," Kane says. "I will see you soon." With that he leaves. Interesting guy.

"What do we do with him?" Rick asks, pointing at Nathan.

"Just give him a couple hours," Mark says. "He'll be really cranky when he wakes up, but basically fine."

"And have a major headache," I add. "Oh, and if he's lucky, he'll be in the middle of a really dangerous jail break."

"And forget to use his brain and fly when he jumps out of a transport," Dac feels the need to add.

"No, he'll remember, just not right away."

"What are you guys talking about?" Jinn asks. I have a feeling he already knows, but it's still weird.

"Yeah, what are you talking about?" Sarah asks, confused.

"Oh, nothing," I say.

Brainless. Dac says in the privacy of my head.

You're just as much at fault, I argue, *You could've reminded me.*

I didn't think you were that stupid.

You know me! And besides, it looked really cool.

Can't argue there.

Sarah watches me staring off into thin air as I ramble on with Dac in my head. "Are they still fighting?" she asks anyone who's listening.

"You get used to it," Jinn says.

"I'm not sure I ever will," she says.

"That's what we all thought," Jinn says. "It's probably worse for you, though, because Dac actually has a body now, which makes things even more confusing."

"No kidding," Sarah says, and disappears up the stairs to her room. John, Rick, and Fred also disperse. Jinn and Mark carry Nathan up to his room, leaving Dac and me to "talk." Even though we're not talking. Close enough.

Who's bright idea was it to put a water trough in the Sky Nation anyway? It's not like they have horses! I continue going with Dac.

I was wondering that. And what are the odds of you landing in probably the only one up there?

I know, right!?

We should have a serious talk with Nathan about that when he wakes up, Dac remarks.

No kidding.

We both sit here in the living room. Dac still has his body down here with me. It's hard for me to see it though. Not literally, I mean, I know it's there and I see this big mass of metal easily, but it's different. I've always thought of Dac as being inside the boots, and when I heard him for the first time without them on, I started thinking of him as part of me. Even then, I kind of came up with my own version of his face and body. He was, and still is, human to me. Human, but different. Not the metal man, I'm sure the others are seeing him as. To me, his new body is more like a suit of armor he likes to wear. I think that John, Rick, Fred, and the kings all believe that Dac's body is like our own, where if it were somehow destroyed, he would die. But I don't believe that's true at all.

What's it like in there? I ask Dac. I don't need to elaborate because he already knows exactly what I'm thinking.

It's weird, Dac says. *It's like I'm here, but I'm not.*

What do you mean? I ask.

I have this body, and I can operate it, and see things around me through it, and talk and interact through it, but it doesn't feel right. It feels like I don't belong.

Then where do you feel like you belong?

Back in those, he says, pointing at the boots. *And stuck in that head of yours.*

147

You like being a copilot more than being the driver?

With you, it's not even being a copilot. It's just being able to insult you every step of the way.

You still do that, I remind him.

Yeah, but it was easier before. More natural.

I let out a loud, long breath. "After all that work I did to get you a body, you go and decide that you don't like it," I say aloud. My voice feels scratchy.

It's not that I don't like it, he explains. *It's just not normal.* Dac is still speaking straight into my head.

"What is normal for you?"

Good point. We sit in silence for a moment.

"What time is it anyway?" I ask suddenly.

I don't know. I'm not your digital clock, Dac says rudely.

"I didn't know," I say. "I've never asked you the time before." I take out my phone, which says that it's about ten at night. Although that's not too late, I realize how long Dac and I have been talking. "Oh shit," I say. "I need to go talk to Gabriel."

"I'll be eavesdropping," Dac informs me.

"I know." Sadly, it's true. There's nothing I could do about it anyway, even if I did have a problem with it.

I go to find Gabriel on the third floor. Dac follows me up to the second, but leaves for his room then. He's probably going to shut his body down for the night so that it can recharge... it's weird to think he's still in my

148

head and on my feet but walked away just now.

My head hurts.

At the top of the stairs to the third floor, there's a fairly large landing, and a single door. The rest of the floor lies behind the Door of Wonders. I don't bother knocking as I push the door open and walk inside.

Gabriel walks in from another room and says,"You could've knocked." He doesn't stop moving as he crosses the room and tosses something into another room, beyond my sight.

"Sorry," I say. "I'm impatient."

He shrugs. "Well come on in, and shut the door behind you." Oops, door. I lean back over and push the door shut.

It's huge in here. It's not just a bedroom like mine is. This is big enough that it could be an entire house back on the Surface. Without moving I can see a living room, kitchen, bathroom, and bedroom. I could be happy living here. In the center of this room there are two armchairs opposite each other with a small, round table between them.

"Please, sit," Gabriel says, waving me to an armchair. "Can I get you something to drink?"

"What do you have?" I ask him.

"Water, primarily," he says, "but I also have some soda from the Surface. In my youth, I was addicted to Coca-Cola. I still am."

"I'll have some of that, please," Coke is my kryptonite. I could sit back and down so much of that stuff. Gabriel disappears into another room, returning shortly with two glasses of liquidey brown goodness. He hands me one, then sits down opposite me.

"Thanks," I say gratefully before taking a sip of my drink. I'm trying really hard not to chug it in two seconds. Gabriel smiles. It's a warm smile, like one your grandpa would give you. Well, I suppose he is my some-number-of-greats grandpa.

He takes a sip of his drink before speaking. "Now," he says, wiping his mouth with the back of his free hand, "I believe I owe you a story."

Chapter Twelve

"I'd appreciate that," I say. Gabriel leans back in his chair.

"Where to begin...," he says to himself, thinking. I sit patiently, waiting.

"You could start at the beginning," I offer.

"I know," he says, "but knowing when the beginning truly was is proving difficult. I've never been quite certain."

"What do you mean by that?" I ask.

"There are so many points where the start could really be. You see, The War didn't start because of some whimsy of mine, or of anybody else. Before actually being in one, my idea of war itself was that it was fought by soldiers who were different than me in every way and happened thousands of miles away. In my mind, war was on a foreign planet. I was safe and happy living where I was."

"Where did you live?" I ask.

"Georgia," he replies. "I was raised a good southern boy."

"Ah."

"That was centuries ago. I'm not even sure if that expression is used anymore.

"It still is," I say. "You don't hear it very often, though. At least not where I lived."

"Where did you live, Sam?" Gabriel asks.

"In California."

He sighs. "That used to be such a lovely place all those years ago."

"I wouldn't know," I remark. "Now it's all factories and industries... it's not exactly the best place to settle down."

"It seems the entire Surface has met that fate, thanks to my son." I choose not to answer, afraid I'll say the wrong thing. Instead, I take a nice, long sip of my Coke. Gabriel does the same.

"Anyway, I haven't even started my story yet," he continues, setting his glass back down. "Where I would say it started was during a war."

"A war started during a war?" I say, confused.

"Well, yes," Gabriel says. "You see, back before we had three kingdoms ruled by three seemingly eternal kings, many nations elected their own presidents. A president could only be in office so long, a few years at most, and then the next one would be elected and so on.

"That had to be weird," I say.

"No, not really," Gabriel explains. "It was perfectly normal and actually worked very well at first. It was called 'democracy'. And the presidents' power would be balanced by other parts of the government, so that no one man could become a tyrant." Wouldn't that be nice to have right now, "It stopped working as soon as it became a rigged democracy. Politicians always had a way of messing up things like that.

When the Americans became fed up with being jerked around by their government, they had their second revolution. It was a bloody, bloody fight."

"How did it end?" I ask. Even though that's where I live, the schooling I had was very limited, and history was never a big topic. Besides, nothing extends back to the days before *King Logan* was in charge. Even the stuff with Gabriel and all the others in it is only considered a fairy tale. Logan himself is considered to have stepped straight out of legend.

"I ended it," Gabriel says. "I was an upset, emotional man. All odds were against us. The government had their well-trained army to fight for them, and many revolutionaries were afraid to fight. I myself wasn't any fighter. We had few guns, but many swords. We had to learn to make them ourselves at one point. We used to laugh about how it seemed the worlds timeline was flowing in reverse. We even figured out a date we thought things started moving backwards, the midway point between America's revolutions and the revolution I myself ended. We called that 'the day the world started dying.' We believed the Earth had reached the halfway point in its life."

"Wait, rewind for a second," I say. "You ended that war, too?"

"Yes I did," Gabriel replies. "It was considered the first step toward my goal of global conquest."

"How'd you end it? Did you start it?" I've always known that Gabriel fought and killed many people, but I never really knew any details other than what the legends and a few kids' books told me. Now I have the actual guy, who was there, telling me about his past. There's no way I'm wasting this opportunity.

"I did not start it," Gabriel clarifies. "I didn't fight for a good, long while in fact. The days I entered the second revolution were the last days of that war. Altogether, I believe it waged on for five years. I was involved for the last two."

"Only two years?" I ask. At first, I'm surprised by the short length of time he actually fought to end the war, but then I think about my own track record. Apparently I cleaned up the Sky Nation in only two months, and now I'm down here.

Two years doesn't seem so long after all.

"I had an unfair advantage," he says with a shrug.

"The nation was already in shambles by the time I came around."

"So how did you get involved?" I ask.

"I got involved against my will. I tried as hard as I could to stay out of the fighting, and managed to do that for three years. Then the fighting came closer to home." Gabriel's eyes glaze over, he's lost in his memory. "My entire neighborhood was burned down. The two sides were the Standards and the Revolutionists, or Revs for short.

"The Standards had the Revs pushed back at first. It didn't seem like much could be going well for the Revs, and nothing was. The Standards came into our town and took possession of our homes, using a law passed long ago. They threatened us with death and violence if we defied them.

"The Revs made a desperate play. They set fire to the entire neighborhood. I still don't know if they cared that they took thousands of innocent lives. My family was taken from me. My mom and dad died in the fires, and my baby sister was shot dead right before my eyes. It was just me and my kid brother left. I was twenty years old, he was only thirteen." Gabriel's eyes start to well up, and I see streams of tears on his cheeks. I respectfully avert my eyes, busing myself with my Coke.

Am I a horrible person? It's obvious that this is excruciating for him to remember, and yet I want him to tell me what happened. I want to know.

"We ran," Gabriel continues. "We ran and ran and ran. We headed north due to the blockades to the south. After five days, starved, not feeling like much more than walking skeletons, we found our salvation. It was the city of Chicago.

"Chicago was the first place hit by the fighting. Some Rev leader had a grudge against a government bigwig from there. But the city was beginning to recuperate. It was the farthest along as far as recovery goes, and by the time we got there, a refugee hideout had been set up. Nobody took sides there, it was just a congregation of people who had been left with nothing. The refugees had taken over an entire city block, and workers had connected all the different buildings to create one 'super building.' We banged on their doors. We were desperate… my brother was sick. Someone opened the doors almost instantly. They took my brother to medical. They tried to take him from me, but I wouldn't let them. Even though he wasn't being taken far away, I wouldn't separate from him, not after all of this. The people that were helping us understood how I felt and let me follow him.

"We lived there for a time, Tie and me," Gabriel sighs. I'm guessing that Tie is his brother. "Then I had a crazy idea. An idea that would end up changing the world." Gabriel looks up at me, not bothering to wipe the tears

156

from his eyes. "I had an idea to win the war. Put an army together of refugees and volunteers and put a stop to this."

Gabriel stops talking for a moment, gets up and says, "Excuse me." He leaves the room, and shouts to me that if I want more Coke, there's some in the fridge. Why not, I've already drained mine dry.

I peek into a few rooms before I find the kitchen. In the refrigerator, there's a brand-new six-pack of Coke, and another with only four cans left. I grab the one with four.

Back in the main room, Gabriel is already back. It looks like he went hunting for tissues. That's more than fair. The guy doesn't have to be strong all the time.

I sit back down and pop open one of the cans of Coke. I pour it out into the glass Gabriel brought me before, only out of respect. Normally I would just drink out of the can. I have a feeling those four cans will be empty soon. I notice that Gabriel's glass is also down to icy sludge. I pop open another can and refill his as well. In silence I wait for Gabriel to continue, if he wishes to continue. I learned a long time ago how to be comfortable with silences.

"Thank you," he says, taking a sip. "I think I'm going to get a little something to add to this," he tells me as he goes to the kitchen. He returns with another glass and a bottle of Jack Daniels. I have no idea who Jack Daniels was, but apparently he made one hell of a drink. Gabriel pours some of the Jack into his second glass, adds some Coke to it, and swirls it around.

"Sometimes stories require a little whiskey," he explains. This is going to get heavy. He offers the glass to me.

"No thanks," I say. "I don't drink." He retracts the glass without looking offended, which is cool.

"You're a good kid," he says. "Don't change that strong character. It's a hard quality to find."

"I won't," I say, and I mean it.

"Now," Gabriel says, still holding his drink, "back to my story." I put my listening ears back on and shut up. Speaking of shutting up, I'm amazed Dac hasn't said anything this whole time.

It's called 'being polite,' Dac inevitably answers. *Remember I tried to teach you about manners months ago?* Oh yeah...I had to say "please" to get him to work with me. I can feel that he's done talking for now, thank goodness. We both sit silently.

"My idea for organizing a better resistance drew a mixed response," Gabriel says. "Most people were reluctant at first. 'It's stupid, crazy, and suicidal,' they'd say. But the people who joined me went along with it for those very same reasons." Gabriel chuckles softly and I repress a laugh myself.

"We weren't exactly Revs," he continues. "We did

fight for a revolution and for the end of the fighting, but we took a much different approach. We put the civilians first, and if someone was injured – no matter who they were – we offered them medical care and refuge. To those left homeless, we offered shelter. And for families who had been separated, we helped them look for their lost relatives. If they were the same as me and their family was gone, we were their new family.

"Very quickly, we took control of all of Illinois. With that, our name spread far and wide. My name became a household term. Everyone had heard of me, the man both dumb enough and brave enough to fight against both the Revs and the Standards.

"With our notoriety came many followers. They flocked from all over the country to join with us. I accepted every person willing to fight. Even if they couldn't fight, we would protect them. All men and women were equal." Gabriel is smiling, seeming to enjoy this memory, like he's seeing old friends. I bet if I asked him, he could tell me hundreds of names.

"Within a month, we had enough forces that I could deploy units of hundreds of thousands to fight in critical areas. I could even send reinforcements when they were needed. I sometimes sent them even when they weren't, to keep the casualty count down. I had so many volunteers that our numbers were enough to populate states. Revs and Standards alike joined us, unhappy with

the way things were being handled within their ranks."
Looking directly into my eyes, Gabriel says, "I took
personal accountability for every single life. I grieved for
each one lost.

"Tie was at my side the entire time. We didn't just sit
back and command. We fought on the front lines. People
put Tie and me up on pedestals, thinking we could
never get injured, that we were somehow invincible.
Well, we got plenty injured, believe you me. That was
the point we tasked scientists with developing what is
now Blue Elixir. At the time it was nowhere near perfect,
and it tasted horrible, but somehow, my youngest has
perfected it.

"I didn't necessarily like having my brother fight, of
course. He was only thirteen... no, fourteen. He'd had his
fourteenth birthday by then. I threw a huge party for
him. The entire Solution did." Gabriel grins. "That's what
we called ourselves, The Solution. Oh we were more
than a little arrogant, but we didn't care at the time.

"Then came one of the hardest days of my life. This
was about one year after I started The Solution, even
longer from when my brother and I were uprooted
from our home. It was the final siege in Washington,
the Battle of Seattle. Tie and I were on the front lines,
like so many times before. We were on top of the world,
confident that by the end of the day, the state would be
ours.

"We fought well. We won the battle, but it wasn't the victory I was expecting."

"What do you mean by that?" I ask.

Gabriel sighs deeply. "I suffered a great personal loss." He takes another long drink of his Jack and Coke, finishing the entire glass. Then he grabs the bottle of Jack and takes a swig from that as well.

"We were in the midst of the battle. Things were going our way. Everything seemed to be going well, and the end was in sight. Nobody in the battle was using guns. Months before this, all the armies had decided there wasn't enough metal to keep making more and more bullets. This was an agreement reached at the one and only meeting of the Revs, Standards, and The Solution. We called it the Limiting Agreement, because it limited the use of a valuable resource.

"The Standard forces were surrendering. The battle was ours. Neither Tie nor I were hurt much at all. That's when my life changed... I was looking over at Tie and there was a loud crack. Deafeningly loud." Gabriel's words start to fade away. Barely whispering, he says, "I can still hear that shot.

"And then he fell. In the blink of an eye, my smiling brother was taken from me. I rushed to his side as he fell to the floor in slow motion. My world cracking around the single image of him." Gabriel pauses to take in a shaky breath, "He was shot in the chest. There was so much blood, I was covered in it. I tried to make it stop, to save him." Again, Gabriel's words choke off to nothing as he's now sobbing openly.

Finally, he goes on. "I just couldn't look at his face. I kept telling him it'd be okay, that we were going to finish this together. Finally one of my soldiers put his hand on my shoulder and said something I'll never forget, 'Gabriel, stop. He's gone.' I looked into Tie's eyes then, and I knew it was true. There was no life left in his young face. He was only fourteen, just a week away from his next birthday. We were going to throw him an even bigger party than the year before, thinking we'd celebrate his birthday and our victory together. And because it was supposed to be fun.

"Cradling my brother in my arms, I said four words that made everybody move, even those who had just surrendered to me."

"What'd you say?" I ask.

Gabriel's face is hard and cold as he says, "'Bring him to me.'"

I hang on Gabriel's every syllable. If the hate and anger he had just now is even close to what he was feeling then, I would've moved, too.

I audibly gulp.

"While the shooter was fetched for me, I sat with my brother. I was on my knees and he was dead. I held him in my arms." Gabriel holds his arms up, looking at them as though he can still see his brother there. "When the shooter was brought to me, I gently set Tie's body down on the ground and stood up. 'On his knees!' I ordered. I was never big on giving orders, but this time I didn't mind. The men who had grabbed him forced the shooter down onto his knees without a moment of hesitation. I picked up my brother's sword and did horrible things to that man. I let him beg me to kill him, and I wouldn't. He kept pleading, and when there was nothing left, that's when I killed him. I earned the name, 'The Bloody Avenger' that day." Gabriel looks indescribably sad and angry, but I know this is nothing compared to how he must have looked that day. I imagine him looking just plain evil.

"I put Tie's sword in my sheath and walked back over to him. I fell to my knees and let myself weep. I don't know how long I sat there crying as I held my brother's body. I noticed he was wearing his necklace, something I had made for him years before for his birthday. I took it from his neck and placed it around mine. This is it." Gabriel says, digging into his shirt. He Pulls out a metal gear strung on a chain. It's old and beat up, nothing special, but it means more than anything in the world to him.

"I kissed Tie's head and said to those right behind me, that I wanted his funeral and a memorial built for him right on this spot. I told them to stop the campaign for now. We did just that. One of my generals took over for me while I worked on my brothers funeral and began the memorials construction. Even today a giant statue still stands guard above his body. I make a point to go there and visit him every birthday of his. I'd still give anything for him to be alive." Gabriel mumbles something after that, but I can't make it out at all.

"At his funeral, I promised him this would never happen again, not to anybody. I decided to force peace on the world. I did when I finally took control. The rest you should know from your stories."

I look at him, not saying anything.

After a long pause, Gabriel says, "If you'll excuse me, I must be a religious man now. Goodnight Sam. I hoped this helped you understand."

"It has," I say. "Thank you for sharing with me." I don't wait for him to respond. I don't want him to have to. I walk soundlessly out of the room.

Wow.

Chapter Thirteen

After my talk with Gabriel, I head back to my room. I try to fall asleep, but I can't. I lie awake, staring at the ceiling. Dac doesn't bother trying to help me sort out my thoughts. It wouldn't do much good right now anyway. Maybe he knows that just as much as I do. Or maybe he's in just as much shock as I am.

Gabriel's story was everything I wanted and more. It was the truth, and it told me that he fought for a good cause. That he really should be considered a savior, not a conqueror or a tyrant. I always believed that, but now it's been confirmed.

That said, he gave me more detail than I wanted to know. It sounds like it was almost as bad then as it is now. At least, that's how Gabriel made it sound. I bet it would be like comparing sunshine and rainbows to an acid rainy day. I'd prefer then over now.

The thought that really keeps me awake is what Gabriel said about his brother. I can't imagine how it must feel to lose someone so close. Maybe I can. I thought I'd lost my dad forever, back before we hated each other and I still idolized him. But that's still different. I never lost hope of getting him back. Gabriel couldn't bring his brother back to life... Not unless he starts the Zombie Apocalypse, that is. Personally, I hope he doesn't try that. Even if he does, I used to know this one kid who did nothing but prepare for exactly that. "One day you'll all see!" he'd always yell at us.

With my thoughts diverted to a Zombie Apocalypse, I find sleep.

"The boy still lives," a very familiar voice says from darkness. Oh great, not this *hearing-other-people's-conversations-in-my-sleep-thing* again. I was hoping to get a good night's sleep tonight, but I guess I'm just lucky like that.

"The one that you were telling me about before?" responds another voice, one that I don't know.

"Yes," grumbles the short tempered voice of the one and only Steven. The jerk tried to kill me before. A couple of times, actually. "I have undercover soldiers patrolling the Sky Nation day in and day out."

"Why undercover?" the second voice asks.

"The Ravens' victory over me seems to have boosted the confidence of both their soldiers and other civilians," Steven says. "It's a dangerous time to openly be a member of the New Power up here." Sounds like everyone finally got themselves together. It's about time!

"I can't say I understand how you feel," the mysterious voice replies. "Down here, it's glorious to be a member. I have volunteers and recruits running to me at all hours." Hold on.... If two plus two equals fish and you divide that by thirty-four... this guy's Lynch!

"How fortunate for you," Steven says. "The master wants me dead because I lost the Sky Nation *almost* as much as he wants the Cutter boy dead." Ha ha ha ha ha, I'm more important than *you*. That was really singsong.... Nobody must ever know of this.

"It is your fault," Lynch says. I try to memorize the sound of his voice. It's clear and medium-deep, I'd say. It sounds like it belongs to someone who could be related to both my dad and Steven. That would make a really weird couple. All of them with serious anger management issues. Who would their parents be? The Hulk and a cage fighter?

Lynch continues. "You were given responsibility for securing control of the Sky Nation. You kept delivering reports that it was 'within your grasp' and that the resistance was a 'weak and broken force.' What a joke. If anything, I have exactly what you promised."

"Be careful what you say," Steven says suddenly. "I still haven't found the Cutter boy anywhere up here—"

"It's a big place," Lynch cuts him off. "You'll find him."

"*If* he's not up here," Steven continues on, irritated by the interruption, "then he may very well be down in the Water Nation with you." There's a pause before he adds, "Have there been any strange disturbances down there?" Oh crap.

"Not particularly," Lynch says. "Well, actually, something out of the blue did happen last night."

"What?"

"Some of my soldiers were attacked. A kid ambushed them, they said."

"It could be Cutter!" Steven exclaims. "Tell me exactly what happened."

"Hold your horses. Let me find that report." There's silence as Lynch finds what he's looking for. I don't bother to try to say anything. Either no sound will come out of my mouth, or these two will hear me, and both my cover will be blown and they'll know I'm able to hear them talk. Even though being able to listen in on these conversations kills my dreams of sleep, it has proved very useful before.

"Here it is," Lynch says, returning to the conversation. "Okay, so it looks like my boys went out – three of them – to pick up another runt for the privilege of bringing them onboard the New Power. Yada, yada, yada...ah, here we go. So they were escorting some girl back to base, when some punk kid showed up. It seems he knew her and forced my boys to release her. It seems like it should've been an easy match, three against one. Not so much. It left one of my guys dead and another injured."

"What else? Was there anything else? Tell me about the boy. Every detail," Steven demands.

"Let's see. The kid was about seventeen," Lynch replies. Cool! I look older than I am. "He had black hair. Tall. Fought with a sword—"

"What kid of sword?" Steven cuts in.

"A sharp one?" Lynch says, not understanding the question.

"Was it glowing?" Steven asks, almost yelling.

"Let's see...," Lynch murmurs, pausing apparently to look at his report. "How did you know that?"

"What color was it?" Steven presses. Uh oh.

"White. Why?" Dammit. Maybe he forgot that mine is white?

"You *idiot!*" I'm boned, "You let Cutter slip through your grasp!" No he didn't... shut up!

"Oh yeah?" Lynch says. Man, I wonder if this guy gets excited about anything. He probably wouldn't even smile if a girl kissed him. "Well, don't worry about this little kid, this Samuel Cutter, anymore." I roll my eyes. Please don't use my full first name. "I'll take care of him good and quick."

"Don't get overconfident," Steven warns, coming down from his full volume. "Cutter is crafty. Suicidal."

Am not! I only wanted you to think that.

"Right. I'll believe it when I see it," Lynch says.

"He crashed and destroyed a precious, *impenetrable* War Ship into the ocean with himself inside of it."

"Okay, so maybe he's a little nuts." You *know* I am! "What do you propose we do about him?" Shake my hand, say, "You win," and go on with your evil lives?

"Kill him! He has a tendency to ruin everything," And damn proud of it. "If he lives much longer, you'll lose the Water Nation to him."

"I wouldn't worry about that," Lynch says. "I have my own ways of keeping order down here."

My eyes shoot open and again I'm wide awake. I try to look out a window to see if it's daytime yet. It's dark out. Wait, I'm underwater. There's no sun down here.

I'm going to hope nobody noticed that.

I noticed, Dac chimes in. Ignoring that.

I still feel exhausted, like I haven't slept at all. I will think about everything I heard tonight, but not right now. I close my eyes, and after what feels like an hour or so, I fall asleep.

"Wakey, wakey!" Ugh, what? I open my eyes to find John shaking me awake. I'm going to kill him.

"What?" I ask.

"Wake up," is all he says. Why did I save him again?

"Why?"

"Well, breakfast is only going to be good for a little while longer, so I figured you would want to eat."

"I'm not hungry," I say. I pull my blanket back over me and turn away from him. Maybe he'll go away if I'm quiet. Sure enough, John gives up and leaves. Before I know it, I hear someone screaming. I don't have time to sit up. I hear heavy footsteps charging towards me. If I was on the Surface, I'd assume it's the peace-keepers coming after me. With that reflex, I go to attack them, but they're faster.

I gasp as I feel a huge weight, like somebody just jumped on top of me. All my injuries from yesterday and before that instantly remind me of their existence, as my head starts pounding and pain courses throughout my body. The weight only stays on top of me for a second.

I hear John yell. I sit up to see what happened. It looks like, and sure feels like, he tried to jump on top of me, but slid off. Strangely, I'm okay with that.

"What?" I ask him.

"Get up," he says insistently. "You can't stay in bed all day."

"Wanna bet?"

"Just get up!"

I tell him, "I'll give you twenty bucks if you go away." John is quiet for a second, actually debating his answer.

"Deal."

"Well, I'll give it to you in the future," I say, falling back to the pillows. "I'm broke."

"Deal's off, then." Damn, I thought that would work.

"I'll get you for this," I grumble, getting out of bed and head to the shower.

The rest of the day, I do nothing. I'm supposed to be sitting around and healing so that I can go back to Hub Fourteen with Kane and some others. Since we didn't bring a whole lot of Blue Elixir down here, I can't get a miracle healing like I have been lately. I'm going to have to get well the old-fashioned way, slowly and painfully. I'm used to it. It's not like I've had Blue Elixir going for me my whole life. A concussion and a sore body are nothing.

Over the next few days, I mope around, not fully taking in much of what's around me. It's not that I'm sad, really, just dialed down. Maybe I'm still digesting everything Gabriel told me. He bounced right back to normal the day after telling me his story. He has a couple hundred years of emotional maturity on me, though. That, and a long, long time to deal with what happened.

It's freaky how close his story is to my own...at least, the fighting part. I guess we're both a couple of angry, upstart, punk kids. That's what people call me, anyway. They also use much more colorful language, but that might offend someone.

Who would it offend? Dac asks. *They are your*

thoughts.

Good point.

I avoid Gabriel for the next few days. I don't mean to offend the guy, and I'm not entirely sure it's a conscious choice, but it's hard to look him in the face after learning how he earned the name, "The Bloody Avenger." I know I'm not handling this so well, but I can't help it. His story was pretty horrible.

Kane checks on me each day, eager to go to Hub Fourteen. Every day I tell him I feel fine, and he tells me I'm not healed yet. He would rather rely on information he gets from some devices he's invented that measure certain things about my physical condition, than listen to how I, the supposedly injured one, feel. Talk about being dependent on technology.

It takes about two weeks for Kane to be satisfied with all his meters. I felt *fine* two weeks ago – the day after the fight, as a matter of fact – but *nooo*. That's not good enough. Stupid machine.

You watch your mouth! Dac jokes.

I wasn't talking about you, I assure him.

Finally, I get the "okay" from Kane. We're going to head out to Hub Fourteen tomorrow morning, so I better be up early. Blah. I go to bed that night before anybody else without saying a word. Am I anxious? Maybe. Tired? Not really. I don't know for sure why I want to go to sleep early. I get to my room and attack my pillow with my face. I don't change my clothes, figuring I'll just lie down for a minute. Sure enough, though, sleep has other plans for me as I pass out right then and there.

"Oh good, you're awake."

"What?" I open my eyes and see that I'm not in my room. Did someone take me? No, but there is someone here. "Hi Armando," I say, recognizing my guest.

"Hello, Sam. How've you been?" Armando says with a smile.

"Just wonderful, and yourself?"

"As you can see, the AI still isn't out of me," he says, clearly not happy about it.

"I noticed," I say. "Do you know if Arthur is at least getting any closer?"

"He almost has it," Armando says. "That's why I'm talking to you."

"Why? Isn't it good that Arthur almost has it out of your head?"

"Yes, but it'll be strange. I've gotten used to it, you know? The constant struggle in my head. You're the only person I know who has ever been separated from an AI before—"

"How did you know that?" I ask, cutting him off. Seriously, it didn't happen until after I escaped from prison, and Armando and I haven't talked much since then. I'm pretty sure he's been out cold, strapped to a table in Arthur's back room.

"I tried to contact you at one point, but I couldn't reach you or your Digital Artificial Core Processor. I assumed you died for a while, but when I heard Arthur talking to you over the phone, I knew you were alive. It only made sense that you and your AI separated for a time." Creepy. But not wrong.... How is it that he's this smart?

"Uuuuuh."

"So, one reason I'm talking to you now is that I want to ask what it's like, being separated," Armando explains.

I'm the only one? With how easy it was, you'd think that it would have happened plenty of times before. Armando's face tells me he's genuinely scared. What harm could there be in telling him what it's like?

"It's weird," I start, "like you're missing a part of yourself. At least for me, I'd gotten so used to there being another person inside of here," I tap my head, "that the silence was deafening. It was disorienting at first."

"What do you mean?" he asks me. "Did you have to re-learn how to walk?"

"No, nothing like that," I say. "It was more like the sun was too bright, and the ground was shakey, and everything seemed really weird. I didn't have a lot of time to get used to it, because maybe only a minute after it happened, I got kidnapped and thrown out of a flying limo."

"What's a limo?" Armando asks. Of all the things he could ask me about what I just said, he asks what a limo is. "It's a Surface thing, basically a really long car." He still looks confused. "You know how cars normally only have a few seats, and everyone faces forward?" I attempt to illustrate using my hands as I go along. "Well, a limo is if you take the whole thing and stretch it out so that a bunch of people can fit in there. Only rich people drive in them, usually. When I say rich, I mean *really* rich. You're rich if you can even afford your own car." Armando looks completely mystified.

"What's a car?" he asks me. Right, Surface thing. He wouldn't know.

"It's like a small, personal transport," I say, trying to think of the Sky Nation's closest equivalent to a car.

"Why wouldn't you just get a bigger transport then?"

"Because it's not the same. It's...forget it." This is getting ridiculous.

"So why were you thrown out of this 'limo?'"

"Steven decided he didn't like me."

"I should've figured," Armando says, sounding totally unsurprised that someone doesn't like me. Do all the people I know expect me to end up in a cage match with everyone I meet? Do I piss people off that much?

I wait for a witty remark from Dac, but none comes. I guess he doesn't want Armando to hear him. I'm not sure why he's being cautious, but I'm okay with it.

"I can't hear their call anymore," Armando says randomly.

"What?" I ask, confused by his odd comment.

"I can't hear their call anymore," he says again. "They can't control me. It's only my voice in my head. Maybe Arthur should leave the AI in. That'd be better, wouldn't it? We could communicate from any distance." He sounds like he's trying to convince himself that it'd be better if the thing that is trying to take over his mind stays in his head. I don't know if he's afraid of what'll happen when it's out, or if the AI is making him think this, or if the AI is making him more talented, or what. Basically, all I'm getting is that he's losing it.

I hope he can get his head screwed back on straight when the AI is out of him.

"No, it should still come out," I say. "I don't want you randomly trying to kill me again. That's not fun."

"But it doesn't have to," he argues.

"Yes," I say, "it does." I'd rather talk to relatively sane Armando than to crazy, ninja-meets-juggernaut Armando.

"But they can't control me."

"How do I know they're not controlling you right now?" I say. I feel a buzzing in my skull. That's probably

Dac agreeing without saying anything. He's a lot smarter than me. There's another buzzing from him. Oh am I gonna hear it when we get out of this.

Armando looks panicked, like I found out exactly what's going on and he's frantically trying to come up with some way to keep his cover.

"Samuel Cutter," says a disconnected voice. I'm guessing it's Armando's AI. It has a low, rumbling voice. "Be forewarned. Your time is soon." For some reason, I remember that my birthday is coming up. Armando starts to transform into a huge, grotesque-looking monster. It's like his bones are shifting and growing under his skin. I know it's not really him, but it's still weird.

"Sam," I hear Dac's voice say so that everyone can hear it.

"Yeah?"

"Run."

"Okay," and I bolt. As soon as I take off, Armandozilla comes after me. He actually roars. If he wasn't trying to kill me, I might think that's cool.

"You still think it's cool!" Dac yells. In here, that's a lot louder than you'd think. He's not wrong. We're in a room, so when I reach a wall, I frantically hunt for a door. Luckily I find one, and run out. I stop short, though. I'm only a few steps outside of the room when the sidewalk ends. In front of me is a swirling mass of...

something.

I don't know how to describe it. It's like a giant storm cloud. Nothing exists past the point I'm standing at. I could stick my hand out and touch it, but I'm afraid that if I do, I'll lose my hand. I like my hand.

Before I have time to do something stupid, Armando-the-Ripped breaks through the wall. He's not running through the opening or anything. It seems like he just didn't like the door and decided to make one for himself. He rips off another piece of the wall and hurls it at me.

I duck out of the way. The bit of wall collides with the storm cloud. As soon as it touches the mass, it spontaneously combusts. Fragments of wood splinter off and fly full-force in my direction. I shield my face with my arms.

Hmm. So that's what happens if you touch the mysterious mass. No touch-ee.

HOW IS HE THIS STRONG!? He was tough before, but not able to destroy a house because it offends him!

"It's this place," Dac says. "Because he called you here, he can alter this portion as he sees fit."

"How do you know this?" I ask him, running around the house, trying to stay away from his muscles with legs.

"I am an AI," That must've hurt him to say. "This place is kinda home to me. This is where I existed before you and I bonded." Wow. If this is all the AI's get to look at, I can't completely blame them for trying to get out and stay out. This place is depressing.

"Talk. More. Later," I say between breaths while running. Armando takes out another section of the building. I turn my head and see that he's running out here with me now. For some reason or another, he keeps smashing the wall with his fist at random intervals. I think it's just to show off. I turn back around so that I can pay attention and make sure I don't run into the cloud of death. The banging on the wall stops, but it doesn't sound like a person running behind me anymore. It sounds like Armando decided that he can use his hands and arms to help him run. Fantastic.

I swerve and start running around the third wall of the house. I glimpse back and see that *Arm*ando has problems taking turns. I gain a little bit of distance on him.

"Wake him up!" I yell to Dac.

"And how do you expect me to do that? Offer him gorilla treats?" That could work.

"You have a body now," I point out. "Use it to get Jinn to call Arthur!"

"Good idea," Dac says. "All I need to do is split my awareness between operating that body and keeping you from getting lost in here."

"Yes, please!" Dac mumbles something else, but I can't make it out. I hope he's trying to get Jinn to get

Arthur. He'd better do it fast. I'm just about to get my ass kicked.

"Worthless vessels will perish!" Armando's AI howls at me.

I run toward the next turn and stop. I pull a one-eighty to face Armando. I stare down this overly strong gorilla-on-steroids monster thing and wait. Time for another stupid idea. As he comes closer, he starts running on only his feet again, raising his left fist to hit me, setting himself off balance. When he's near enough to throw the punch, I duck out of the way and run down the last side of sidewalk we haven't been on yet.

An ear-piercing shriek rings out. I stop and turn around to look. Oh no. His fist went into the cloud. Oddly enough, there's no smell of burning flesh. He pulls his arm away, and there's no hand attached

At least it didn't kill him. I wonder if his hand just disappeared into the real world. That'd be weird to see.

Monkey-Godzilla-Armando looks over at me, hate in his eyes, and then he vanishes. I blink and rub my eyes to make sure I'm not seeing things.

I fall to my knees, knowing that Dac got him to wake up.

Chapter
Fourteen

I'm on my knees in silence for a time. I'm not crying.
I'm not really doing anything except choosing not to move.
All I want is sleep...real sleep, not this fake twilight, AI-
world sleep. I'm more exhausted when I wake up than
when I fall asleep when I go into one of these things.

I move without getting up, so that my back is against
the wall of the house. I watch the massive cloud. It's
swirling, not like regular clouds in the sky that move a little
with the wind. This one is actually moving, like a giant
snake coiling around itself. It's interesting to see, this black
giant with bits of color shot through it. There's purple,
red, dark blue, all the colors of the rainbow are in there
somewhere. I don't see any white, though. I wonder why
there isn't any?

I continue to watch the swirling cloud, trying to see any
pattern to it, but I can't find any.

I almost fall asleep here, watching the black storm-
cloud of death, but I find motivation to get up. I get up off

my knees and start walking around the house, the long way around so that I can see the damage left behind. Armando left dents in the ground when he started running with his fists. When I get to the point where he was pounding the walls, there are holes clean through. I'm suddenly even happier that I didn't let him get me.

I look out to the swirling blackness again. The colors make it bearable, but it's still unsettling. It feels like the world itself isn't stable.

I look for any sign of white out there, but I can't find any. It's almost as if it's all been erased. There is no white light here. I stand and stare for a bit, but when my stomach starts churning and it feels like someone turned the heat up a couple degrees, I decide I'm making myself sick from looking at it. I move on.

I stand in front of the door into the house. I turn the handle and walk in. Why do I choose to open the door instead of stepping through the giant hole right next to it? I honestly don't have the slightest clue.

It looks like a tornado decided to throw a party and invite all its friends over. That doesn't bother me though. I walk over to the remains of the couch and plop myself down on it. I lie down and fall asleep. I fall asleep in this ruined hellhole. I fall asleep with the threat of Armando coming back at any time. Isn't it great being tired and fifteen?

As soon as I close my eyes inside that dream-world, I wake up in the real world. Well, I'll be tired, but at least I'm not dead. I look around me and see that everyone is in my room. I didn't even know we could all fit in here.

"What's up?" I say, trying to play it cool.

"How long have you been having those dreams, Sam?" Jinn asks me.

Jinn has warmed up to Dac for the most part, but mostly because he didn't have to see him in the beginning. Jinn isn't the biggest fan of AI's. He doesn't even like the autopilot on some transports.

"A while," I say.

"How long?" Jinn repeats.

"Almost as long as Dac and I have been connected," I say.

"I've never even heard of these dreams," Jinn says. "Nathan, have you?"

"No. But then again, most times when individuals were connected to an AI, they were constantly in a dreamlike state, being controlled. Either that, or they were fighting themselves not to give their body and basically everything over to the AI," Nathan says.

Suddenly everybody but Dac and me start shooting around ideas, talking about the dreams as if they're some disease. Rick even proposes that Dac has been trying to take over my body this whole time.

"It's a way to communicate," I say loudly, before things

184

get even further out of hand. That shuts everyone up.

"You know what it is?" Sarah asks me. I almost forgot that she's here. I should set aside some time to talk with her later. She is one of my oldest ancestors. Not that I'd ever call her old to her face. That'd be a good way to get killed.

"Yes," I say. "It's a way to talk. Steven has been using it non-stop to communicate. And because I can use it to eavesdrop, I know that they both hate me personally and..."

"They?" Jinn says.

"Steven and Lynch. Aren't you paying attention?" I say.

"You never mentioned a 'Lynch'."

"Well, he was there too, and now both of them know I'm down here because Steven recognized my sword."

"I hope you were at least putting it to good use," Jinn comments.

"I was," I reply. "I saved some girl."

"Always the lady's man, aren't you?" Sarah teases.

"Sure seems like it," I say. I have gotten in a lot of trouble recently for helping girls... Aha! I have found the root of my problems!

No you haven't

I know. It'd be a nice thing to know, though.

"Sam. Sam!" Jinn yells at me.

"What?" I ask, snapping out of my thoughts. Oh well, I'll work on finding the origin of all evil later.

"Could you not talk to Dac like that when we're all trying to have a discussion with you?" Jinn says.

"I wasn't talking to Dac," I say. "I was just thinking."

Liar.

Shush.

"About what?"

"About my life." And how it's only getting marginally better as I go.

"Oh," Jinn says. There's silence for a bit. He probably doesn't know what to say. Apparently the fact that I think about my life is weird.

"How long did it take you to get used to him blacking out to talk to...um, himself again?" Sarah asks the group in general.

Everyone gives an answer at once. Rick and Fred basically say they're still working on it. Fair enough. They've only known about it a few days more than the royals. John says he's always realized I'm weird, so that doesn't help. Jinn and Mark say it took them a while.

"Got it," Sarah says, no more informed than she was ten seconds ago. It gets quiet again.

Kane's voice breaks the silence. "So are we ready to go?"

"Yeah," I say. "Let's go." I can definitely use a change of scenery.

"Excellent. I'll finish loading the equipment." Kane leaves. The sound of heavy footsteps on the stairs echoes throughout the building.

I get my butt out of bed, feeling less rested than I

did when I lied down. I push past everyone, not saying anything, and head downstairs. Kane isn't anywhere in sight, but I hear something going on outside, so I head out. There I find him, busily putting a whole assortment of things I don't recognize into what looks like a giant bubble. It reminds me of an oversized hamster ball... I don't know. It's weird.

"Are we rolling that all the way to Hub Fourteen?" I ask him.

"No, why would you think that?" he replies.

"Because you're putting a bunch of stuff into the world's largest hamster ball," I tell him.

Kane looks from me to his stuff and back again. "What's a hamster?" he asks.

"It's—" I begin.

"Never mind," he cuts in. "This is not your 'hamster ball'. It is the storage unit for a personal watercraft." He says this in such a superior tone, like he can't believe I have no idea what he's talking about.

"Okay," I say. What the heck is a 'personal watercraft'? I poorly mimic his voice in the security of my own head, making him sound way worse than he was.

"So what's that?" I ask using my normal voice.

"Water vehicles are transportation devices we have down here. You could compare them to your Surface motorized vehicles, or Sky Nation aircraft."

So it's their car down here. Why couldn't he have said

that before? That would've made things easier!

"Well, do you need any help loading any of that stuff?" I ask, reaching for something lying on the ground outside the bubble.

"No! Don't touch it!" Kane exclaims, smacking my hand away. "You'll break it. You have no idea how to handle this delicate equipment."

"What do you expect me to do then?" I ask him.

"Just stand there and don't touch anything," he says, not even looking at me. I raise my hands up like I'm being accused of a crime and back away. Just stand here and don't touch anything. I can do that.

No touch-ee. Nothing.

Just stand here... I can do that... I have never wanted to touch something more in my entire life.

You're so weak, Dac feels the need to point out.

I know, I say, slumping over, defeated.

Kane glances over just long enough to see me slump over. "Are you getting ill again?"

"No, no, I'm fine," I say. Just really want to touch something. No big deal.

Can you do anything you're told? Dac says to me.

Not really, no.

Did you ever consider maybe that's what gets you into trouble all the time?

Obviously not, I say.

Maybe you should. I stick my tongue out at the house

188

where Dac's body is.

That's not going to work, Dac says. Meh, it makes me feel better, though.

Everybody drifts outside on their own time as Kane finishes loading up his bubble. I'm sitting with my legs crossed in the middle of the hall, away from everything.

"What are you doing?" Sarah asks me.

"Not. Touching. Anything," I say, trying not to even move my mouth much.

"Did Kane yell at you?" Nathan asks me. I look at him, moving only my eyes.

"Maybe," I say, dragging out the word.

"I thought so," Nathan says. "Whenever he started getting bossy when we were younger, I would keep pushing his buttons until Dad had to break it up."

"Don't remind me, or I'll punish you all over again," Gabriel says, smacking Nathan upside his head. Is Gabriel even allowed to do that? Would grounding someone who's a couple centuries old even work?

"Sorry, Dad," Nathan says, rubbing his head where Gabriel hit him. When Kane finishes putting the last of his mysterious, space-age stuff in the bubble, he turns toward us.

"Is everybody ready to go?" Kane asks. We all mumble that we're set.

Kane walks over to the edge of the tunnel we're in pulling a small, shiny, silver something out of his pocket.

He pushes some button on it, and it starts blinking. He returns the now blinking shiny thing to his pocket and calmly steps away from the edge, positioning himself behind his bubble of junk. The royals are the only ones who look like they know what's going on.

A moment later, what appears to be a light comes speeding straight towards us. Uh, are we in trouble? This light thing looks like it's going to crash into us! I look over at the royals, who still look perfectly calm. Either they're insane, or we're safe. Everybody else looks just as nervous as I am. Dac stands motionless.

What happens if you get wet? I ask him.

I have no idea, he says. Interesting. I wonder if Arthur knows.

As the light gets closer to the tunnel, it bends and turns away from us, further illuminating the ocean floor. It looks like somebody goes out there and sweeps the floor.

The light is attached to a hulking mass of metal which is now backing into the tunnel wall. The glass wall of the tunnel is about to shatter, yet the royals remain unfazed.

But instead of the big crash and instant flood I was expecting, the metal thing is actually fazing through the glass wall, like it's not there at all. It's unsettling to watch, but I can't bring myself to look away. The glass is perfectly reshaping itself around the metal with no gaps. The first parts to push into the tunnel are two identical, rounded beams set on opposite sides of the metal mass, empty space between them for their entire length. They look similar to an electrical plug on the Surface. They are followed by the larger body of metal, which gets taller on the top then bottom, looking like it's growing as it pushes through the glass, eventually revealing a set of doors. The front portion of this vehicle stays out in the water, never passing through the wall. It's still weird to see, but not as much as before when the glass was distorting and shifting around. It looks like the glass was made around the thing.

With a grunt, Kane heaves the storage bubble between the two poles, the items inside never shifting an inch. The side of the beams facing the bubble light up a bright green.

Satisfied, Kane says, "Okay, everybody get in."

He walks up to the front left side, closer to the wall of the tunnel, and opens a door. The door opens vertically so it doesn't hit the tunnel wall, which I'm not sure would be a problem considering everything that has happened already. Kane climbs in without another word. He's not a very patient man.

I look inside and notice that there are only six seats. I look around and count eleven of us "How are we going to fit?" I ask Kane. "There are eleven of us, and only six seats."

Kane pushes a button on the steering wheel and without looking at me says, "There. I called a chase PWC. It'll follow the route this one takes. It may deviate a bit, but the destination will be the same."

To save you the trouble of asking, I'm pretty sure PWC stands for Personal Watercraft, Dac tells me.

Thanks… Couldn't he just call it a boat? That'd make things so much easier.

Nathan, Gabriel, Jinn, Mark, and Fred get into the first car with Kane. I want to ask Fred why he's going with a bunch of people he doesn't know, but I don't bother. He's probably got some weird reason of his own. Maybe he wants to ask Nathan for a job.

"I'll drive us over to Hub Fourteen," Kane says. "When your chase craft gets here, climb in and press the green button once everyone is inside and the doors are secure."

"I know," Sarah says, leaning her arm against the open door on the right. "Just get out of here." She closes the door, and Kane takes off. The boat passes back through the wall much faster than when it arrived. As soon as it's entirely in the water, it picks up even more speed, leaving a trail of bubbles in its wake. I watch them until the green lights holding the storage bubble in place fade in the distance.

"Why did you stay with us?" I ask Sarah.

"What, I'm not allowed to go for a drive with my great-grandson?" I'm pretty sure there are a few more greats in there, but that's beside the point.

"Is it because you want to know more about me?" I ask.

"Yes, for starters," she replies. I look over at John, Dac, and Rick while she answers.

Would you mind keeping them busy for a bit? I ask Dac. *Do I look like a babysitter to you?*

No, you look like a clown, I say, then hear an audible growl from Dac in response. *Just tell them the story of what happened to me – to us – while they were in prison. Please?*

Fine, he says. I can tell that he understands why I'm asking. He's just giving me a hard time.

"So what do you want to know?" I ask Sarah, returning my gaze out the window. I hear Dac in the background, starting to talk to the others the same time I do.

"Everything," she says, "I want to know who you are, not just that you exist."

"Let's see, I'm fifteen, tall, have no luck with girls, go to Renaissance fairs every now and then, and seem to make enemies on a daily basis. Oh, and I hate your brother."

"What?" She asks.

She regards me with amusement. "I'm not telling you how old I am," she says. What is the big deal with girls and their age? "I can help you with your girl problems," she goes on. Doubtful. "And what's wrong with which brother?" she says finally.

"*The King,*" I tell her, feeling a familiar coil of hatred in my gut.

"Oh, right. You're from the Surface. You must mean Logan."

"That's the one," I confirm. "Are you guys so cut off from the world that you don't even know what he's doing?"

My eyes flick to the reflection of her eyes in the glass. She looks away quickly.

"It's impossible to know everything," she argues.

"Yeah, but this isn't something small," I say with a hint of anger.

Sarah doesn't try to come up with an excuse. I'm glad that she doesn't try to defend her brother. That'd probably just piss me off.

"What does he do to you?" she asks.

"Some things are really trivial, like the forced child labor, poverty, and crappy living conditions. The pollution from the factories isn't so bad either, once you get used to it. At least most of us have electricity and some sort of roof over our heads. But some things are bad, like when you are 'politely invited to a discussion' by anyone from Logan's forces. Everyone knows it's torture, literally. You go in when you misbehave or the enforcers are bored, and come out changed. Suddenly you have new scars and a black line tattooed across your wrist." I trace over the inside of my left wrist with my thumb, feeling the familiar bumps of the veins, imagining that perfectly rectangular line there, as black and ugly as the shell you become. I never want one of those. "Without fail, horrible things have happened to those people, and that's only for minor offenses."

"Is there anything…" She stops, letting her sentence trail off. I know what she was going to ask. *Is there anything I can do to help?* No, short of killing your brother,

194

and finding a do-over button for life, I don't think so.

"What's your family like?" Sarah asks me, changing the subject.

"I had to work in the worse factories to support my mom after my dad disappeared ten years ago. I haven't known my dad most of my life and now every time we speak, we take turns threatening to kill each other." I turn to my head look at Sarah. "Life sucks, huh?"

She looks shocked. It's almost like these are new concepts to her.

I continue, "Even coming up to the Sky Nation, I was forced to fight in an arena, joined a resistance group, killed more people then I care to count, was arrested again, orchestrated a jail break, and singlehandedly took down a Warship after being kidnapped by some creepy dude in a limo. As soon as you guys showed up again – *after* all the fighting– all the friends I made, my new family, instantly fell to their knees and weren't the people I knew anymore. It's taking forever to get them back, which I don't know if it'll ever happen. I was in awe of you guys initially, but really, I think I hate all royals."

"You are technically a prince," she chooses to point out. Why is that the only thing she can think to say!?

"And I hate that about me!" I say, punching the glass. The thud echoes through the tunnel.

"Yet you still wear my necklace," Sarah says flatly.

"I've had it since I left the Surface. I can't get rid of it, even if it used to be yours." I say, my fist still resting on the glass. There was an attack on my life *again* less then five hours ago by someone I thought I had saved, someone I could've just killed. And in my dreams even! Excuse me if I'm not in a good mood right now. Talking about my history always seems to put me in a mood like this.

"Well, this isn't how I expected our talk to be going," Sarah says, pushing a rogue strand of hair out of her face and tucking it behind her ear.

"When you ask questions about a history that isn't sunshine and rainbows, it's going to get dark." I look over to Dac, John, and Rick and see that they're all staring at me.

You got really loud. Distracting them didn't exactly work, Dac says in my head.

"You tell her!" I call to John and Rick. "You know just as well as I do that the Surface is crap."

"It's true," John says.

"Yeah, and these two actually have it worse than me and Freddy," Rick adds.

"So excuse me if I'm a little pissed," I say to Sarah.

"I-I never knew," she stammers, obviously uncomfortable.

"No, you didn't," I say. "Nobody does, and nobody cares. We're on our own. We thought coming to the Sky Nation would be a fresh, safe, better start. Now look where we're at. This does *not* look much better to me. This looks like the middle of a war."

"I'm sorry" is all she says. It's weak, but I know it's genuine, and that somehow defuses me a little bit. I look out past the glass and see the lights of that boat Kane called for. Perfect timing.

Chapter
Fifteen

We climb into the boat with no problems, except that Dac takes up nearly two seats. He and I sit in the back, behind the others in the front row. There's no legroom back here, and my knees are jammed into the seat in front of me. I'm sitting back here sulking, propping up my head with my fist, as I gaze out into the passing ocean. There's not enough light to see a whole lot, but I can see enough.

Why did Sarah need to go and bring up my past? Now I'm going to be in a bad mood all day. I should probably apologize to her for snapping, but right now, I'm still angry and it'd probably only lead to another one-sided argument... me screaming in her face, and her taking it. Maybe she feels somehow responsible for her brother's actions and thinks taking verbal abuse is partial penance. Or maybe I just shocked her.

Or maybe you're over-thinking this, Dac says. The boat is silent, not including telepathic communication.

Not in a good mood right now.

*I know...that's why I'm trying to talk to you. So listen,
dammit,* Dac says with unusual firmness.

Fine. What? I respond impatiently.

*Just give everybody a chance. They're new to your life,
and you to theirs. Everybody is an anomaly to everybody.*

I find this advice ironic, considering whom it's
coming from. Even my relationship with Dac started
better than having an argument right off the bat. Well,
maybe a small one about manners, but that's different.

*I know you're trying to get away from the Surface, but
I don't think that's going to happen. Get over it.*

"Shut up," I say to Dac out loud. Everybody turns
around and looks at me, but nobody says anything.
Maybe they're getting used to the ball of insanity that is
me.

I look back out the window, bored. There aren't
many fish swimming around right now, but it's cool to
look at the human sized hamster cage of tunnels and
Hubs forming the Water Nation. Light seeps out of the
halls and illuminates this undersea world. I look around
for a mermaid – I hear they're normally redheads – and
I'm actually disappointed when I don't see any.

What? If this whole place is possible, why not
mermaids?

I wish I could fly right now. That'd clear my head.
I wonder if my boots would work out in the water? As

cool as that would be, I really don't think it's a good idea to test it out. It probably wouldn't end all that well.

I close my eyes and remember the Sky Nation. Oddly enough, the first memory that comes to me is of Jinn pushing me off his platform. I wonder why that's the first thing I think of? The memory continues playing in my head, past the whole screaming faze and right into me flying for the first time. The first time I flew with Dac. The first time I felt freedom in its rawest form. The wind rushing past me, howling in my ears, the speed, the insanity, the sheer one hundred percent terror of it all. What was I more afraid of, the potential for falling to an excruciatingly painful death, or that I would have to land soon? It just felt like nothing could touch me.

My next thoughts are like flashing pictures in my brain of all that has happened to me. I see the people I've met and the battles I've fought, but my mind freezes. I get stuck on Rose. I imagine the smile on her face, her blond hair lying in a sort of perfectly uncontrolled mess. She was probably the one part of prison that made it okay. I was with her all the time. We were cellmates. When I wasn't being abducted by my dad and running around, we would stay up late and talk throughout the night. I would be okay with being arrested again if I had another chance at that.

Still, prison overall was *not* fun.

I start grinning like an idiot as I look out the window

without seeing anything with my eyes right now. All I'm seeing are memories. Horrible, terrible, unhappy memories intrude, and I shiver involuntarily.

"Is he alright?" Sarah asks, turning around to look at me.

"Don't worry about him," Dac says. "He's just in his happy place right now." Sarah gives me a concerned look before turning back.

I'm entirely zoned out, occupied with planning how to get rid of Todd. I have so many deliciously horrific ideas. I'm brought back to reality when the boat shakes. I look around and see that we're backing through a Hub wall. Next to us is Kane's boat. If I twist my head around enough, I can see the others waiting there next to Kane's Science Bubble of Doom.

I watch as my seat goes through the Hub's wall. It's almost like passing through an illusion projected onto smoke. From in here, it feels like the wall isn't real. I want to hop out straightaway, but I wait until the boat stops moving.

"All right, everybody out," Sarah says. We all climb out of the boat and stand around awkwardly.

"Follow me," Kane says. What, no hello? He starts to walk, and the Ball of Doom rolls after him. I pause in my tracks to watch it for a moment.

"Weird," I mumble to myself. I jam my hands into my pockets and bring up the rear of the conga clump with

Dac beside me. If I could melt into the shadows for a bit, that'd be great. I feel like being alone right now, but talking and explaining why seems like too much of a pain.

Just as I start to stealthily fall behind, Kane says, "Sam, where is it you saw these people?" Everyone turns around and sees me a good ten paces behind the second farthest back. Well, there goes that plan. I look up from my feet and let out a puff of air.

"Just keep walking," I answer. "They'll find us soon enough."

"Will you navigate for me?" Kane asks.

"There's no need to navigate," I tell him. "They'll find us. We might as well sit down and wait." Kane apparently takes this to heart, stopping at once. He looks around at the seemingly abandoned buildings, intrigued by them.

"This place will do, then," he announces. He places his palm against the ball of junk and says, "Open lab." The place his palm is against lights up and a grid like a circuit board illuminates all around the ball. Then the ball itself cracks into multiple pieces, folding out to create a long desk with all of Kane's science things on it. I don't even want to know how it works.

Wow, you're really out of it. No kidding.

Kane immediately gets involved in the lab desk, grabbing a wand-like object attached to the table. He walks over to one of the buildings, the sphere-table still following after him. As he runs the wand across the exterior wall of the building, he looks at a screen on the table. His face is lit up by the monitor, making him look truly like the mad scientist he is. Maybe I should call that ball thing "Minion" from now on.

"Would you tell me when the Hub residents arrive?" Kane says, not really as a question, and without looking up from his monitor. I stand around for a bit, watching Kane, before Jinn comes up to me. He doesn't say anything, just stands next to me. I'm the first to speak up.

"What?" I ask him. I don't sound aggressive or inquisitive. Really, my voice sounds distant.

"Are you okay?" he asks back.

"I'm fine."

"You sure? Because you're acting like a moody teenager."

I let out a single, semi-forced chuckle. "I'm still fifteen," I point out. "It's normal for a bit of moodiness every now and then." We both smile because of the stupidity of this conversation.

"So I may have heard about your little temper tantrum with Sarah," he says, to my extreme annoyance.

"It was not a 'temper tantrum' and it was entirely justified."

"I'm not saying it wasn't," Jinn says. "I've never asked

you about the Surface, and I don't plan to. I figured that if it was bad enough that you were willing to run away to the Sky Nation, you wouldn't want to talk about it."

"No, it's not that," I say. "It's just how she asked me, I guess. You see, I can't say that I'm much of a fan of the Royals, and the fact that she doesn't know anything about what her brother does," I raise my arm, gesturing at Sarah, "pisses me off."

Jinn nods his head. "And why does that bother you?" Great. He's starting to sound like a therapist.

"Because of how cruel her brother is," I say. "She has the same never-ending life as him, and she has no idea of how horrible he is. She's probably had hundreds of years to fix the Surface, or at least learn something about it, but she hasn't done anything." Yay me, I'm actually controlling my voice right now, even though I want to scream

"You know," Jinn says, perfectly calm, "my opinion of the royals is much different then yours." I open my mouth to say something, but Jinn adds, "Just hear me out." I shut my mouth, making a nice little popping noise when my lips reconnect. "I've had a much different experience then you have. Although Nathan may seem extremely childish and immature a lot of the time, he is still a good king. He listens to his subjects and keeps the peace."

"Only problem is when he disappears for a decade

and the New Power tries to take over," I interject.

"Well, there is that," Jinn says. "But do you see what I'm saying? I don't know what Logan is like, but Nathan is a very good king when he's around." In spite of everything, it sounds like Nathan is probably normally there, and has the Sky Nation people's best interests at heart. Even though he sometimes acts my age, he is alright as a king. "You get it?" Jinn asks.

"Yeah, I think I do," I say. "We are what our lot in life makes us. I just happened to have been born in the wrong world."

"You don't have it," Jinn says almost immediately. "You're whining. That's not the Sam I know. Besides, what I'm really trying to tell you is that our experiences give us a different outlook. It's our choice how we live and what happens in our lives. You're living proof of that. You're willing to tear down the whole world and rebuild it just so that you can live a better life."

"That's not fair. You're not allowed to use me as an example against me. That has to be cheating."

"No it's not. It's in the rulebook, page seventy two. 'Make them feel stupid at all costs.'"

"Real funny," I say. Jinn smiles at me, enjoying his own sense of humor.

"You need anything?" he asks, done poking fun at me.

"I think I just want to be alone for a bit," I reply.

"Alright. Mark and I will cover for you," he says. "Give

me a call in a bit. I'd say no fighting, but I'm pretty sure that's impossible for you."

"Thanks," I say, "jerk." I silently stalk off, ducking behind a building. As far as I can tell, nobody notices my escape.

Wrong, Dac says.

You don't count, I say. *You know everything I know. I can't really keep anything from you.*

You were still wrong.

I hear Jinn start talking as I walk away. Good job keeping them busy, buddy. I pull my hood up as their voices fade the farther I walk away. This place seems really quiet when you're by yourself. I guess I didn't notice while I was trying not to be spotted by loony New Power agents.

I don't know which streets I'm taking, but I keep walking for a good half hour or so. Hopefully, I'll run into something that looks familiar. Where's that trashed-looking library? I debate flying, which would be so nice right now, but I see something on the building next to me. It's another burned "XIV" like the one in the amphitheater I'd been taken to earlier.

"Now we're getting somewhere," I say to myself. I check out the surrounding buildings, looking for more branded XIV's. Sure enough, I find one. This building is further in the Hub than the one I saw before. I check the buildings further down from this one and see yet another marking. I follow mark after mark until I see the amphitheater. "Looks like I can find you guys pretty easy," I say to myself. The knowledge doesn't do much for me, though. If I recall correctly, the majority of them don't like me too much.

I wander along, content with knowing that I can find my way back here if need be. All I need to do is look for the XIV's in a circle, and a really well-drawn circle at that.

I look back and decide that I'm far enough away that I can fly for a bit. I kick on my boots and feel like a weight has been taken away from me. I don't go much higher then the average building height, but it's enough to change my entire perspective on the day. I don't know how I ever got along in life before without being able to fly. I pull a loopdy loop before shooting straight up. I cut the boots' ignition off just in time to flip and have my feet press against the top of the Hub. I can't make out anybody I know from up here. I can't see anyone out and about at all even.

I push off the Hub's roof and can't resist letting out a shout of joy as the normally stagnant air stings my face. I activate the boots again, propelling myself faster before I stick my arms out and start to spin. At the last second, I pull up and land on my feet. It's a running stop, but I don't eat dirt.

"I need to do that some more," I say to myself,

grinning like a madman, my chest heaving. If I wasn't trying to keep a low profile, I would probably fly some more, but now's not the time. I probably shouldn't have done that just now. My ecstatic screaming doesn't help either... Okay, so it was all a pretty bad idea, but it's in the past. I should probably get away from this spot in case anybody spotted me.

I jog away, not really paying attention to where I'm going. I didn't land anywhere near where I took off, so I'm incredibly lost right now. And I get tired of jogging pretty quickly. It's not that I'm out of shape. I just don't care to run right now. It's amazing how a little bit of flying can make your whole day

I turn a corner, running my hand against the edge of a building. For an instant, I see a flash of feminine blond hair before it disappears behind another building. I don't know why exactly, but I head that way. What if it's another New Power geek? I jog a few steps to catch up, but soon slow down to a fast walk. With heavy footsteps I continue forward. Shut up, feet!

I'm still here, you jerk! Dac yells at me.

Well, can you take quieter steps? I ask.

How does that even make sense? You're the one that's walking!

Stop trying to make me look dumb.

You don't need any help with that one. Harsh.

That one went a little too far, I tell him.

Sorry, he answers after a short pause. I can tell he's not really that sorry, though. Regardless, I keep moving forward, looking for that girl. All I'm catching are split-second glimpses of her, just enough to point me in the right direction. I see nothing a few corners later, and it looks like I've lost her.

"Dammit," I say, slowing down. "Now how am I supposed to find her?" As soon as I come to the edge of the building, something hits me from the side. I fall to the ground hard, landing on my back, a weight on top of me. I instinctively close my eyes as a reflex to the pain. Adrenaline shoots through my veins, prepping me for the fight that's already begun.

When I open my eyes, I see something that I really didn't expect. The girl on top of me leans down and kisses my forehead. I instantly freeze up, unable to do anything or even form a complete thought.

"Heya, lead-foot," Rose says, smiling.

Chapter Sixteen

"R-Rose?" I stutter. I can still feel the outline of her lips on my forehead. Please don't ever go away, tingly feeling.

"Who else would it be, genius?" she asks, pushing herself to her feet.

Wait. A rough diagram appears in my head with stick figures and everything. There are bubbles for the water, a rock for the Surface, and clouds for the sky. Stick figure me is standing on the Surface with one arrow leading to the clouds and another pointing from the clouds down to the bubbles. A stick figure Rose is standing on the clouds with an arrow leading to a question mark on the bubbles. Geez...even my imagination can't draw.

"How'd you get down here?" I ask. She sticks her hand out to help me up, and I take it.

"I came with Arthur," she answers as she gives me a pull.

"Arthur's here, too?"

"Yeah. He said he needs to kick your ass or something like that." That sounds about right.

She's telling the truth, Dac tells me. *Arthur's over here talking about how much he wants to wring your neck.*

"So next question," I say, now back on my feet. "Was that a tackle or a hug?" I know it seems insignificant, but I really care about this answer!

"It was a hug," she says, clearly seeing how pathetic I am.

Do I really have to give you dating advice? Dac says in my head.

No! I say back…. Maybe?… *No! I think I got this.*

Don't choke! Call for me if you need help.

What dating advice could he give anyway? I've been alive longer than him, as far as I know, and the only memories he can access are his own and mine. Between the two of us, there's no good dating experience.

Rose wraps her arms around me, less violently this time. "I missed you, blockhead," she says, burying her head in my chest.

"I missed you, too," I reply instantly, putting my arms around her. Hold on, hold on, why did I do that? Do I care? I could just stand here like this and probably be happy with how life turned out. Well, maybe doing this in the sky would be better than down here, but this is still pretty good.

Rose doesn't seem like she's going to pull away any

time soon, so neither do I. "How'd you find me here?" I ask.

She laughs. "You're the only knucklehead I know that can fly down here! I just followed the speck in the sky."

"That makes sense," I say. "Why did you miss me?" No, no, no! Stupid! Why would I ask something that dumb!? "I haven't been gone that long, have I?"

"After living with you for a week, I'm lonely without you," Rose tells me softly, her head still pressed against my chest. She starts loosening her grip around me, and I reluctantly do the same. I almost start whimpering.

"Let's walk for a bit," she says. "I've been sitting on a boat for a while and feel like stretching my legs." She starts walking without getting an answer from me. I jog up two steps so that I'm next to her.

"So what've I missed while I've been down here?" I ask.

"Nothing big," she says back. "My dad's okay with me fighting now."

"When did that happen?"

"A day after you left. He said I did a good job at Jinn's house and that if I ever did get into trouble, he was sure you'd protect me. I told him that'd be a little hard while you were in the Water Nation, but he just said that you'd find a way." Wow.

"I didn't know your dad thought that highly of me," I say.

212

"He said he met you when you first came up to the Sky Nation, and that you've been special since the moment he talked to you. He said you're the kind of person that can move the world if you feel like it." Well, thank you, Jackson. I had no idea you thought that highly of me.

"He's right," I say, smiling at her. "If you're in trouble, I'll help you."

"That's a pretty big promise for someone you haven't known that long," she jokes.

"Doesn't matter. I mean it." Rose smiles, and it's even better than what I remembered. There are some things that can't be done any justice.

I force myself to look around, just to see where we are. When I look up, I see something I really don't want to. There's a group of about ten New Power goons patrolling the streets of Hub Fourteen.

"Fantastic," I say. Rose follows my line of sight and sees them as well. I pull her behind a building so there's no chance they can see us. I look Rose up and down and notice the distinct lack of a sword. Fighting them right now would not be a good thing.

"What're they doing down here?" Rose asks me in a hushed tone.

"They've kinda been down here," I whisper back. "The whole problem we came down here to fix is them."

"But I thought you killed their leader," Even though

that could've been true, it's still a grim way to put it.

"Not their leader, and he's still alive," I say. "Sucks, right?"

"Not really," Rose says. "That means I've got a chance to get him before you do."

"Okay, I don't think defeating an entire evil organization should be a race between the two of us."

"Why? Are you afraid you're going to lose to a girl? Don't forget who beat you in the arena."

"Are you really going to bring that up *now*?" I ask.

"Sure, why not?" The New Power guys are getting farther and farther away when I come to a spur of the moment decision.

"Let's follow them," I say.

"Why?" Rose asks.

"Well, maybe we could find out something useful," I tell her. "Come on, it'll be fun. Finding their secret hideout would be a good first step in shutting them down." I start sneaking down the street and check over my shoulder to see if Rose is following. She is.

Should I call in the cavalry?

Not yet, but let them know what we're doing.

On it.

We follow the New Power patrol out of Hub Fourteen and down a tunnel. Luckily they're not looking behind them, which is kind of stupid on their part, but I don't care. If it means we don't get caught, then I'll go with it. We get to a crossroads in the tunnel that opens up taller and wider than usual. The goons turn right but Rose and I don't have to round the corner to see where they're heading. The only thing in that direction is an industrial warehouse looking thing in a slightly smaller Hub all of its own.

"Well that screams evil hideout if ever I've seen one," I say.

"Have you ever seen an evil hideout before?" Rose asks me.

"No, but it looks similar to some of the small factories on the Surface."

"That's small? That's not that small."

"It's all relative," I say. "And they're all pretty evil, in my opinion." Rose shrugs.

"You wanna go try to take it on?"

I stick my hand in my pocket and pull out my Sky Iron sword, letting it grow when I have my hand at my side.

"Ready when you are," I say. "Maybe I should get you a sword first, though."

"Nah, I'm good," she says. I give her a funny look. "You're not the only one who can do magic tricks." She reaches into her pocket and pulls out nothing with her hand in a fist. She stairs at her fist, scrunching up her nose in concentration. It takes her a bit, but out of nowhere, a sword forms in her hand. I'm not surprised at all because I just did the exact same thing a second ago.

Her sword glows a shade of pink. The light's not like with mine. Instead of having the whole subtle foggy thing going, hers just radiates the pink light.

See, you're not so special," she says with a smile, twirling her sword.

"You're a little slow shaping it," I say stupidly.

"Well I may not be as fast as you, but I've been working on it," Rose says, pointing her sword at me. It's been so long since somebody aimed a sword at me that it feels kinda good.

I'm entirely insane.

I push her sword away from my face. "You ready to go?"

"Race you there," Rose says before taking off running. A race to destroy the entire New Power hideout? That's a little too much. A race to see who gets to the warehouse first? I think I can get behind that.

I take off after her, not far behind. I decide to cheat a little. I kick on my boots and shoot ahead.

"Hey!" Rose yells as I rocket past her.

"See you at the finish line!" I yell back. I pour on some more speed. As I speed along, I see the backs of some New Power soldiers up ahead of me, wearing the full armored get up. "BEEP, BEEP!" I yell as I shoulder one of them and keep going. I look back and see he's flat on the floor.

Dac says, *I'm telling the others you're attacking a New Power base.*

Tattletale!

There are only two soldiers where I just was. One standing and the other now prone. The soldier standing is shouting something into a radio. I double back. Whatever he's doing can't be good. I cut my boots off and fly feet first into the one still standing's chest. He falls back, arms flailing, and the radio goes skittering across the floor. It didn't even hurt to hit the armor that time! Maybe the Water Nation branch of the New Power has worse armor? Or maybe they just made it squishier so that I can hit it!

Doubtful, Dac interjects.

"Both of you do me a favor and stay down," I say to my knocked out friends. Rose is almost here so I decide to wait for her.

"Not fair," she says as soon as she reaches me. "Not all of us can fly whenever we feel like it."

Jinn, Mark, and Arthur are coming. Arthur seemed like he wanted to fight, too, but Jinn just wants to get you out of there. He figured something like this would happen.

"Timer's on," I say to Rose, completely disregarding what she said. "The others are on their way over here." I look over my shoulder at the warehouse. "I go high, you go low?"

"How about you give me a lift and we stick together?" Rose says.

"Fine," I say. I shrink my sword down and stick it in my pocket. I get behind Rose and grab her around the waist, then activate the boots and fly us to a walkway higher up on the warehouse. It's only about ten feet up, but flying makes things easier.

A deep thud comes from inside the warehouse that shakes the ground beneath us. What the hell was that? I run over to a window, hoping to see inside. I press my face up against the glass and cup my hands around my eyes.

Inside, I see a fire starting to grow, and all rubble scattered around the place. People are running everywhere in panic. Most of them have some variation of the New Power armor on, but a good amount look like normal people. Maybe those are the people the New Power have been kidnapping from Hub Fourteen?

The masses inside are heading toward the front side of the building. The side Rose and I are at. The sounds of screaming and stampeding feet becomes audible in the blink of an eye.

"What's going on?" Rose asks me, the joy of a moment ago gone.

"Give me a second," I say, still looking inside. I see that there are a lot of busted open cages and cells, but there are still a lot of unopened ones filled with panicked people. So the New Power is caging people now too? It's like they're trying to make me hate them.

"Hang on," I say to Rose, turning away from the building and grabbing her. I fly us safely back down to ground level. I have to watch out for the running, screaming mass of people pouring out. There's no where I can see without people. Amazingly, I don't hit anybody, and nobody seems to react to the fact that I can fly. Well, this time was more like a well-controlled fall, but whatever. With a successful landing, a little pocket free of bodies forms around us as everyone else tries to run for the tunnel out of here.

"Get out of here!" I have to yell at Rose in order to be heard.

"You're not coming?" she yells back.

"I'll come find you in a second. Just get back to the Hub you found me in! The guys are coming. They'll find you first." I take off my jacket and shove it into her hands.

"But what about you?" she says, her face a picture of fear.

"There are still people inside! I have to help them! Go! I'll be fine." She nods reluctantly and lets herself be carried away by the stampede. I hope she knows enough to shrink her sword so that she doesn't hurt anybody. I turn around and start forcing my way through the oncoming crowd. I push and shove my way forward, yelling, "Get out of the way!" Nobody listens. Of course. Fed up with shouldering through people and getting nowhere, I activate my boots and fly over their heads. The door is only big enough that I have to suck in my gut to fit and still somehow manage to hit a few people in the head. I pull up once I'm inside so that I don't collide with all my fellow tall people.

God, it's hot in here.

The fire has grown into a roaring inferno. Or maybe it just looks bigger in here than it did outside. No, no it's definitely bigger. I start hacking and choking because of the smoke and am forced to touch down to stay lower. I pull the front of my shirt up over my mouth and nose as a kind of makeshift filter.

We're moving faster and keeping an eye out for Rose, Dac feels the need to say. His voice becomes faster as he goes along, *But I can tell you really need to concentrate right now. Sorry. Bye!*

Fires weren't that uncommon back at the factories, so I know how to handle them just long enough to safely evacuate. Hopefully the same principles apply when you're trying to stay near the fire longer.

Where the hell are those cages!?

I frantically look around for the trapped people, but I can't find them anywhere! Dense smoke and flames obscure my vision, and without the same vantage point as before, I can only vaguely guess where to look.

Already sweating, eyes burning, I plunge deeper into the burning building. I dance around the spots where there are open flames. I'm not dumb enough to think that I can walk straight through it without suffering any consequences. At least, not any more. Phantom pain courses through my left leg and I struggle to ignore it. Hopefully the pain isn't because of something new.

Go left, go left!

So much for being quiet!

You're useless without me. Not true! *Go left! I have better memory than you do.*

I do what he says and veer left, running up a short flight of five steps without touching the metal handrail, which I'm sure is hot enough to melt my skin. I feel that spot on my leg throbbing again, and I glance down to make sure my jeans aren't on fire. So far so good.

What now? I ask Dac.

Go right. You need to get to the back of the building. I should've realized that myself...

I can't run anymore. It hurts to suck in full breaths. I'm breathing as shallowly as possible and moving at as fast of a walk I can manage. Seconds later, I come face-to-face with a wall of flames. Well I can't walk through that, and there's no way around it. I look around. There's got to be something. Anything.

I spot a metal table sitting nearby, unharmed. This is going to hurt.

I take off my shirt and wrap it around my hands as best as I can, creating as much protection as possible to shield my flesh from the red-hot metal. Please don't be bolted down! I grab a leg of the table and pull. Thankfully, it moves. I drag and position the table in front of the fire so that its length points in my direction. Coughing violently, my only junk filter gone, I position my hands in the center of the edge of the table and lift. It starts to slide out to the side and I involuntarily reach out with my left hand to keep the table balanced. I scream as the hot metal sears my skin. My throat rips itself to shreds with the force of the scream. Through the smoke, I smell the familiar, sulfurous, gut-wrenching aroma of burning flesh. Adrenalin pushing me through the agonizing pain, I manage to push the table forward and up the last of the way and flip it over onto the fire, letting gravity take it down. As I planned, it creates a perfect path for me to get through the flames. I don't waste any time and run through. I really really really hope that path is still there when I get back.

I squeeze my left hand into a fist and cradle it against my chest. I have a feeling it'll be pretty useless for a while. It feels like the fires of a thousand suns are trapped inside my clenched fist. My hand all on its own feels hotter than the rest of me, even with flames on all sides.

You're almost there, keep going! Good, I don't think I

can keep this up much longer. *I think.* You son of a—

Something cracks overhead and falls right next to me, crushing whatever was beneath it. At least it wasn't me! I keep pushing forward, trying desperately to put the pain in my hand out of my mind. I have plenty of experience ignoring pain, but this is pretty bad.

"Next time, somebody else can be the hero," I grumble to myself as I stumble along. I start feeling really sympathetic for hotdogs when I see the first cage. Somehow I actually manage to run the rest of the way to it.

The people locked inside crowd closer to the bars, but are careful not to touch them. I wouldn't want to either. "Help! Help us! Get us out of here!" I hear a chorus of pleas coming from the cage in front of me as well as from all the others. I look at the door and see a thick lock. Of course. I need a big key... or a *really* sharp sword. That'd probably work.

"Stand back! Get back!" I yell at them, drawing my sword out of my pocket. Aiming at the lock, using only one hand—the other is still tightly clenched against my chest—I bring my sword down with as much force as I can muster. The lock breaks open. "Kick it open! Don't touch it with your skin!" The bravest man in the group lifts his booted foot and does as I say. The door swings open and slams against the wall. The freed prisoners surge out in a panic.

"Go, get out of here!" I yell, pointing my sword in the direction I just came from. As soon as this cage empties out I move on to the next cage in the row.

"Watch out!" I yell to the group inside as I again bring my sword down on the lock. It slides through it like there's nothing's there. I make sure I really it before yelling, "Kick the door open and follow the others!" I keep going down the line to the next group. The prisoners are already backed away from the door, probably having already heard my shouting.

I cough like crazy as I walk down the line. I spit on the ground and see that my spit is entirely black. That's probably not good. The spit starts to sizzle. Yeesh. Looking ahead, fire roaring in my ears, I see that there are another three cages. Almost done.

I weave around a bundle of fire to get to the next cage. Heart pounding, the sound of the fire deafening me, I cut the lock. A man kicks at the door seemingly in the same instant, forcing me to jump out of the way to avoid getting griddled.

"Watch it!" I yell at him.

"Sorry," he yells back. I want to be mad at him, but I want to get out of here just as much as he does.

Two cages to go. While trying to get to the next cage, I trip over some rubble and fall to the floor, scraping myself up further. But my left hand never moves from my chest, clenched at all times. I'm coughing uncontrollably, squinting through tears.

Don't die dumbass! Dac yells at me.

"Easier said than done," I say between coughs. This stopped being fun a while ago. Why didn't I just leave with Rose? I could've avoided all this playing-with-fire crap.

But then all the people in here would've died.

"Get up!" I hear someone scream at me. "Please, get up. You need to get out of here!" I blink my eyes open and see that I landed right in front of the second-to-last cage. There's a little girl standing close to the front, ahead of the others, a concerned look in her eyes.

I get my right hand under me and push myself up so that I'm sitting on my knees. This officially sucks. I thought the Surface was hell and that it couldn't get any worse. Surprisingly, I'm proven wrong. If you take the Surface and set it on fire like this, that'd be the lowest circle of hell.

I grab my sword and use it to help get to my feet. I cough into my shoulder as I weakly bring my sword down on the lock. It doesn't budge. Dammit. I raise my sword again and grit my teeth as I bring it down a second time. The lock falls away this time, broken.

"Go," I say in a feeble voice, nodding my head. The adults that were in the cage head for the hills. The children, led by the little girl, walk up to me.

"Come on, mister, we have to go," she says, tugging

on my pant leg.

"I...not...yet," I manage to get out between coughs. I'm almost completely unable to breathe at this point. "One more cage." Ugh, I'm going to throw up and pass out soon, I can feel it. "I'll be right behind you," I assure the kids. I try to smile at her, but I'm sure I look worse than Arthur wearing Mark's pajamas. I touch my hand to her face to comfort her, making sure the sword doesn't hurt her. I leave a big, black, sooty handprint on her cheek. I see her move her mouth to say something, but at the moment all I can hear is the crackling of the flames that are probably going to barbeque me. As the kids head off, I try to make it to the last cage.

Why does fire spread so fast? It's stupid. I don't like these rules. Does fire care if I like it or not? I wish my head would clear up, but with the serious lack of oxygen, that doesn't look likely.

I'm on it, I vaguely hear Dac say in my head. My left hand feels wet. I peek down at it and see that it's coated with a layer of blood and—

"OW!" I yell in shock. It feels like I just got smacked across the face with a lead pipe and I... I... I actually feel relatively good. For some reason, I can think clearly again!

It worked! I hear Dac yell.

Tell me what you did later, I say, rubbing my eyes. One cage left.

When I look into the last cage, I see there's only one guy inside. He looks like he's in his late twenties or early thirties. He's calmly sitting in the middle of the cell, glaring at me.

"Not this one," he says. I completely ignore him and cut the lock anyway. He jumps to his feet.

"Are you deaf?" he shouts at me. "I told you to leave me locked in here!"

"Not a chance," I say. "Hurry up and kick the door open. We're leaving."

"No," he replies stubbornly. Ugh, I do not need a problem child right now. "I am prepared to die. I deserve to die."

"Yeah? Well I don't' think so," I say. I cut the hinges of the door on the other side and let it fall away. "I'm risking my life to save your stupid, ungrateful butt, so you're going to be rescued, like it or not."

"I want to die. I refuse to go."

"This is not a discussion, nor is it *your* decision. *You* are being rescued and that's final!" I shrink my sword down and shove it in my pocket. I grab this guy's wrist and pull him after me.

"Let go, you stupid wet-head! I want to burn!" he says, tugging back. I release him for a second and slug him in the jaw.

"Shut up and come with me," I say. "I don't care what you did. You can complain until your voice gives out later, but for now let's get out of here. Got it?" He stares at me for a second, a precious second that forces me to cough harder than before, and starts walking toward the exit. Thank God! I walk alongside him, but I'm doubled over, coughing, barely able to get any air in. The guy that was reluctant to be saved is now essentially dragging me along as I cough to death from smoke inhalation.

Funny how that works.

The fire is continuing to engulf this place, eating the ceilings, walls, floors, and everything unlucky enough to be inside. Like me and this guy.

I can't tell exactly where we're going, seeing only the floor and the bases of flames. With the way I'm coughing, I expect to see my lungs lying on the floor in front of me. The heat is excruciating, blistering my skin. My lips are long split and I can taste blood. When I finally manage to look up, I see the exit, as well as a wall of fire covering the entire thing. Great. Can this day get any better?

"Jump through it," I wheeze out. "Run and jump through."

"Are you crazy?" the man asks me.

"Probably," I say. "On three?" He nods.

"One. Two. Three!" On three, we both run forward and take a leap toward the wall of fire. I squeeze my eyes shut as tight as I can and clench all my muscles. The different parts of my body burn even worse, pain playing with my senses, as I pass through the flame. I hold in my scream because I don't want to let any fire get into my mouth.

I slam against the ground, hard, unable to brace myself being completely unaware of my surroundings. I suck in a breath that's considerably cleaner than any I've taken in what feels like an eternity. I cough and spit and scramble forward, heat on my back, hopefully away from the flames. I feel hands grab onto me and pull me to my feet. I stumble the first few steps, as I get back into a miserably forced run.

"Keep moving, wet-head! We're probably almost out of time!" I drag the back of my arm across my eyes and open them. We're in the tunnel, running away from the burning building. This is good. This is very, very good. I could laugh hysterically if it wasn't for the concern in my new friend's voice. What are we almost out of time for? I see that he's in a full sprint and a good amount farther ahead of me.

"Come on, wet-head! Hurry!" he yells back to me, gesturing me forward with a wave of his arm.

"Why are we hurrying?" I shout back. Before he can say anything, the ground shifts underneath me. It feels like the entire world shifts to the right. Suddenly, torrents of water crash into me. I can't even suck in a final breath before I'm entirely submerged.

I try to open my eyes, but they really sting when I

do. It's a different sting than before, but it still hurts. Although, it seems to be helping the pain of my burns. The fire in my hand finally starts to feel like it cools down a bit, as does the rest of me. There are small pieces of something black seeping off all parts of my body. I try to look around, but my body doesn't turn like it normally does. Lungs burning from lack of oxygen, I try to walk, but it doesn't work. Odd.

I turn my head and see a giant, monstrous looking thing heading straight for me. I can't make out any details at length, but it scares me enough that I involuntarily scream. Not much of any sound comes out, but plenty of bubbles do.

My lungs feel like they're entirely collapsing, my head's throbbing, and my vision is spotty. Am I about to drown to death just to be eaten by a giant sea monster?

As the monster comes closer, my world turns to black.

Chapter Seventeen

"Is he dead?" I hear somebody ask.

"No, he's not dead. His chest is still moving, see?" another person says. The voices sound familiar, but for some reason, I can't recall who they belong to.

"It's possible you are imagining things," yet another voice says. "I extracted a large quantity of water from his lungs, and he still hasn't awakened. It is probable that he's brain-dead due to the extended lack of oxygen. Really, it was quite foolish of him to run into a burning building and end up drowned." Wait, am I dead?

"He was saving the lives of *your* people!" another voice yells.

"I understand, but logically, it makes no sense. If he had never left and gone into the building, he would not be in this condition." Stop talking about me like I'm not here!

"Maybe I'll shove my foot up your ass," I say weakly. I open my eyes as fast as I can, which is pretty slow at the moment. I'm blinded by a bright light and squint for a moment until my eyes adjust. I'm lying on a wonderfully cold, hard floor, and see that pretty much everyone I know is standing around me, arguing with each other. Even Arthur and Rose are here. Rose looks like she's screaming in Kane's face, pointing fingers at him, talking with her hands, the whole bit. Mark and Jinn are next to each other, looking just as ready to rip Kane limb from limb, but holding each other back either because they don't want to attack a royal, or because they're competing to get to him first.

I keep trying to tell them that you're alive, but nobody believes me. I'm standing behind your head. That's why you can't see me, he adds, already knowing my question.

I like being alive, I tell him. *Too bad it hurts so much.*

Well at least you followed my directions and didn't die.

You didn't have to tell me that. I could've figured out 'don't die' all by myself. I look and see that Arthur is staring directly at me, wearing his usual pissed-off expression. I give him a little nod.

"Dammit, you're still alive," he says. He comes closer to me and crouches down so his eyes are inches from mine. I can't look away if I want to. "You owe me money." Good ol' Arthur. That's the tender love and care I've been missing from my life.

"Put it on my tab," I tell him.

"Did I mention how much I really wish you died?"

Arthur says.

"Would it make you feel any better if I told you every part of my body really hurts right now?"

"Humph. It does, actually. I think I might go throw a party." Arthur slaps my cheek and I wince. "I like the ash on you. Makes you look like a real blacksmith." Arthur stands up and shouts a booming, "HEY!" over all the arguing. That was painfully loud. Rose stops yelling. Jinn and Mark look right over. "Your boy's still alive." He jabs a thumb at me and walks toward the tunnel wall. All eyes shift to me. Creepy.

"Sam?" Rose says, breathless. She flies over, drops to her knees and kisses me, seemingly all in one motion. I vaguely hear a couple awkward grumbles and coughs, but they're a million miles away. Right now all I know is that Rose's lips are pressed against mine. It doesn't last anywhere near long enough, as she pulls away long before a couple years pass.

"What did I do, and where can I get another one of those?" I ask right after her lips leave mine.

"Maybe later," Rose says.

"Hey, you finally kissed a girl!" John exclaims. I roll my eyes.

"Real smooth. Thanks a lot, buddy," I mumble. Rose smiles at me.

"Fascinating," Kane says. "It's curious that you're still alive with no apparent brain damage. May I examine you? You were technically dead for a long period of time, even before you drowned." I look at Rose, really look at her, and see that her eyes are red and puffy like she's been crying. How long was I out?

"What the hell is your problem?" Rose yells at Kane, standing back up. "He wakes up and the first thing you do is ask if you can use him as a science experiment?"

"Just his brain," Kane answers calmly, "but potentially his entire nervous system, and his organs as well. It would depend on my initial findings." As much as I don't want to become Kane's plaything, the question doesn't shock me at all.

"You're unbelievable!" Rose says.

"My apologies," Gabriel says, stepping in and silencing Kane with a touch of his hand. "While my son is very inquisitive and intelligent, he lacks many social graces."

"It's not the first time he's asked Sam if he could experiment on him," Sarah says under her breath. Rose looks at me with a horrified expression, having crazy good hearing.

"I'm used to it at this point," I say from the floor, sounding like a chain smoker. My throat is killing me, being raw and split open. Honestly, I probably couldn't get up right now even if I wanted to.

"I got you," Dac says, stepping forward and tucking his arms under me.

"Cold!" I say, surprised. His metal arms are freezing!

"Sorry," he apologizes, picking me up and placing me on my feet.

"No, no. I like cold. Cold is good. Cold is my friend," I reply, liking anything but heat. "I'm moving to the North Pole after this." I start to put pressure on my legs and suck in a breath between my teeth. Finally getting a chance to look myself over, I see that my skin is charred black in places and badly blistered in the others. My jeans are ruined, burn holes spotting them and the bottoms burned up and torn. They're a good couple inches shorter.

"Sorry, what hurts?" Dac asks me.

"Everything," I answer back. "How many people got out?" I can't keep the sense of "holy crap" out of my voice as I tentatively poke my blackened skin. I'm a Sam-kabob! I should be in way more pain than this. I must still be in shock. Yeah, that's it.

"We all did," somebody says. I look for the owner of the voice. I quickly spot the last guy I saved, the one that was locked up by himself, sitting with his back against the tunnel wall.

"What're you still doing here?" I ask him. "Go home already."

"They would not welcome me back."

"And why's that?" The others aren't paying attention, still busy arguing. I'm just choosing to ignore them.

"I did a horrible thing," he tells me. "I betrayed my entire Hub, and I let my Hub Runners down." What's a Hub Runner?

"Eh, that's nothing," I say. "What's your name? I went through all that trouble to save you, the least you can do is share."

"Eli," he says. "Yours?"

"Sam. Nice to meet you. Please don't get stuck in any burning buildings again." I try to smile at him, but I'm not sure it comes out as sincere as I intended. For some reason, my brain decides at this exact moment to feel self-conscious about my lack of a shirt. I look and see that Rose has my jacket on. "Um, Rose, could I have my jacket back?" She turns away from a new one-sided argument with Kane, and looks at me.

"Yeah, sure," she replies, exhausted from yelling, she pulls off my jacket while walking over to me. "What happened to your shirt anyway?"

"Burned up in the fire," I say, reaching out to grab my jacket. I see a really ugly sight...my left hand. There's an ugly, brown burn mark covering the length of my palm, extending from between my thumb and other fingers to the opposite end. I recall the metal table edge and resist wincing. The scorch mark on my hand looks like a design someone might burn into a piece of wood. Also on my palm are cuts where my chewed-down, nubby nails bit into my skin. There are a few blisters among the other damage, but that's nothing.

"Ow," I say, transfixed, feeling the ghost of pain. It's weird that I'm not screaming bloody murder right now. There's this weird sensation of lingering heat, and yet it feels like I'm holding onto an ice cube that's tearing my skin off.

Rose gasps when she sees my hand. "Oh my God, what happened?"

"I think I accidentally branded myself," I say, raising it for closer examination.

Switch sides, I say to Dac, who's standing to my right. *I don't think that hand'll do me much good right now.* Without a word, Dac swaps over to my left and leans slightly to let me put my arm around his neck. It's a good thing I'm tall, since he's especially massive. With my right hand, I take my hoodie back from Rose. I pull my arm away from Dac, suddenly feeling silly for having put it there a second ago. Very carefully, I first put my left arm into the left sleeve. I can't avoid scraping a few blisters, but it doesn't hurt, not really. I pull on the other sleeve without any problem, and zip it up. Somehow, I feel a lot better with clothes on. The jacket covers most of the blackened splotches on my arms and chest. A few marks are poking out on my neck and hands, though. It's weird how destroyed and wounded I look and then I have this pristine jacket with the subtle smell of perfume on. Maybe I should cut some holes into it, just so that it matches the rest of me.

"You don't have to keep fighting with Kane," I say to her. "He's not a people person, at least as far as I know." Rose still looks distressed, but there's a tiny bit of calm starting to return to her. I turn my attention to Eli. "Come on, let's get you home."

"Are you sure?" he says, unwilling to believe that I'm serious about helping him.

"Yeah, let's go," I say, nodding my head in no particular direction. He climbs to his feet. "You lead the way," I tell him, "because I have no idea where we're going."

"It's this way," he says, pointing down the tunnel.

"That way it is, then," I answer. I try to take a step forward on my own and find out that I can do it! At first, it feels like my limbs don't want to listen to me, but after a few zombie-esk steps, I can walk fairly normally again. It hurts, though.

"You look like death walking," Dac remarks.

A memory of the fire suddenly comes to mind. I ask Dac, *How did you clear my head back in the fire? It sounded like you did something.*

It was quite simple, actually, he answers. *You know how slapping someone can sometimes clear their head?*

Yeah?... Where's this going?

Well, I had Jinn hit me with a metal pipe so that we could clear your head. What?

That's not simple at all, I say. *Why would hitting you do anything to help me?*

I don't get it either, but you're not dead. Are you really going to argue?

No, I think I'm happy with the end result. Maybe that's what Kane was talking about when he said I was "dead" before I drowned. Maybe I was. Is it possible that while my own body was dead, I was essentially running off any life force Dac gave me?

That's creepy and crazy, Dac comments, *but probably true. With all the screwed-up things that have happened to you lately, I wouldn't be surprised.*

My legs are really starting to hurt. I'm forced to stop walking for a moment and catch my breath. Even though I'm hurting, it still doesn't make sense that I'm not worse off. Far worse.

"Hey Jinn," I yell up to him. "Do you have any Blue Elixir on you?"

"It's back at the house," he tells me. "Somehow, I wasn't expecting to need it today." I don't know why he sounds so accusing. It's not like it's *my* fault someone set that building on fire.

"Not a problem," Kane says, butting in on our conversation. "Just call Bean and he will get it here. I took the liberty of programming his number into your phone for you while I was fixing it." I awkwardly use my right hand to dig around in my left pocket. When I get my phone out I hit the button to turn it on. Nothing. The screen remains dark. I try shaking it, hitting the button a bunch of times, and slapping it against my leg, but it stays dead. As I beat it against my pants, I notice drops of water coming out of it.

"I think it's broken," I say.

"Aw, all my hard work!" Mark complains, running up and ripping the phone out of my hand. He looks at it, examining every inch. "It's okay, baby," he says. "Daddy'll get you all fixed up and pretty again." Wow. Mark is baby-talking to a cell phone. He holds it up to his cheek and seems to be stroking it.

Even I *think that's weird,* Dac says. That's saying something. Mark hangs onto the phone, shoving it in his pocket. I check to make sure that I still have all my stuff. It would suck if I lost anything on the ocean floor.

Necklace, check.

Sky Iron sword, check.

Everything else, inconsequential.

Touching my sword reminds me that Rose has one now, too. "So what's the story?" I say to her. "How'd you get a Sky Iron sword?"

"Arthur made it for me," she says, falling into step alongside me.

"Are you rich?" I ask. The last I checked, Sky Iron swords were extremely expensive.

"No," she says with a little giggle. I'm relieved to

240

see she's not in the mood to stab someone in the neck anymore. "It's kind of a long story."

"We have time," I say. We're following Eli to whichever Hub he's from, and I have no clue how far a walk it will be.

"Okay," she says, pausing a second. "Well, after you guys left, Todd and I started having issues." Pause. Is there any way to get out of this conversation? I don't want to hear about *Todd.* I pronounce his name in the weirdest voice my brain can manage. "We started fighting and were growing apart."

Still want her to stop talking? Dac asks.

Shut up, I'm trying to listen, I say impatiently.

"One day he called me and told me to come to the Market District," Rose continues.

"And somehow they ended up in my shop," Arthur interjects from behind us. "The little prick wanted to buy a Sky Iron sword for her, engraved with something sickening like 'Love you, babe – Todd.' Blaugh." Arthur makes a fake vomiting sound.

"He thought it would make me like him more," Rose explains. "He thought he could buy me." Does that actually work? I've never had enough money to try. To me, "buying" a girl would be sharing some bread with her. Maybe. If I was feeling generous.

Arthur grumbles, "I gave him a price ten times what I normally charge. Insult my work, will he? Comes crying

241

to me expecting a discount? HA!"

"Todd left, offended by the price," Rose says. "He also called Arthur an 'inferior life form' or something like that." Arthur lets out a deep rumble from his chest. Is he growling? It sure sounds like it, like a convincing don't-mess-with-me growl.

"I told your girl here to wait up a minute," Arthur says. Wait, did he just say *my* girl? "Told her that I'd make her a sword, but she'd have to tell that punk-ass that it's from you. I charged it to your account, so it's only fair." Wow, Arthur hates Todd enough that he was willing to make Rose a Sky Iron sword.

"When I told Todd, like I promised," Rose says, "he left me. He said that I could go be with you, then."

When it's clear that's the end of her story, I say, "Wow." I'm very articulate.

Now what do you really think? Dac asks me, knowing there's more behind my one-word response.

That was the most beautiful story I've ever heard.
You're pathetic.

Shut up! I know, I think back in a whiney tone.

"I was planning to break up with him anyway," Rose says. "Something made me realize how big of a jerk he is."

"And what would that be?" I ask her.

"Secret," she says with a devious smile. I raise an eyebrow at her.

242

"And so why are you down here?" I ask, frustrated by not knowing.

"I came down a few days after Todd and I broke up," Rose says.

"Oh?" I say back.

"For the love of Pete," Arthur says, "the boy's dense as a hammer. Just tell him!" Such grace. How does he do it?

"We all know where you're going... well, everybody but Sam," Fred says.

"We do?" Kane says. "I do not understand."

"Don't worry, sweetie, boys are stupid," Sarah says to Rose. What is everybody talking about? What am I missing?

"Congratulations, buddy," John says, bringing his hands down on my shoulders. I wince in pain. "You just got your first girlfriend."

"I did?" I say. I look at Rose, and see that she's blushing.

"Only if you want," she says, looking at her feet.

Say yes, stupid!

"I just got my first girlfriend," I say to myself in disbelief. I get a round of applause from everyone around me. I'm not sure if it's pity applause, sarcastic applause, or genuine applause. It's probably a mix of the three. There are butterflies in my stomach, regardless of the fact that my body is one big ache.

243

But now something new is gnawing at me. What do I do now!? I've never had a girlfriend. What am I supposed to do? Do I hold her hand, do I kiss her, or do I just keep smiling at her awkwardly? Should I ask somebody what to do? Yeah, that's what I'll do. I'll ask John later.

"We're here," Eli says. Saved by the bell. "Welcome to my home, Hub Fourteen."

"Wait, this is where you're from?" I ask.

"This was my home, but now I don't know anymore. I did some horrible things." Eli looks down, sounding remorseful.

"Do you want us to go somewhere else while you go to the amphitheater?" I ask him. The people from this Hub are kinda touchy. I don't know how well they'd react if the group of us appeared at their super-secret headquarters out of the blue.

"You know about the council house?" Eli asks me, sounding genuinely surprised.

"I've been there once," I tell him. "They wanted to kill me."

"Sounds about right," he says. "In that case, you're more than welcome to come with me, but I don't think the others should. They can wait nearby, just not inside the house."

"No need to bother," Kane says. "I will be returning to my research site. I believe I'm close to a breakthrough."

"Wait, Kane," I say. Something else has been on my mind. "Before you go, what was that monster I saw out in the water?"

"Oh, that's Billy. I developed him years ago. He's a guard-and-retrieval squid. He put you back inside the tunnels. He's two hundred feet long and one of my most fascinating developments." Without another word, Kane turns and walks off on his own. I see him turn down an alley. Does he even know where he's going?

So I was saved by a giant, two-hundred-foot-long squid that kills people? That's extremely creepy.

"I'd best be going with him," Sarah says, heading quickly after her brother. "Someone's got to keep him out of trouble. You coming, Nathan?"

"Hm? Yeah, sure. I don't need to walk them back. Dad?"

"I'll stay with these youngsters," Gabriel says. "Take care of your brother."

"See you soon." With that, both Nathan and Sarah leave, chasing after Kane. The rest of us continue towards the "council house." I still think it's a wrecked library or something, but I understand using what you have.

When we're a few blocks away from the building, Eli says, "Okay, you guys wait here. Sam and I will go ahead and talk to the council." Eli and I keep walking. Dac follows along.

"Why are you coming?" I ask him. "You've never been here before."

"No, but I don't want there to be another chance of you dying again," Dac replies. "It gets annoying rather quickly."

"I'll say," I agree. The three of us walk to the broken-down council house. We pass through the broken doors and see a huge amount of people already standing on the floor with us. The elevated seats are filled. A hush comes over the room as all eyes turn to us.

"So, the traitor returns." The presider says.

Chapter Eighteen

"Whoa. Wait...what?" I say. Traitor? Who's a traitor?

The speaker is the same guy I talked to before, when Britney brought me here. "What did you think? We would welcome you back with open arms?" He sounds pissed.

"No, I didn't," Eli speaks up. He's the traitor? What did he do? "All I hope for is a chance to explain. After that, you may pass your judgment, and I'll do as you say."

"Mister!" I hear a suspiciously familiar little girl's voice. The next thing I know, something crashes into my legs, almost knocking me over. I look down and see that it's the little girl from the fire.

"Hey, you didn't get hurt, did you?" I ask her, using one of my more gentle voices.

She looks up at me. "No, I'm okay."

"That's good to hear," I say with a smile. I'm talking gently to this little girl, but in my head, I'm slaughtering that jerk of a presider. He didn't seem like this much of a jerk the last time I was here, but he really doesn't like Eli.

You have a dark imagination, Dac says to me.

"So this wet-head is the one that saved our citizens from the Snatcher's warehouse. You look like hell," the leader says to me. I nod. "From the whole of Hub Fourteen, I thank you. However, even though you saved a great number of our people, among them is one of our most despicable traitors." All eyes are fixed on Eli and nobody is gawking at Dac. They all did for maybe two seconds until Eli stole the stage.

I can't hold it in anymore. "Come on," I say, annoyed. "What could he have done that's so bad?"

"He sold us out to the Snatchers," the presider nearly shouts. I look up into his worn, gray, clouded eyes, and besides wariness see nothing but the truth in them.

"Just let me explain," Eli pleads. "I didn't do it on purpose, I swear." The presider turns his attention and contained fury to Eli. To me, the presider isn't that intimidating. But apparently, he absolutely terrifies Eli, who can't even look at him.

"Are you trying to say that you did not sell us, the people of Hub Fourteen, as well as your fellow Hub Runner," the presider barks, jabbing a finger at Eli for emphasis, "to the Snatchers? Are you trying to tell me that you are not the reason we live in terror every single day of our lives?" Some question. The presider isn't listening. He's just listing Eli's accused crimes.

"Hey jerk-face," I cut in, raising my voice to shout across the large room, "would you shut up already? The guy's trying to speak." It's subtle, but the presider seems furious. Probably because he thinks that Eli is the epitome of evil right now.

"Presider Rido," Eli says, stepping forward. "I did not, nor would I ever betray my comrades. The true story is that I was captured. Initially, the Snatchers followed me when I was coming here, but lost sight of me a few blocks away. By the time they found me again, I was asleep for the night, and they took me." That's even more pathetic than any of *my* stories. "I was brought back to their hideout and when I awoke, I was already caged. They kept trying to get information out of me, but I misled them. Evidently, I couldn't lead them far enough away. I began to worry when the first prisoners arrived. It was torture to see them bringing more and more prisoners..." Eli's voice trails off here and he looks down, as though fighting his emotions.

Finally he lifts his head. "There was nothing I could do, they started investigating on their own. I wanted to die. I watched friends of mine join them. They became volunteers, just to be freed from their cages." A guilty look takes over Eli's face. But it's combined with something darker. "In secret I planned to destroy the place, to kill everyone there, myself included, to stop the evil!" There is a collective gasp from the entire room. I don't pay any attention to them. I slug Eli in the jaw. He falls to the ground, tripping over himself, surprised by the unexpected blow.

"You idiot!" I yell at him. "If you could've waited another five stinking minutes you would've all been out of there! New Power idiots are much easier to handle than a burning building! What would you've done if I wasn't there to save all your asses?" No matter how many times I've wanted to die and be done with the factories, the Surface, my miserable existence, everything, I've always had to live on. For myself and for others. Eli doesn't get to die over a misunderstanding. "Hey, Rido," I yell at the head dude, skipping the title crap, my eyes never leaving Eli, "I know what you can do."

"Oh, and what's that?" he responds.

"Put Eli in charge of your defenses," I say. I turn to look at Rido. "He's so big on protection, give him a way to do it. Give him a team, call them the 'Hub Runners' or whatever."

"*We* are the Hub Runners," Rido points out, referring to the whole of Hub Fourteen.

"Then call them the Sprinters," I continue, rolling my eyes. "I don't really care what you call them. Just make this guy do something he cares about. Put that devotion to use." I keep my eyes trained on Rido, and he meets my gaze, pulling at his lower lip.

"You know what, wet-head?" Rido says, bouncing his finger at me. "I like your style. Eli'll get his Sprinters! Nice punch, by the way. No wonder the Snatchers fear you." He bangs his fist against the arm of his chair, as do the other counsel members in the room. "It's done," he says grandly. Apparently when they make big decisions, chair destruction finalizes things.

I help Eli clamber to his feet. "You're welcome," I say under my breath.

That was actually smart, Dac says to me.

I have my moments, I reply.

"One more thing," I say to Rido.

"Yeah?"

"Can somebody teach me how to swim?" I really don't like this whole drowning thing. If I'm going to be hanging out in the Water Nation, knowing how to swim might prevent it.

The entire room bursts into tear jerking laughter. I should probably be embarrassed, but I really can't force myself to care.

"What's with you, Wet-Head?" Rido asks through his laughter, wiping a tear from his eyes with one hand and holding his gut with the other. "What planet are you from?"

I look back over my shoulder at Dac. *Should I?*

Reading my thoughts, he shrugs. *Might as well.*

"The Surface," I say flatly. The laughing gets harder and louder, but I don't flinch. When Rido opens his eyes and sees me, completely serious, the laughter in the room dies down a little.

"You're serious?" he says, finally catching on. Took him long enough.

"Yup," I say, over accenting the word, dragging out the "*y*." I wish it weren't true, but it is. What's a guy to do?

"A-Alright...alright," Rido stumbles, trying to swallow that pill. "So who's going to teach our Wet-Head to get a wet head?" He addresses everyone present. There's an awkward silence.

"I'll do it," a familiar female voice finally says. I look around and see her standing in the back of the room, her older brother seething next to her and trying to pull her back into her seat.

"Hey, Britney," I yell up to her with a wave.

Rido twists around awkwardly in his seat to get a look at her. "That's easy, then," he says, going back to his normal slouch. "Britney will teach the Surface dweller, soon to properly be a Wet-Head, how to swim."

Chapter Nineteen

Britney works her way around the mass of bodies and disappears to an out of view staircase. Her brother remains in his chair, wearing a less than pleased expression.

"Eli, today, rest. Tomorrow you and I will set up your Sprinters," Rido says. He turns his gaze to the clump of people in front of him that isn't Dac, Eli, and me. "All of you, return home. I'm sure it's been hard for you. We'll organize things in the morning." Is it late right now? I have no idea how to tell time without the sun.

Why do you even go anywhere in the body? I ask Dac. *It's not like you do much of anything.*

You know how it is when you think you want something, then realize you don't really care?

Obviously.

This body is like that for me, he admits. *Don't get me wrong, I love it, but it's overrated. Bossing you around in your head is a lot easier and so much more fun.* Alright then. *But keep in mind, I'm able to fight like this. I guess that's what I use it for.* Britney comes around a corner to where we're waiting.

"Your brother doesn't look very happy," I say, pointing up at him sulking.

"He's not," she says, "but that won't stop me from teaching you how to swim."

"Thanks," I say. "I've got some friends waiting like a block away. Just let me go grab them, and then we'll have our lesson." For some reason it sounds more like I'm asking permission than telling her.

"That's fine," she says. "It shouldn't take long for you to learn anyway." I head for the door with Britney and Dac.

"See you later," I tell Eli as I walk past him. He gives me a relieved smile, looking like a weight has been taken from his shoulders.

While we're headed to meet back up with the others, Britney asks me, "Are you afraid of water?"

I take a second before I respond. "I don't think so. I mean, I drowned to death and back again earlier today, so maybe subconsciously."

"You drowned?"

"Apparently I died, too," I say. We turn a corner and I see my friends still waiting there.

The first comment I hear is from John. "You traded that Eli guy for a girl? Teach me your ways, oh master!"

He mock bows over and over, begging for my secret of how I trade guys for girls.

"Don't mind him," I tell Britney and anybody else that's creeped out by John. "He's normally like this." It's true. If John can find a way to get closer to girls, he will study and perfect it.

"It's fine," Britney says, sounding totally accepting and okay with John's weirdness. Her face, though, gives the clear impression that she thinks he's weird. "I volunteered to come by the way."

"So it wasn't kidnapping?" John asks, somehow sounding surprised.

"No, not at all," Britney laughs. "Sam asked if someone would teach him how to swim, and I thought it might be a start on paying him back."

"Pay him back for what?" Jinn breaks in, suspicious. "Have you two met before?"

Britney nods, "Sam saved me from the Snatchers."

"The Snatchers?" Jinn asks.

"New Power," I clarify for him. The jerks are everywhere.

"What have I missed all these years?" Gabriel asks himself in a hushed tone.

"There's a lot you've missed," I tell him. Gabriel is silent, and gets a contemplative look on his face.

"So shall we go start the swimming lesson?" Britney asks, trying to change the topic.

"Yeah, let's go," I agree.

"Wait," Rose says. I look at her. Please don't be the jealous type. Biting her lips, and nervously twisting the edge of her shirt, she asks, "Can you teach me, too?" Red touches her cheeks. She's embarrassed that she, apparently, doesn't know how to swim either.

"Same here," John interjects. I look around and see that everybody else looks like they know how to swim. What does that look like? Well, for one, they don't look super awkward right now like Rose and John do.

"Sure," Britney says. "I can teach all of you. Follow me." She starts walking and the we shuffle along behind her. "Do any of you have swimsuits?" she asks while we're walking. When she sees our blank looks, she adds, "Got it. You can borrow Connor's and mine."

"Who's Connor?" John asks.

"My older brother," Britney says.

"Oh. Good, good," John says, smiling to himself behind Britney's back. Oh no.

I grab John's arm and whisper to him, "Are you really going to try and ask her out?"

"Well, you just got yourself a super hot, awesome girlfriend from another nation. I figure it's my turn." He's grinning like that somehow made total sense.

"Please, just don't mess with her while she can really easily drown us. Trust me, it's not as fun as it looks."

"I don't see the problem," John says. "Your girlfriend

could probably kill us anytime she wants to. She doesn't even need water to do it."

"No," I say. "She could kill *you* whenever she wants to. I could beat her in a fight."

"Is that so?" Rose says loudly from behind us, making both John and me jump. She rests her elbows on both of our shoulders. "If I recall correctly, I'm the one that beat *you* in the arena." She and John both give me one of those *uh hu, she's got you* faces. Stop being on her side John! Some best friend.

"That's only because you snuck up on me," I say, reaching for a comeback, "and I was distracted."

Smooth.

Nobody asked for your opinion.

"So all I need to do is distract you?" Rose says, plotting. "Well, that's easy enough." She grabs my face and kisses me. My brain turn to mush. All this brain melting and reconstruction probably isn't good for my health.

Smooth. Dac says, this time actually sounding impressed.

Thanks, I say, giddy.

"You're dead," Rose exclaims, her lips an inch from my face, smiling.

"Yup, that'll do it," I say with a short, two puff laugh.

"That's how I want to die," John murmurs, staring longingly. "Um, did I just say that out loud?"

"Yes. Yes you did," Rose says.

"Why am I not embarrassed?" John asks nobody in particular.

"Because you're you," I answer. "Chasing girls is your life. Oh, and don't think kissing me will work for you. That's a "Rose only" thing." Well, chasing girls would be John's life if it weren't for the factories, and having to take care of his family, and making sure he doesn't get killed, and so many other happy thoughts. For those of us with that situation, we generally avoid talking about it. We all know we have craptacular lives. Why mention it when we already know it's there?

"Oh, and I was so looking forward to trying it. What does he taste like?"

"That's a secret," Rose laughs, sliding her hand into mine. "So how does the life of 'girl studies' work for you, Creeper?" She uses "Creeper" as a nickname, not primarily an insult.

"Pretty well, actually," John replies. "Want to know what one of my best pick-up lines is?"

"Will I regret saying yes?" Rose says cautiously.

"No, it's nothing bad," John argues. "I just say that I'm Sam's best friend. He is kinda like a celebrity at the factory we work at."

"Factory?" Rose asks. Good going, loudmouth! She doesn't know much about the Surface, and I was hoping to keep it that way for as long as possible. Besides, if I was going to to tell her about it, I would've at least had better timing than right now!

Dac suddenly appears behind John and whacks him upside the head.

"OW! What was that for?" he yells, rubbing his head.

"Glitch," Dac says simply, and falls back.

Was that really a glitch?

No. That was a favor. I thought it would look weird if you suddenly hit him.

Thank you. I think it, Dac does it. That's pretty awesome. Well, more like I ask, he *sometimes* does.... When he's in the mood... Okay, almost never.

"So what factory?" Rose asks. Damn. I was hoping she would be distracted.

Want me to hit her too?

No! I think we're good. I'm at a loss here. Normally, punching someone resolves any issue (Any of my issues anyway), but I don't think hitting my new girlfriend would be good.

"It's, uh, bad," I have a way with words.

"What kind of bad?" Rose persists.

"The really bad kind," I say unhelpfully. Lucky for me, the others are politely engaging in their own conversations so that it doesn't look like they're paying attention.... Even though I know they are. Rose glares at me, not letting me get away with this.

"There are factories down here," Britney says. "Are

the ones on the Surface different than ours?"

"Oh yeah," John says. I glare daggers at him. "The ones on the Surface are pure evil. They don't care about us. It's basically work until you die. Injuries don't matter, if you're sick it doesn't matter, if your friend just died it doesn't matter. You work."

"What do you mean by that?" Rose asks. Oh man, John started talking. Everything's going to come out.

"Well they don't really care. It's basically slave labor," John. Shut up! "I mean, Sam and I have both almost died a couple times and we had to keep working." He lifts his shirt up to show off his nonexistent abs. There's a giant crescent moon scar that runs from right under his ribcage to just above his pelvis on the right side. "I got this one a few years ago," he explains. "I lost one of my ribs in the process. Only reason I'm still alive is because of Sam." He nods back at me, "While I was on the floor screaming in pain because of losing part of my stomach and ribs, he took over for me. He did my work in the factory, neglecting his own. They punished him pretty severally for that."

Rose turns to me. "What did they do?" We've stopped walking.

"We're going to got get you some Blue Elixir. You haven't stopped limping and you wince whenever your shirt moves," Jinn says, meaning everybody there except for the three of us needing to learn how to swim are going to leave. He clearly still hasn't heard our conversation.

"Alright, we'll meet you back where Kane is as soon as we can. Worst case, we'll see you back at the house." I say.

"Try harder to die this time," Arthur says, lumbering off. The four of us, John, Rose, Britney, and I, wait until they've left before we speak again.

I'll be sure to get you that Blue Elixir, Dac says.

Thanks, buddy.

"What happened?" Rose asks again, really wanting to know the answer, almost shaking me. Britney is running her hands over John's scar, following it from top to bottom. That's one of his favorite moves, let them play with the scar. God, he's an idiot.

"Torture," I say blankly. "It's really no big deal. It happens all the time. I just received the *'proper'* punishment for not doing my work." I can't help but mockingly use the word proper. The enforcers use it so self-righteously. We all know they're full of it.

"Tortured how?" Rose asks.

"You didn't see before?" I ask her. I've been shirtless around her before, she should've seen the scars. Jinn and Mark have seen them plenty of times around Jinn's house, they've just had the courtesy not to ask how I got them. When Rose shakes her head no, I say, "You'll see when we get in the water then. I'm probably too burnt up for you to get a good look at it right now."

"Let me see," Rose says.

"Really, it can wai—"

"Let. Me. See," Her eyes are fire. With a sigh, I unzip my jacket and shrug it off. The inside of it has been further mucked up by the charred skin and ash from my burns. I turn so that my back is to Rose, John, and Britney.

"Can you see anything?" I ask, my head hanging so that my chin is almost against my chest.

"No? What am I looking for?" Rose asks.

"Here, let me show you," John says. "Look here." Even though he doesn't touch me, I can feel John's hand tracing lines on my back.

"They're mostly faded," I say.

"Oh my God!" Britney gasps when she sees them, a hand flying to her mouth. I guess it's even shocking to someone from the Water Nation.

It's official.

The Surface is the worst.

"How did you get these?" she asks.

"Knives and chains mostly," I reply. "None of the mark from the beating generally stuck around past a bruise, and you can't really see broken bones. Sometimes they would heat up some rebar until it was glowing red and hit me with it. The factory managers would play a game where they'd each get twenty seconds to do as much damage as they could. None of them were allowed to use the same method, though."

One of the girls puts their hand against my back. Pain races through me from my burns. But instead of screaming out like I want to, I clench my jaw.

"They wailed on him for a week," John says. "He covered for me for a week before they finally decided I was unfit to work." They're all staring at my back. I don't need to see it. I know what it looks like. Silver and whitish-pink lines crossing everywhere, covering most of my skin. I wonder what it will look like with the new scars from the fire.

"Makes my little injury look like nothing, doesn't it?" John continues. "When he got those is also when he became the most respected kid in the entire factory. He didn't have to do that. Nobody else would've if it was one of their friends on the line."

"Don't you ever think about your own health?" Rose asks, tracing her fingers over the patterns on my back.

"Not really in my nature," I say.

"Sam had to keep working through all the 'discipline sessions,' and even after them. He didn't get a break like me. We normally get abused, but that was a special kind of discipline," John says. "They really hated Sam. A few months later, there was this kid, younger than both of us..."

"He lost his arm working in the factory," I say, taking

over the story. "When the managers kept pushing him to keep working, I punched one of them in the jaw and shoved him down onto the conveyer belt. I hit him over the head with a wrench so he'd lie still, and let him be carried away into the furnace. That was the first time I ever killed someone." I look Rose in the eye, then Britney. "Before he burned up, I stole his 'Unfit for Duty" slip – all the managers carry just one, or I would've taken more – and filled it out for the kid. He was sent home and even got medical treatment. By the time the other managers figured out what I did, the kid had mostly healed up and nobody could deny that he wasn't able to work. After that, though, I had to run both our stations. They would've cut my hands off if it didn't inhibit my ability to get the job done. But I got a stab wound in the back and a punctured lung."

"They still didn't authorize lethal force against him," John interjects.

"What?" Britney asks, shocked, "So what's everything they did to you then, all the, the—"

"Punishment for a lesser offense," I say. "All they did was scar my back and make it hard for me to breathe. Don't worry, the lung healed. They basically healed it themselves with some sort of treatment. I wasn't spared any of the pain, though."

"Lesser offense?" Rose asks.

"That's right," I tell her. "If I ever go back, I'd

probably be killed. Even though they still haven't authorized lethal force on me, I've caused them a lot of problems and sabotaged the factory so many times I lost count. I have a bit of a rebellious streak."

"So than what are the New Power like to you?" Rose asks.

"Annoying," I answer immediately. "They're evil, yeah, but you guys have never been to Hell, where John and I were born. There's worse out there."

Rose wraps her arms around me, resting her head against my chest. I try to ignore all the stinging sensations and pain. After a moments hesitation, I put my arms around her, too. Like a dork, John wraps his arms around Britney. Just had to get in on the hugging, didn't he? "I'm sorry," Rose says quietly. "I didn't know."

"There's no way you could have," I reply. "I'm a little surprised you didn't notice my scars in prison, though."

"You're not funny," she says, squeezing tighter. Ow. Ow. Ow. Ow.

"Hurts," I say, giving in. "Sam kabob in pain."

"Sorry," she says, easing up. It feels wet where her cheek touched my chest.

None of us moves for what feels like a good long time. Finally Britney breaks the silence. "We should go. It's really late. I'll teach you guys how to swim in the morning. Let's head back to my place." She peels herself away from John. "It's this way. We were heading in that direction anyway." She pulls John along by the hand. How the heck does he do that!? He decides he's going to get a girl, and like magic, he gets one! I don't get it! It's so not fair! Those aren't the rules of "save the world, get girl!"

Okay, I'm accepting it. John gets girls, I don't. Rose is an extremely bizarre exception.

Rose untangles herself from me. I take a moment to put my jacket back on, excruciatingly conscious of my freshly-branded hand. It's nothing like when I was beaten with the red-hot rebar. That just seared like a knife, but cauterized the skin right away. The thing on my hand is so different, a kind of pain I never experienced before.

After I carefully get my jacket on, I take Rose's hand. That's right, *I* grabbed *her* hand. How's that for initiative!

It's a good start, Dac says. *You still need some work, but with my training you can become a lean, mean, dating machine.* Is it sad that I'm almost willing to take his coaching? Almost.

We follow Britney back to her place, and I spot a few circled "XIV" markings along the way. It's amazing how many there are. While Britney walks up to the door, John in tow, I stop short and hold Rose back.

"What's wrong?" she asks me.

"You'll see," I say. Britney positions John safely away

266

from the door. He looks confused, but doesn't move. She pulls open the door and immediately steps to the side. Within the same instant a cannonball comes flying out of the opened door and lodges itself in the building directly opposite us. Rose jumps, and I see John take a quick step back. Only Britney and I don't flinch. What? Isn't it normal for small cannonballs to come flying out of houses?

"Sissy!" I hear Britney's younger brother, Gus, yell from inside.

"Hi, Gussy," Britney says, going in.

With Britney out of sight, John mouths to me, "What just happened?" with a wild look in his eyes. I shrug at him as if to say, "You sure know how to pick 'em." Britney comes outside and digs the cannonball out of the wall.

"You guys coming in?" she says with a smile.

"Yup," I answer, following her.

"Sam!" Gus exclaims, throwing his hands up when he sees me.

"Hey, kiddo," I say, limping inside.

"Did you see my cannon?"

"Sure did. Is it more powerful than before?" I ask when I see how excited he is.

Gus looks at his sister, wearing a proud expression. "Told you so!"

"What? Who's here?" A sleepy Connor comes out of

the bedroom, rubbing his eyes. He looks wide awake as soon as he sees me. "Them? You brought them here?" He immediately comes down on his sister. "Why did you bring him back? I told you before that he was trouble."

"Calm down, man," I say to him. "Britney was just saying she's tired, so she's going to teach us how to swim in the morning. Apparently I was dead long enough that it became pretty late." He looks at me like I'm insane, which might be true.

"You can't stay here," Connor says harshly. "There's no way that you can be here. You attract trouble." He hasn't even known me that long and already has that figured out? I need to be sneakier.

"If it makes you feel better, I'll just find a nearby abandoned building to sleep in," I tell him. I don't really want to cause any trouble here. All I want to do is learn how to swim. Is that too much to ask?

"It would, actually," Connor says.

"Here," Britney cuts in. I'm sure she's trying to avoid a screaming match. It's not like we were headed that way anyway "At least take this with you." She hands me a folded-up blanket, which I tuck under my arm.

"Thanks," I say. "Any recommended buildings?" I ask both Connor and Britney.

"This one was best," Connor says. "I don't remember much about the others." At least he's honest.

"Alright," I sigh. "I guess I'll see you guys in the

morning. Either look for me in one of the buildings around here, or I'll come back and wait out front." I try to drop Rose's hand as I walk out, but she refuses to let go. Okay, I guess she wants to come along.

"'Bye, Sam," Gus says.

"I'll see you tomorrow, kid," I say with a smile. "John, you staying here?"

"Um, can I?" he asks Britney and Connor.

"It's fine with me, and Connor will be okay with *one* of you staying. Isn't that right, Connor?" Britney gives her big brother a fiery look.

"Fine," he says grudgingly.

"Alright, I'll see you tomorrow then," I tell them.

"You sure?" John asks. I know what he really means. He's asking if it's weird if he stays behind. Trust me, he's overjoyed to be getting the chance to work on Britney. I'm not worried about much happening with both of Britney's brothers there, so it's no big deal.

"Yeah, it's fine," I answer. "'Night." I close the door with my good hand before grabbing Rose's again. We walked to a couple doors of nearby buildings. The first is locked, but the second opens into a structure that looks completely empty. This could work if we don't find anything better. We try a few more doors until we actually find a bottom-floor room in an abandoned building. The best part is that there's an old couch, apparently quite a luxury here. I'm guessing that

Connor, Britney, and Gus had to pick through a lot of places before they found as much furniture as they have.

"You can take the couch," I say.

"Maybe it opens up," Rose says, letting go of my hand. She lifts up the cushions and gets an "aha" look on her face. Throwing the cushions to the side, she pulls out a couch bed. We're living the high life now! It's just an old queen-sized mattress, but I can't count the number of times I would've killed for one of those. Okay, maybe I wouldn't have killed for one, but I really wanted one.

I try to throw the blanket over the bed, but only using one hand, it isn't going so well. Rose has to set the blanket up. She takes the cushions from the floor and puts two on the bed like pillows.

"A real five-star resort, huh?" she says, joking.

"You have no idea," I say. Now that Rose knows some things about the Surface, it's probably okay to let more slip. I carefully take my jacket off and throw it over the arm of the couch. I kick off my shoes and peel off my socks. Oh, mama, that's good. My socks are still soaked from earlier, and I wring out a few drops of water. "Well, that's kinda gross," I comment.

"Anything else you're going to take off?" Rose asks me.

"Nope," I say, climbing under the blanket. "That's it for me." I look over at her as she also takes off only her shoes and socks. She throws the blanket over herself and lies on her side, facing me

"These pillows are pretty horrible, aren't they?" she says, laughing.

"Just a bit," I say, throwing the seat cushion to the floor. Rose does the same. I flip over so that I'm facing Rose and use my arm as a pillow. The mattress really stinks, but I'm not going to complain.

"How do you do it?" Rose asks me.

"Do what?"

"Keep going," she shrugs. "Keep living. I don't even know that much about your life on the Surface, but I already know I couldn't have taken it."

"It's not easy," I say, "I would dream of dying sometimes. It's not an easy place to live. I guess that I'm still me because I rebelled. I never did anything monumental, but I wasn't a willing cog in their machine." I close my eyes, exhaustion hitting me like a wave. "Who knows, maybe I would've been different if I grew up somewhere else. I wish I did." I fluff my arm, avoiding the tender spots, and try to let sleep come.

"I'm glad you're the way you are," Rose says.

In what feels like another second, sleep finds me.

Chapter Twenty

"CUTTER!" I hear somebody howl murderously before a loud crash and the sound of glass shattering. My eyes shoot open, and I'm staring at Steven in a fit of rage. The room looks like a storm blew through it, with shards of broken glass all over the place. It looks like Steven just swept everything off the top of a cabinet violently. He doesn't look anything like his normal prim and proper self. He's more feral now.

"Perhaps you should calm down," suggests another man sitting in the room. Despite the destruction around him and Steven's violent anger, the second man looks unsettlingly calm.

"Calm down?" Steven spits at the second man. "How can you expect me to calm down? Cutter is still alive, and he destroyed one of our warehouses!" Who, me? Aw shucks.

"There's a chance he died in the fire or drowned in the resulting flood," comments the second man. Well, technically I did both, but that's beside the point.

"No, he's alive," Steven says, pacing. "I can feel it. He's like a constant nagging pain." One of Stevens hands shoots to the back of his neck and he starts kneading the skin.

"Maybe your feeling is wrong. I don't know that it's possible to tell if someone is alive or not from a tingle in their neck."

"Quiet, Lynch!" Steven mutters. Wait, isn't Lynch the guy in charge of the New Power down here? I suddenly get really interested in what this guy looks like. First of all, he's ripped! He could probably tear someone like Steven in half if he felt like it. He's wearing a loose-fitting blazer over a black shirt with an offset, red vertical stripe. The shirt is similar in design to the New Power armor. Does the New Power have its own clothing line now? Chez New Power-ay? I don't know, clothes aren't my thing.

Unlike Steven, Lynch is not clean-shaven. His facial hair seems more lumberjack-like, as opposed to wild-and-wizardly. Barely visible under his scruff is a scar that extends diagonally from under his jaw to his collarbone. I don't really want to know how he got that. It looks painful. He has hard eyes that warn against messing with him. Lucky for me, I'm don't usually take warning to heart.

"It's just one warehouse," Lynch reasons. "It's not

like they conquered our headquarters nor am I defeated. As long as I am here to lead our forces in the Water Nation, we are functional." Good news! All I need to do is take Lynch out and everything will be fixed down here. "Our army grows larger by the day. "Why are you so concerned with one boy?" And there's the bad news.

"That's what I thought, too," Steven says, clenching and unclenching his fists agitatedly, walking towards Lynch, "but that's just what he wants you to think. DON'T BE FOOLED! He is a Surface warrior, more powerful and resourceful than any from the Sky. His reckless abandon with his own life makes him unpredictable. That means he's dangerous." Hey, I care about my life… sometimes. "You've seen this for yourself. He burned your warehouse and hid himself inside to release our potential recruits. He's building his own army. We must act now!" I didn't know I scared Steven this much. It's pretty sweet. And since when was I building an army?

"How do you even know it was him that attacked the warehouse?" Lynch asks. "We've been going off your suspicion, but you haven't told me how you know for sure."

"His sword," Steven says, his hands trembling on either side of Lynch's face. "Cutter carries the only white Sky Iron blade in existence. It is unmistakable."

Lynch pushes Steven away, clearly thinking that he'd

gotten too close. "So let me get this straight," Lynch says incredulously. "You're more afraid of one child than you are of the king of the Water Nation."

A glimmer of calmness and rationality comes across Steven's face.

"No, no. I suppose you're right," he replies. Steven straightens up and combs his fingers through his hair to fix it how he likes. "King Kane is a much greater threat than the Cutter boy." This sudden change in Steven is suspicious. He pauses, then asks, "How far along are you on that project?" What project? What's going on?

"It won't be long n—"

I wake up with a thud, my head aching. I'm looking up at the ceiling of the room Rose and I commandeered. I'm mostly lying on the floor, except one of my legs is still on the mattress, tangled in the blanket. What just happened?

You woke up, Dac says. *Nothing I can do about that. Ask somebody to hit you over the head if you want to go back to sleep.* Good morning to you, too.

I think I've got enough bruises at the moment, I tell him. I lift my leg off the bed and, keeping my left hand cradled against my chest, climb to my feet. Rose is sound asleep on the mattress, taking up as much room as humanly possible. Well, at least I know whom to blame for waking me up.

You know what you could do? Dac says with a hint of slyness.

What? I say weakly.

Dump a bucket of water on her! It's only fair. She did it to you in prison. Imagining her reaction, I accidentally let out an evil chuckle. Rose stirs in her sleep and I shut up, covering my mouth with my hand. Well, there's no room for me there. Floors can be comfortable.

Since I don't have a blanket, I put on my jacket and socks. I sit with my back against the wall and try to sleep again, but unfortunately, I can't...looks like I'm awake for the day. I put my boots on and head outside. With ease I fly up to the top of the building. I take a seat, letting my feet dangle over the edge. I lean back on my right hand, the rough roofing material leaving dents on my palm. My left hand is cradled in my lap. I notice that all the rooftops here are flat, and the lights illuminating the entirety of the Hub are slightly dimmer than when it's "daytime."

Throwing my head back, I look up through the glass ceiling of the Hub. A giant squid swims by, alarmingly close. But since the warehouse fire and drowning incident, I have a different feeling about this monster sea creature. "Thanks for saving my life, Billy," I say to the squid, knowing full well that it can't hear me. Who in their right mind names a giant killer squid "Billy" anyway?

276

I lay back on the sandpaper-like roof and dream of the sky. As great as all this water is, it feels confining to me. I liked the open skies and floating platforms of the Sky Nation much more than these oversized, drowned hamster cages.

After lying around for what feels like a few hours, I fly back down to the ground and head back inside the building. Rose is still fast asleep, but the sound of me coming inside causes her to stir. She rubs her eyes, then lowers her head back into her arms. "What time is it?" she says.

"How should I know?" I say. "I haven't had my phone and there's no sun to go by."

"Lame," Rose says. She takes her free arm and starts feeling around in her pocket for her phone. When she finds it, she throws it onto the mattress, where it lands and bounces just short of the edge. "Now you can see what time it is." I take a look at it and see that it's about seven in the morning.

"Time to get up," I say, dropping her phone back onto the mattress. I'm suddenly reminded that I haven't checked to make sure my sword is still safely in my pocket. I dig down and feel it there. Good, that's one less thing to worry about. One day I'm going to forget it, and then I'll be in deep trouble.

Rose goes through a series of stretches before getting up. She climbs out of bed and as she ties her shoes, she asks me, "How did you sleep?"

"Pretty well," I lie. I really only kinda slept before you pushed me onto the floor, and then I decided to lie around on the roof for a while. "Ready for a swimming lesson?"

"Ready as I'll ever be," she says. Once Rose gets herself together, we fold up the couch and blanket, and walk back over to Britney's place. Standing in front of the door, I can't decide if I should knock or not. Instead, I put my ear to the door and listen for movement. I hear a rustling inside, so I guess they're awake. I knock, and in no time flat Britney opens the door.

"Morning," she greets me, looking and sounding refreshed. Well, at least *someone* slept.

My offer to hit you over the head is still good, Dac brings up.

Stop hanging out with Arthur, I tell him. Britney is holding a bundle of clothes in each hand. She shoves one into my chest and hands Rose the other.

"Go put those on," Britney says. "They're swimsuits. Clothes meant for the water." Okay, then.

"Where should we change?" I ask Britney as she takes the blanket from me.

"There's not a lot of room in here," she says. "Just go use an open room somewhere, there's plenty of those around. We'll wait right out here for you." Rose and I turn around as Britney steps back into her house. We go to one of the buildings we remember being open, and head inside. There's more than one room so Rose and I split up to change. It looks like Britney gave me a pair of shorts. Easy enough. I put on the faded grey shorts, transferring my sword into a pocket with a zipper. I ball up my ruined jeans and shout over to Rose, "You done changing?"

"Almost, give me a second," she says. I hear the gentle sound of fabric against fabric. I lean up against the wall to wait. She comes out a minute later.

"You don't look like you changed," I say to her. She's wearing the exact same thing she had on before.

"I did," she insists. "We just need to come back here to change again after, okay?"

"Okay," I reply, throwing my trashed pants into the corner. "Shall we go?"

Britney and John are in front of Britney's house. John's in a pair of shorts similar to mine, and Britney looks exactly the same as before, just like Rose. Britney has a stack of towels tucked under her arm.

"You guys all set?" she asks.

We nod our heads, and Britney proceeds to lead us through a maze of buildings until we reach a small connecting Hub. Inside are multiple pools of varying sizes and depths. The miniature Hub has a blue tint to it that I haven't seen anywhere else down here. It's better lit in here, the pattern of the water reflected on the floor and walls. Next to the pools are lounge chairs. I think I might've seen one of those on the Surface, but I'm not sure. Maybe the factory managers had one.

Britney walks over to the smallest pool and throws the stack of towels onto a chair. "Alright, take off everything but your swimsuits," She say, taking her top off.

Wow. What!? No, must fight it! Come on Sam, you can do it! ARRGH!

I can't help it. I stare.

After kicking off her shoes, Britney also slips out of her pants, putting her bunched-up clothes on another chair.

I kick my boots off and toss my shirt onto a chair, just in time to turn and see Rose pull her shirt off over her head. It's a crying shame that she's facing the other direction! Then she wiggles out of her pants. Maybe facing away from me isn't so bad after all.

Stop being creepy, Sam. But that's nearly impossible right now. I mean. Wow.

Apparently John stripped at some point without me noticing. I was preoccupied with Britney and Rose's, uh, assets. I clear my throat as Britney tells us to get into the water. The first thing I notice is COLD! The second is that I'm walking on mud. There's no base for these pool, they're open to the ocean. Britney wades out ahead of us as John, Rose, and I shuffle after her, quickly getting used to the water. Once my body is used to it, it feels almost warm. Nobody better be peeing!

The mud feels good between my toes. Weird, but in a good way. I look at the others to see if they think this is as cool as I do. I see that John is still ogling at Britney.

At least you're not that weak, Dac says approvingly. *Or if you are, at least you're not that obvious.*

Agreed. Rose, on the other hand, looks really shy and like she's trying to cover herself up. *Should I say anything?* I ask Dac.

Why are you asking me for advice? Dac responds. *I'm in your head, and neither of us have any experience what so ever. Just push her into the water or something.* While I take a split second to actually consider that, Dac adds, *I was kidding. Try putting your arm around her. Girls like that, right?*

How should I know? I ask as I get closer to Rose. *Shoulders or waist?*

Guess! Dac says, sounding annoyed. I wrap my arm around her waist and hope that I guessed right. She jumps a little when I touch her, but calms down right away and gives me a weak smile that doesn't quite reach her eyes.

I guessed wrong! It isn't helping!

Maybe you should push her into the water, then, Dac says.

No, I realize that's a bad idea now.

You didn't before?

Well...

Never mind. I let go of Rose, accepting that touching her is not helping.

"I think I love swimming," John says. "I'm going to be a professional swimmer as soon as possible. Maybe I'll even be the best in the world."

"John, you know we haven't even started the swimming yet, right?" I point out.

"I don't care," he says back, absolute bliss on his face.

When we get waist deep in the water, Britney stops and turns around. It's obvious she heard John because she's grinning at him. "So you guys know nothing about swimming, right?" We all nod our heads. "Can any of you open your eyes underwater?" I awkwardly raise my hand.

"When I was dying, I did," I add to give the setting.

"Okay, good," Britney says, "So how did you close your second eyelids?"

"My what?"

"Eyelids. Your eyelids!" she says like I'm stupid, "So you can see underwater."

"I only have one pair of eyelids," I say. "Do you have two?"

"Doesn't everybody?" Britney says, snapping closed a translucent film over her eyes, which makes their color look even more unusual. John, Rose, and I instinctively

282

recoil back at the strangeness of it, making not so flattering sounds.

"That's weird," I say like an idiot.

"No," Britney says, hands on her hips. "What's weird is that you guys don't have them."

"You're not going to sprout gills next, are you?" John asks. That's even worse than what I said.

"I don't know," Britney says, straightening, "you tell me." She squeezes her eyes closed and flexes the muscles in her neck. I shield my eyes with my hand as the three of us make strange, grossed out noises again. "Kidding!" she says. I slowly move my hands down and see that her neck still looks normal—no gills—and even her eyes are back to normal. "Can we go back to being serious now?"

"Uh huh," we all mumble.

"So, wet heads, it's time to get wet heads. Put your faces in the water and slowly let out air to blow bubbles as long as possible."

"Sounds easy enough," I mumble, as I get to my knees and take a deep breath. I stick my head in the water with my eyes closed, and I can hear John and Rose doing the same. I start letting air out from my nose. The bubbles tickle as they crawl up my face to pop at the surface. I keep going until my lungs start to burn and I can't force any more bubbles out. I lift my face out of the water, loudly sucking in a deep breath. I wipe my hand down my face to get rid of some water on my face and see that John came up a while ago. Rose is still face down, blowing bubbles. I sit back, soaking as much of me as I can in the cold water as we watch Rose, waiting patiently. The water feels so good on my raw, burned skin, my hand especially. Water is magical. After a good two minutes or so, Rose calmly lifts her head out of the water.

"How long are we supposed to be doing this again?" she asks.

"I think you're good," Britney says approvingly.

"How can you hold your breath for that long?" I ask her.

"Everyone in the Sky Nation can. We have really big lungs. Don't you?" What is it with everybody from the other Nations getting cool superpowers! Why am I the loser who doesn't get anything? My eyes flicker over to the lameness that is John, and suddenly I feel better.

"Not like that, no," I say, half grumbling.

"And you called me weird," Britney says. "Moving on, I want you guys to try to float."

"How?" I ask.

"I'm going to show you," she answers. She lies back on the water so that she looks like a star, somehow not sinking. "This won't save you if you're ejected out of a Hub, but it's still a good skill to have." Okay, I can do that. Standing up, I stick my arms out like Britney's were.

I proceed to fall back like a log.

I crash onto the water. The burns on my back sting maddeningly to the point I'm ready to scream my throat raw. My butt hits the mud and apparently I'm underwater. What happened to the floating thing! I quickly bring my head back up above water. Well, this water. I'm still on the bottom of the ocean.

"It didn't work," I say, shaking my head like a wet dog. Seriously, what did I do wrong? I did what Britney did, didn't I?

"Of course not," Britney says, shielding herself from the water I'm splattering. "You need to gently lie back, not fall over like that."

"Oh," I say.

"Like this?" Rose asks, floating almost as well as Britney was, looking like a rag doll.

Want to be romantic? Dac asks me.

Depends, I answer cautiously.

Tackle her under the water and kiss her. That's actually not a horrible idea. *It's sad that I'm more romantic than you are. Do you think there are any hot AI babes out there? Then I could really use this power for good.* Not answering that.

I jump on top of Rose, pushing her down beneath the surface, and plant one on her. My left hand is killing me because I'm pushing it against something right now, but I can mostly ignore it right now. I have something really good to take my mind off the pain. Somehow, by some miracle, she kisses me back! It's still a mystery why she would want to be with me, but I don't really care, at least not right now.

Out of nowhere, the skin on my back feels different than the rest of me. I hear someone talking, but it sounds like shouting through a wall. I know they're talking to me, but I can't make out a single word. What do you want? Can't you see I'm busy? Somebody taps on my back, hitting one of my burns, and I spasm. Freaking out, I shoot my head up above the water and flub to the side.

"Well, that's one way to learn," Britney says, smiling.

"Uh, yeah," I mutter, scratching the back of my head from where I sit as a wave of water crashes into my face. I peer out from under the wet mop known as my hair. The water's calm so somebody has splashed me, but who? Another wave slaps me in the face

"Warn me next time before you do something like that!" Rose says, delivering another dousing.

"It was Dac's idea," I defend myself.

Tattletale.

"Sure, blame Dac," Rose says, sending yet another barrage of water. I can almost tell that she wanted to add some comment about me being crazy in here. I glance at her.

"This means war!" I yell, dragging my arm through

the water and splashing her with a wave bigger than any she has sent at me. OWWW!

Don't hurt yourself, Dac says. *I'm almost back with the Blue Elixir.*

"Hey!" she shouts as she retaliates. Expecting it, I close an eye and turn my head away from her. I keep flinging water and she tries to get me back. Missing entirely, she drenches John.

"What was that for?" he asks, going after Rose. She makes a shocked face as the water hits her and uses both hands to attack John. Sitting off to the side, temporarily forgotten, I execute a sneak attack on both of them. Now they turn their attention to me, and it's two against one. With my eyes closed, I start wildly flinging water everywhere.

"Stop it! You guys are acting like children," Britney yells. The water temporarily stops flying. The surface of the water still churns as an aftereffect of our water battle. John, Rose, and I all look at each other and a consensus is made. If I didn't know any better, I'd swear we just used telepathy. Turning towards Britney, the three of us unleash a vicious barrage of water upon her. She lets out a playful squeal as she gets soaked.

Why does hurling water at each other matter? Dac asks. *You're all soaked anyway.*

This is the most serious battle of my life!

I see Britney carefully take a deep breath before

raising her fists above her head, hands together, and smashing them down into the water in front of us. A torrent of water shoots in all directions. There's a two second pause before it turns into a free-for-all.

Eventually the water fight dies down, and Britney gets back to the job of teaching us to swim. We get through flailing around, which Britney calls "treading water." It keeps my head up above the water so it works for me. After that, she shows us what she calls the "front crawl" and "breaststroke." I feel like a frog doing the breaststroke, but apparently that's the best way to move underwater.

Dac shows up while we're practicing swimming underwater. I swim over to where he waits by the chairs. "It looks like you can swim," he says.

"I'm not great at it, but at least I can move in the water now. John and Rose are much better than I am."

"That's good," Dac says. I notice he is wearing a backpack—which looks pretty weird on a robot—and holding a container of familiar electric blue drink in his hand.

"Can I have that?" I ask him pointing at his hand. He hands me the Blue Elixir before I have to give it back to him because I can't open it. My hands are still hurt to use.

How're you feeling? he asks me in my head.

Terrible, I tell him honestly. *It all hurts really badly, but I don't want anyone to worry about me.* I raise the Blue Elixir to my lips and greedily drain the entire thing. Comforting warmth spreads through my body as my injuries start to stich themselves together. I relish the feeling of my back returning to normal, the intense pain there receding. I watch as the massively hindering burn on my hand seals together to leave a thick, ugly white line across my hand. I figured that at least one thing would scar. I watch as the black, scorched areas of my skin heal, for the most part, to a raw, pinkish color. With a night or two of sleep, I figure I'll be good as new, plus a few new scars.

I let out a massive sigh of relief as the pain evaporates from my body. "Thank God," I say, a weight off my shoulders, muscles relaxing. I didn't realize I was tensed up to begin with.

"It was that bad?" Dac asks. I wonder if he can feel pain...

"Let's just say that food should be glad it's dead when it's cooked."

"That's grim."

"So is being burned alive." I stop talking when I see that John, Britney, and Rose are swimming their way back over here. They step out of the water, and once again my mind is completely captivated by the sight of Rose and Britney in their swimsuits.

Think you can save a picture of that, but take John out

of it? I ask Dac.

    You're acting like a teenager.

    So?

    Got it.

Chapter Twenty-One

"So, what've we missed?" I ask Dac as we walk towards Britney's house. As absolutely amazing as it is to have a fresh set of clothes, with the exception of my same old jacket, everybody else wants out of their swim suits. Britney is leading the way, John at her side. Dac, Rose, and I follow far enough behind them that I don't have to listen to more of "John getting the girl" again, which gets old fast! Can't the guy *not* get what he wants, just once?

"Everybody is back in Hub Fourteen. Kane wants to do more research, so instead of letting him ask the locals for permission to dissect them, Jinn was able to convince Kane to let him be an ambassador. He figured it would be better that way."

"He's probably right," I say, jamming my hands into my jacket pockets, staring directly ahead at John's back. Something's off about the way he's walking. I can't tell exactly what's wrong, but at least it doesn't look like he's hurt. What's wrong with him? Is he finally going to choke on asking a girl out?

"Last I know, everybody split up," Dac continues. "Most went to meet the locals, but a few stayed behind with Kane."

"Do you know who went where?" I ask.

"I only know where a few of them are. I was more concerned with making sure you stayed alive."

"And I really appreciate it," I tell him sincerely.

"We all appreciate it," Rose says, smiling.

"Speak for yourself," I remark. "I'm pretty sure there are a lot of people who want me dead, Arthur being one of them."

"He does not!" Rose argues. "He does nothing but sing your praises."

"Arthur sings?"

Rose elbows me a bit harder than what would normally be playful. "You know what I mean."

"Sure," I say, rubbing my ribs. "I still think Arthur would find it funny to see me dead." Rose lets out a harsh puff of air and throws her hands up.

He might get a good laugh out of it, right before it starts to bother him, Dac says before continuing aloud for Rose's sake. "Anyway, somehow we were able to make it through the night without any more fighting." That's a miracle in and of itself. On the other hand, I guess I'm normally the one who starts things, so it makes sense. "Kane brought his assistant along, that Bean guy. He's not very exciting. He does everything Kane tells him to, so he's mostly a research aid."

"At least he's not in charge of a torture center," I mumble. Then more loudly, "You know, if you were bored you could've talked to me."

"I figured I'd give you some privacy," Dac replies, "and I did. Remember how I said—"

"Shhh! Stop it," I frantically say, putting my hand up to where his mouth would be. It doesn't impede his speaking at all. I'm doomed. "—that you should push Rose under the–" Mentally, I give him a kick and miraculously, that shuts him up.

What's wrong with you? Keep quiet about that.

Then never leave me with such boring people again, Dac bargains.

Deal, I say, eager to change the subject. I look over at Rose and see that her frustration with me has been replaced by embarrassment, her cheeks reddening.

While we walk, I busy myself by looking outside the tunnel to the open water. In the distance, among the tangle of passageways comprising the Water Nation, boats and chasers buzz about in every direction. Really, it's the first time I've noticed how many there are. There are real people moving around and going about their days. Sure they're half crazed New Power freaks right now, but still. Every place I've seen down here seems so far from being normal life. From life in general, actually. How does Kane live so far away? What if there's a problem or sadness? How will he know? Do the kings even care? How long has there been a problem down here before Kane noticed? It seems like there have been people living here in Hub Fourteen basically since it was created and he thought it was abandoned.

I should probably stop trying to relax like this. I end up depressing myself.

Lost in my thoughts, I jump when I hear, "Hey, Sam?" John is standing next to me. It must've been him saying my name.

"Yeah, buddy?" I say, willing my heart to stop racing.

"Can I talk to you about something?"

"Sure, what is it?" John's eyes shift around uneasily.

"In private," he finally says.

"Oh, okay," I respond, a little curious now. "Would you guys give us a minute?" I say to the others and fall back with John. I expect him to keep walking but he stops altogether. "Shouldn't we keep moving?"

"I can't do this anymore," John says in a barely-contained hush. Now that I look at him, I can clearly see he's freaking out.

"Wow," I try to say reassuringly. "What's going on?"

We're probably going to be a while. Think you can guide me back?

Sure, it's that big one over there. I look over and see

Dac pointing toward a Hub still a bit of a distance away.

That works, I say to him. *See you there as soon as I can.*

"I can't take it," John says again, clutching his head, starting to pull at his hair. Now he's starting to look crazy. "It's too much."

"What is?" I pry.

"This... this place!" John says with a shout, throwing his hands up and gesturing vaguely to everything around him.

"It's not that bad," I say.

"Yes it is!" John snaps, whirling around to look me in the eye. "It's trying to crush me. No matter where I go down here I'm stuck. M-my chest collapses," he stammers, "and my heart is going a mile a minute. I can't even breathe right—"

"You've seemed fine up til now," I remark, cutting him off.

"Because I've been able to keep a lid on it! I'm secretly losing my mind!" Well, it's not so secret anymore. John tightly grips my arms and I can really see the madness in his eyes.

"John," I say, trying to sound calm, "are you claustrophobic?"

"YES!" he shouts in my face, shaking me. How did I never manage to know this?

"Okaaaaaaay. Well, what can I do to help?" I ask,

reaching for some way to not be useless.

"Get. Me. Out of here," John says in a strained voice, never letting go of me.

"As soon as I can, I will," I tell him quickly. "I'll talk to Gabriel as soon as we see him. We're going back to where he is now. I just need you to keep it together."

The desperate insanity stays in his eyes, but his features look to be calming down. He takes a few deep breaths, and I squeeze his shoulder reassuringly. I don't know if I've helped him, but it's all I can do for now. How am I supposed to comfort a claustrophobic person while we're trapped underwater with no way out? It's not like I can just break the tunnel and fly John out of the ocean. Even if my boots worked underwater – and I have no clue whether they do or not – there's no way I could hold my breath long enough to break the surface anyway.

"Thanks," John says with at least a semblance of calm. "I just, I-I-I can't do it. It's too much."

"Were you always claustrophobic?" I ask him. So I'm a little insensitive. Get over it.

John looks thoughtful. "No. I don't think so. But I sure found out as soon as we came down here." Good to know.

Sam! Dac pipes up. *Something's wrong. Call it insane man's intuition.*

What's wrong? I ask him.

Get over here. We have a problem. Knew it! Why am I excited by that?

What is it? I try to ask again.

Little busy. Can't explain. Hurry! There's nothing like the sound of a frantic AI screaming in your head. Talk about ear splitting. I look over at John, whose anxious expression could mean that he's either about to have another episode, or can tell something's wrong.

"What is it?" he asks me. Oh good, he's not freaking out again. At this rate, I just might, though.

"I wish I knew," I reply. "Let's go!" I take off jogging towards Hub Fourteen. I can see it ahead, but that doesn't mean we're *there*. I don't bother to make sure John is keeping up, and just pour on the speed. Whatever is going on, if Dac can't even focus enough to talk to me telepathically, then we probably don't have much time to spare. Damn, if I didn't have to worry about John, I could just—

Wait a minute.

"Are you afraid of flying?" I shout back to John, not slowing down.

"Flying?" he shouts back, breathing heavily. I don't know what he looks like, he's behind me. "No. Why?" I drop back so that I'm right next to him, and grab him under his armpits.

"Then hold on!" I kick on my boots, and John and I go screaming down the tunnel. John literally screaming. I

297

make a hard left when we reach the tunnel leading back into Hub Fourteen. "Can we go higher?" I shout to John, who's clutching me for dear life.

"WAAAAAAAAAAAAAAA!"

"I'll take that as a no!" As we enter Hub Fourteen, I wish I could fly above the buildings, but instead, I weave among them toward where Dac is. How I know his exact location, I have no clue. Call it a feeling.

"Stop eating so much, fatty!" I complain to John, whose extra weight is severely compromising my flight balance and control. He responds by screaming louder and holding on even tighter. I think he'll do good living on the Surface, if we can clean it up a little and get a new monarch in place. The guy's claustrophobic and is terrified of flying. His fear of flying might be my fault, though.

We come up to an extremely sharp turn. I try to make it, but with John holding on, I can't do it. I start to shriek almost as loudly as John as we crash headlong into the side of a building. John gets thrown from me as I crumple to the floor. My right shoulder is screaming at me and my neck is none too happy. I look at my injured arm and see that my shoulder isn't exactly in the right place.

"Oh, that's not good," I say to myself as the pain suddenly gets a thousand times worse. I also notice that I can't feel my arm as much. I painfully roll over so that my injured shoulder is away from the ground. I make sure my arm is against my side as I grab hold of my wrist and gently start to—"AUGH!" oh this sucks. Ow ow ow ow ow ow ow ow. Great, I've got my arm to my stomach. Now to push it back. Oh this hurts even worse! I curse under my breath as I start the process over.

I push hard, squeezing my eyes shut, and gasp as my shoulder pops back into place and I suddenly feel relief. Well that'll be sore in the morning, but at least it's working. I look around for John.

"You could have helped me, you know," I say as I look around and see him lying unmoving on the floor. "John?" I say as I quickly half crawl over to him. "John," I say again louder, shaking him. I put my ear right above his mouth and can both hear and feel him breathing. At least he isn't dead. I try shaking him even harder, "John, wake up, dammit! Don't expect me to kiss you to wake you up, you lazy freeloader! Wake! Up!" I start slapping him. Something has to work. He's breathing, barely, but that doesn't mean anything. Okay, it means he's alive for now, but I don't know how bad of a shape he's in, having just had a head on collision with a wall and everything. I'm alive, and I don't feel like moving. I'm sure that when the adrenaline wears off, I'll just pass out no matter where I am or what I'm doing,

"John!" I keep shouting in his face. "John, wake up!" I deliver the hardest slap of my life to John with the word "up" and suddenly he starts to stir.

"Did we get the license plate number of the truck that hit us?" he says, not opening his eyes, but trying to move his arms.

"You stupid idiot!" I yell at him, then hug the oaf. I let go almost instantly, realizing how awkward this is. I glance around, certain someone is standing there watching us be weird.

"Can we just keep sitting here? I don't feel so good," John says, rubbing his head.

"No, we have to keep going. Dac and the others are in trouble."

"Ugh! Fine," John says with a grunt, sticking his hand out. I climb to my feet first, then help him up. "Can we please walk this time?" he asks me. Personally, I think I could fly faster and less painfully, but it's not my goal to scare John to death.

"We can do that," I tell him, and we start walking slowly. I'm still hurting and my leg is protesting big-time. Wait a minute.

Technically, you're in my shoes and have always been able to nag at me whenever anything is going on. Why can you not do that now? I ask Dac. Seriously, it makes no sense.

Focusing more power to body. Hitting harder this way. Get here NOW, is all he says. I'd love to run there and be there five minutes ago, but I'm lacking a time machine.

"Sam, what is that?" Johns asks me.

"What is what?"

"Listen," he says. I focus on the sounds around me, and suddenly I can hear it. The unmistakable sound of fighting, screaming voices, non-descript crashes and thuds. I don't know why I didn't pick up on this before.

"That's so not good," I shout as I start running toward the sound. I'm tired, out of breath, and feel like I want to take a five-year nap, but I have to keep moving. I have a foreboding sense that Dac is near the fight, maybe in the middle of it.

As we run closer, I can better distinguish the shouts of pain and frustration, and the clang of steel on steel. Someone's attacking the Hub Runners and it sounds like there are a lot of them. Now I understand why Dac was in such a rush for us to get back. How many of the Hub Runners can actually fight? It's not like Eli has had enough time to set up his Sprinters yet. These guys aren't fighters, just victimized residents.

An image of Britney putting a knife to my throat forces itself into my mind. Maybe they're not so defenseless.

The sounds of battle get louder and louder as we get closer. I can't pick out any voices that I know. I glance at the sky, but realize I'm the only one here able to fly using just my shoes. I don't think anybody brought a jetpack down, and I know for sure there aren't any sky bikes or transports. We keep running.

Only now, when it matters, am I starting to realize how this place was built like a labyrinth. Maybe this wasn't its original design, but it's a good remodeling job. At any rate, it's completely confusing, and I can't figure out how to get around all these stupid buildings! And what happened to all the alleys? There were tons of them before, and now that I need them to get to my friends there aren't any! Do the buildings move? That would be cool, I'd be asking them to kindly MOVE OUT OF MY WAY!

"John," I yell back at him, "I know you don't like it, but we have to fly over this."

"No!" he instantly yells at me before I even finish speaking. "I refuse to go through that again!"

"Too bad," I say, picking him up and activating my boots. He's not willing at all. He squirms under my arms, trying to make me drop him. Doesn't he realize that I'm flying up and we're both already a little broken? If I were to drop him, it would be very bad. Like, splat John bad!

You're only up about ten to fifteen feet, he wouldn't go splat.

NOW you can talk?

Nope. Still. Busy.

Then get back to fighting! You're not allowed to die.

Wouldn't die. Just. Lose. Body. I refuse to respond to

that one. Let him focus on fighting.

John is squirming so much that I have to land on this roof or I will drop him. I shoot up the last few feet, paying attention only to reaching the roof. I hover above it, then do my best to gently touch down as I unceremoniously drop John. He clambers to his feet and faces me, the direction we just came from.

"No!" he yells in my face, somehow loud enough it drowns the sounds of fighting. "I told you no, do not start flying! Did you even care about my opinion, or did you just want to give me the illusion of choice?"

"John," I say, looking past him.

"No, you can't do that, man. It's not fair," he continues whining.

"John," I say more assertively, shutting him up. "Look."

He turns and sees what I'm staring at. We're on a building overlooking the fighting. It's right at our feet.

Chapter Twenty-Two

I take in the battle before me, a spectacle of clashing bodies, the sparks from the staffs of the New Power visible everywhere. I try to spot anyone I know, but I can't make out any individuals in this madness.

Then again.

Spread throughout the field of bodies, I see glowing colors that don't quite look natural. There they are! I spot the blue of Jinn's Sky Iron, the red of Arthur's armor, the pink Rose must be carrying, and the yellow of Nathan's. I see two other spots of silver and brown radiance that must be Mark and Gabriel. Dac isn't glowing, but somehow my eyes seem to find him with ease. Maybe it's because we're connected, or maybe it's because of the trail of bodies he's leaving in his wake. He's also taller than everyone else.

And made of metal.

He's pretty close to where whoever has the brown sword is.

All the New Power soldiers are clad in their typical armor. The waves against them consist of normally dressed people. Shocker. I can't count casualties from here, but it looks like the Hub Runners are holding their own. Barely. "We have to get down there," I say to John, still trying to take everything in, my eyes never leaving the battlegrounds.

"I can't," John says, sounding as dazed as I am.

"Why not?" I bark at him. Who does he think he is? People are fighting and dying down there, and John wants to do *nothing*? I might just go at him. Coward!

"I don't have anything to fight with. I would be killed instantly." Oh. That's a pretty good reason. A light bulb goes off in my head as I watch the fighting.

"Wait here," I say, pulling my sword out. "I'll be right back." I kick on my boots and go flying through the air, leaving John behind. Getting a bird's-eye view, I see that the New Power are slaughtering Hub Runners. I can't just fly from place to place. I have to help!

Why do I have to see such a good guy?

I pass over a New Power soldier and cut the power to my boots, throwing me into a flying tackle, sword first. I skewer him as we both fall to the ground, blood spraying out of the poor saps wound. I pop back up, not even feeling it, to see a shocked and terrified Hub Runner, looking like he's about to leave a smelly bomb in his pants. I don't have time to say anything reassuring because another soldier from the New Power is coming up behind him, looking ready to drive his staff into the guy's back. Eyes wide, I shove the terrified Hub Runner out of the way, then raise my blade to deflect the sparking end of the staff, just barely avoiding being fried myself.

I bring my sword back around and up while he's set off-balance, and cut from his hip up to his opposite shoulder. The New Power soldier reels back, screaming, and I kick him into the midst of another melee. Now that he's out of the way, I again take to the air. I take a second to reorient myself and continue towards my destination.

But there's another desperate struggle up ahead of me. Of course, I decide to drop in and save the day. I get right above a New Power goon before I cut the power to my boots and land literally right on top of him, driving my feet into his helmet and shoulder. Turns out, though, this isn't one of my best ideas. As the New Power soldier crumples to the ground, I fall with him, my foot seriously hurting due to how freaking hard their helmets are!

Maybe one day you'll remember that they're wearing armor, Dac says unexpectedly.

Doubtful, I quickly think back, climbing to my feet. *Now go back to fighting things!* My foot aches when I put pressure on it, but it's bearable.

It's getting easier, Dac says as the New Power soldier

I had hoped would be out cold clambers to his feet.

Oh? Why's that? I ask, bringing my sword around in a wide arc to attack. The soldier dropped his staff when I landed on him, so he ducks my blow, drawing a dagger out of I don't want to know where. Regrettably, I end up in an awkward position, showing my left shoulder to the New Power soldier. He takes full advantage of the situation and lashes out with the dagger. Unable to stop him, he gets a nice slice across my arm.

Seems like the New Power are terrified by the flying white thing, Dac starts to explain as I feel blood starting to dribble down my arm. Gross. That feeling alone makes me want to be sick. I whip my sword arm back around, trying not to lose momentum, and smash the hilt against this guy's helmet with a satisfying crunch. Well there goes one helmet. *Seems like you have a reputation. Probably for being crazy, violent, and killing a lot of them.* Dac continues, totally unaware, as the crazy, wicked grin this soldier's been wearing now falters. He tries to stab my sword arm, but I grab his wrist, putting my arms in an *X* in front of my face. About zero seconds later someone comes around from behind him and brings something sharp down onto his head with a resounding *thwack,* embedding itself in the guy's skull like an ax in a thick stump of wood. Blood splatters over me, some on my face. If this were a professional wood-chopping contest, whoever did that would win.

I don't see it, I reply, my breathing returning to normal. The New Power soldier's expression softens as he falls over like a freshly-chopped tree. See? Wood chopping contest victory. I'm grateful I can't see his eyes as his wrist is pulled from my hand and the fresh corpse spins to the ground.

"Hi Sam," Eli says, stepping up to pull the sword out of the man's head. He flexes and retrieves it with one sharp tug. Losing no momentum, he immediately steps forward and takes on another enemy. I cover his back and take on the onrushing crowd. For some reason, these guys are considerably worse than the last one I was just fighting. Maybe they're new recruits.

I wish there was some other way to do this. Maybe we could get the newbies out of here.

Question, Dac says.

Answer, I say back stupidly. Isn't my timing for jokes impeccable? *What is it?*

Why does it seem like most of the New Power are moving toward you? Um, what? I don't believe it. Or rather, I don't *want* to believe it. Even if I had the time to safely look around me, at this level I don't think I would be able to see anything. Maybe if I fly up to check it out, I could see what's going on, but then I would be leaving Eli unprotected and he would more than likely be killed.

Maybe it's because I'm just that sexy, I reply offhandedly, forced to take his word for it. Why always the bad news? Couldn't he have said the people are coming towards me bearing milk and cookies? Actually, I hate milk. It's still better than angry, sweaty guys from the New Power, though. Pretty much anything is. Except brussel sprouts. Yuck.

I cut down another New Power soldier, and the bodies are really starting to pile up. The bile in my stomach wants to come up and say "hi," but I can puke my guts up later. Oncoming attackers are forced to stand on the backs of their fallen friends, sacrificing their footing. Speaking of feet, I don't think I can stand on mine much longer. Maybe I hurt my foot worse than I originally thought. Also, it's probably bad that I can't feel my left arm anymore. I swing my sword in a slightly wider arc, just to make sure it's still there. Yup, I'm good.

If it was just me against this entire horde, I probably would be dead a while ago. Luckily, there are Hub Runners dotting the field, and I have Eli at my back.

I hear a scream behind me that I wish I didn't recognize. I look over my shoulder for a split second and see Eli holding his hand over where his left eye should be. There's an ugly cut running from his hairline to the corner of his mouth before it crookedly comes off at an angle. The skin looks like it has been peeled open, and blood's fountaining from the wound. Eli's hand is stained red with it, and it flies gruesomely from his mouth as he breathes. Unbelievably, the loss of an eye doesn't stop him. Clutching his face, he launches himself right back into combat, and takes down the wicked goon who took his eye.

Out of the blue, I feel a shock in the small of my back, and my body spasms into a weird arch before I spin around with my sword extended. I don't hit anybody, but I do manage to knock a few spears away. The shock in my spine doesn't hurt, not at all. Maybe a little... Okay, it hurts like hell.

I bring my sword in, jamming the hilt into the visor of the closest New Power soldier. The glass shatters, allowing me to see his eyes. He falls to a knee and looks up at me. His gaze is one of pure and utter hatred. His whole face is a mask of hate.

There's something wrong with his eyes. It's not that they have the now familiar haziness that characterizes all citizens of the Water Nation. It's something else. Something's off. I know I've seen those eyes before, but I don't know where. He moves to attack me again. I dodge, sucking in my gut, before raising my sword in both hands and bringing it down on his shoulder.

As the, probably, dying man howls in rage and uses his last ounce of strength to try and rip out my entrails, I remember where I've seen those eyes before. It's funny how the mind works. I've seen those eyes twice before. One was when some near cannibalistic creeps were chasing me. The other was Armando. They are

310

the eyes of someone being controlled. As far as things that fall under the category of "not good" go, this one might just take the cake. I might actually need to file it under "*really* not good." The New Power have managed to figure out how to take control of an entire freaking nation! How is this even possible!?

Instead of using my sword to push this dying guy aside, I reach out and shove him aside with my free hand. I notice that I leave a red handprint on his face. I inspect my arm and see that my jacket is nice and bloody the entire length of my arm. Wonderful, another thing to file away under not good. I guess that guy from before must've got an artery.

"Eli, I need to move. Want a lift?" I shout over my shoulder, not willing to turn my attention away from my attackers any longer than need be. At this point, all feeling from my ribs down has gone away.

"I'd love one," he shouts back in a pissed-off, cynical tone. Well fine Mr. Grumpy Pants. I disengage from the New Power trying to kill me, dodge another blow, and leap towards Eli. I kick on my boots and grab him under the arms. He screams as I lift up, but seems to recover quickly as he attempts to kick the heads of the New Power soldiers until I get him above their range. Or maybe he's trying to run on them.

I temporarily abandon my original objective as I fly us over to a nearby rooftop. I don't have the world's most controlled landing, but at least I get Eli down safely before I land myself. The next thing I do is shrink my sword back down and inspect my arm more closely. It's actually a lot worse than it feels. How is it that I'm not on the ground in the fetal position, crying? I pull off my jacket and see that my entire arm has been painted a nice shade of red, normally not a good sign. I look at my shirt and sigh.

"And I liked this shirt, too." I take my pocket knife-sized sword and cut off the clean sleeve of my shirt. After the fabric has been liberated—and another of my shirts destroyed—I put my sword back in my pocket.

Eli studies me with curiosity. "Could you always fly?" he asks, spitting more blood.

"Nof," I try to say with the ripped sleeve clenched between my teeth, tying it around my arm to try and stop the bleeding. The fabric will probably be soaked through and red really soon, but this lame tourniquet is better than nothing, I guess.

Now I look at Eli and see how he's doing. He's sitting on the ground, still holding his mangled face and looking like he's on the verge of tears.

Translation: Bad.

His head looks horrific. He's still bleeding quite a bit from the near-perfectly-vertical gash down his face. That won't be healing any time soon. He moves his hand away from his face, and where his left eye should be is something I don't want to see. My stomach threatens to empty itself again, but I fight to get it under control. Luckily, Eli's wearing a long-sleeved shirt.

Grabbing his arm, I tell him, "Trust me here." I cut his sleeve off at the shoulder and split it open so that it's now a rectangular piece of cloth. I do the same with his other sleeve, and tie their ends together. Sadly, I've had to do this before. With a practiced hand, I wrap the fabric around Eli's head, both to slow the bleeding, as well as to ensure I don't have to look at his wound. Probably it's more about hiding the gash. That was just sick.

"How do you know how to do this?" Eli asks me.

"Long story that we don't have time for," I say, tying the bandage tight. I manage to cover most of the cut, except for some of it extending below his nose. Eli lets out a disgusting, wet cough. He wipes his mouth with the back of his hand and it comes away bloodied. "Are you okay to go back?" Eli doesn't say anything, but instead looks at me and shakes his head. To me he looks like a scared kid whose mom just caught him stealing a cookie. "Then stay here. It's safe," I say, carefully wriggling back into my jacket, keeping my weight on my less-injured foot.

I've learned and been conditioned to work through pain all my life. Eli probably hasn't. It makes a huge difference. I look back over the fighting and make out

John standing on the roof where I left him, a few blocks away. Looking at the fighting itself, I see that Dac, Jinn, and the brown glow are together at this point, and that Arthur has a wide berth around him. He's moving toward Dac, Jinn, and whoever brown is. Nathan and Rose have started to get closer together, but whoever silver is is still pulling a Lone Ranger.

"Don't die," I say to Eli as I take off again, pulling my sword out of my pocket, but not extending it. I make a beeline right for Arthur, landing as close to him as I can and fighting my way nearer.

"What're you doing here?" he shouts at me, taking out a line of New Power soldiers with a long drag of his oversized scythe.

"I need to borrow a sword," I shout back as I counter a high attack and cutting back low. Pain shoots through both my arm and foot, but I do my best to ignore it.

"What's wrong with yours?" Arthur somehow manages to cleave someone in two. The longer I know this guy, the more I learn not to piss him off.

"It's for John," I yell. "He can't fight without a sword!" I try to dodge another blow but stumble, essentially genuflecting because of my bum foot. Somehow I manage to avoid the attack, but I don't like that I'm forcing myself to my knees.

"Fine! HERE!" Arthur screams, elongating a cutlass as he draws it from his pocket. Before I can get it, he drives it into a charging New Power soldier's chest. The impaled man runs a few more steps towards me. I spin out of his direct path and draw the sword from his torso with my free hand as he falls. "Now help me get to Jinn and Mark!" Arthur shouts at me, never missing a beat in his ballet of violence. Actually, he's probably closer to slam dancing than ballet.

I awkwardly cut through a brave New Power soldier with both swords, not using either very effectively. I have no idea what I'm doing!

My left hand has the painful pins and needles of numbness going through it. The rest of my left arm might as well be amputated for all the sensation I have in it.

"Why do you need to get over there?" I shout back, piecing together that the brown glow must be Mark. That means Gabriel is the silvery color.

"I just do!" Arthur shouts back impatiently. A New Power soldier gets too close to Arthur for his scythe to be effective. Arthur holds it aside and uses his free hand to punch the soldier in the mouth. The dazed soldier topples backwards, falling heavily onto a comrade behind him, resulting in a chain of a dozen soldiers fumbling to the ground like a line of dominoes. Somehow, this makes Arthur even more terrifying.

Don't even think about trying to piss him off, Dac tells me, probably saving my life in the process. Temptation to annoy people is too great for me to handle.

"Fine!" I yell to both Dac and Arthur. "Bull-rush them!"

"What's a bull?" Arthur asks. Right. Sky Nation. No bulls.

"Just run and break everything that gets in your way!" I yell over my shoulder.

"I can do that!" he yells.

"Ready?"

Arthur slices through some New Power as if that's an affirmative. That's how I take it, anyway. I kick back another attacker, and Arthur and I heft our weapons up. Well, I lift my normal sword because my left arm really doesn't' want to work for me right now. That's probably bad. I don't know how to use two swords anyway.

We both scream and start running. We try to move as fast as possible, but there are, of course, complications. As we move, we ferociously shove the New Power out of the way. Why are there so many of them!?

My foot catches on I don't want to know what and I start to stumble and fall. Arthur catches my arm so that I can keep moving, stumbling really, taking big, heavy, unbalanced steps while doubled over for a few feet. Before I can right myself, I bowl headfirst into an armored gut. Lights dance in front of my eyes as I push off whatever I hit and keep running. In the chaos, I'm pretty sure I've accidentally cut at least one person. I just hope it isn't Arthur. He'd probably be mad about that.

Up ahead, I see a wide ring that Mark, Dac, and Jinn formed. I can see the glow from Mark and Jinn's swords, but I can't make out either of them individually. Dac's pretty hard to miss. Right before we break through to their circle of protection, with Hub Runners fighting on all sides, maintaining the room in the middle, I take a staff to my side. The high voltage makes me stiffen before pitching forward. I hit the ground tumbling heals over head and both swords are ripped from my grasp, clattering forward.

Now my entire body feels numb, the pins and needles everywhere. It hurts and immobilizes me, but no real damage is actually being dealt. I think. If the New Power are the ones who launched the assault, why are they using, for the most part, non-lethal weapons? I try to get my arms under me to push myself up, but my left arm gives out and I collapse onto my side.

"Dammit," I mumble between gritted teeth, struggling to climb to my feet. I tilt my head back and see my sword lying there, next to a corpse in a pool of blood. It's actually my sword, not the one that Arthur gave me. I roll over onto my stomach and start dragging myself forward using only my right arm. As soon as I can, I wrap my hand around the sword and fight to push myself to my hands and knees, my less injured limbs taking more of the weight. I take a second to glace over at the corpse my sword fell by and my heart leaps into my throat.

"JINN!"

Chapter Twenty-Three

"JINN!" I scream again. I'm planted on one bent leg, my other knee in a pool of his blood. I grab his slashed, blood soaked shirt at his shoulders and partially lift him off the ground. "Jinn! Jinn! Wake up!" He can't be dead. He's just sleeping. Yeah, that's it, sleeping. He doesn't *look* like he's dead. He looks like he's sleeping. His eyes are closed and there's pain on his face.

That's what pain looks like, right? Right!?

"Wake up!" I keep screaming. I can't stop. Maybe if I make enough noise, he'll hear me. If I'm louder, he'll wake up.

Blood. There's blood covering his face. Maybe if I clear it away, he'll come to. I let my sword clatter to the floor and frantically try to wipe the blood from his face with my own blood-stained hands. There's an annoying little buzz in my head that I ignore. I can't make out any detail from it anyway. I don't think I could even if I wanted to.

Wait.

I freeze in place, almost as if the movie of my life was paused. I look at his face, at ho w all I'd done was spread blood around.

I stop trying to clean Jinn's face and reach down to grab my sword. I clutch it so tightly that my knuckles turn white as I slowly rise to my feet. The buzzing intensifies as I raise my head, barely noticing the tight ring of Hub Runners holding off the tides of New Power. All I see are those that need to die.

With a primal, bestial howl, I launch myself forward. NO! You bastards won't take anyone else from me!

I move through the line of Hub Runners, knocking some over. I don't care. What does it matter? They'll get back up.

"DIE!" I roar as I cleave through one New Power soldier after another. Their shrieks of pain and horror are drowned out by my own cries of rage. One by one, soldiers fall. I kill them. I keep killing them. Mountains of slain bodies start to form around me as the seemingly endless ranks of those that need to die keep coming at me. What does it matter who they are, who they were? There's no face. None of them. They're just armored dealers of death. Why should murderers live? HUH?

I scream as I take a New Power soldier's head clean off his shoulders. That annoying buzz in my head keeps getting louder and louder, but I still can't make anything out. All it does it feed my rage.

I'm vaguely aware of all the prods I'm getting from enemy staffs, but I don't feel it. They just make me move faster. Just a moment ago, a single hit from one of those things knocked me on my ass. But now, I can take a thousand of them and not feel a thing. My arm, useless a minute ago, is operating perfectly to help me execute these monsters.

I don't stop. I keep fighting these pieces of trash as long as I possibly can. A head flies here, a limb is severed there, an impaling every now and then. With a spin, I kill, or at least maim half a dozen of them.

Some of the bodies fall on me, painting my whole body with the red of their blood. How dare they cover me in the blood of monsters!

I push harder, killing ever more of them until it seems like all that surrounds me is a pile of corpses. That's what they'll all be soon anyway. All I see are dead men walking. Their time is up.

As I slice straight through another helmet, I vaguely hear someone calling for retreat. Without any hesitation what so ever, the New Power soldiers run. I can't let these bastards get away! I give chase, unwilling to lose them, leaving bloody footprints behind me. I refuse to let them go free to do more evil.

Before I can take more than five steps, I feel a heavy hand land on my shoulder, holding me in place. I bring my sword around using all my strength, fully intending to cut this nuisance's arm off. But my sword uselessly clanks off metal.

I look up at the face of whoever is holding me, rage burning in my eyes.

Dac.

"Stop," he pleads, his voice sounding hurt. I look over to where the retreating New Power are. I can still catch them if I fly over. I start to break out of Dac's grip when he says, "Sam. Please. You can stop now." Suddenly, something hits me like a wall and I can finally make out that buzz I've been hearing. It's painfully loud, almost driving me to my knees.

SAM! SAM, STOP! IT'S OKAY! STOP! YOU'RE OKAY! STOP! The words are a flood of messages, all layered over each other as if all the people in a massive, faceless crowd are shouting at me at the top of their lungs, straining their vocal chords. *SAM, HE'S ALIVE! SAM, PLEASE! YOU DON'T HAVE TO DO THIS! NO! STOP! CALM DOWN! HE'S OKAY! PLEASE! SAM! DON'T!*

My head is spinning faster than anything in existence. I close my eyes and take a few shaky breaths before I can steady them. I don't know how long I stand here with my eyes closed. Miraculously, my head quiets.

"Sam?" Dac says, not sure if I'm okay.

"I'm fine," I reassure him and anyone else listening.

Liar, he says in my head. I wince from the pain of

hearing him mentally as blood drips off me, from my perfect suit of red.

"It's okay," Dac says again, thankfully returning to talking out loud. Why does he sound like he's getting farther away? "You're okay. Everyone's alive." What? What was that? I-I can't hear him. I look around me, but none of the faces are familiar. Just a lot of strangers with something on their faces. Terror? Then I see Arthur looking right at me, concern all but completely masked by his normally his hard features. I see everyone else I know running towards me. What is everyone saying? I hear voices, but I can't understand their words.

I see mountains of bodies lying near me. Not just one pile, but many of them. Rings of them. Entire mountain ranges made of corpses, with rivers and oceans of blood...

I look back at Dac, but he seems to be moving farther away. And before I know anything else, my vision is swallowed by black.

Chapter Twenty-Four

"Finally, I have one!" somebody says triumphantly. I don't know who it is. It's too dark for me to see, and my brain doesn't feel like it wants to work enough to connect the voice with a person.

"Yes and it only took how long? Plus my having to lead an assault?" another voice replies testily. "Do you know how many soldiers I lost in order for you to get one stupid little toy?"

"An inconsequential amount, I assure you," the first voice answers. Why does this conversation seem vaguely familiar? Eh, I'll put it together later. For now, can somebody turn down the volume and let me sleep? "With this one 'toy,' as you put it, I can control many things."

"But my men–" the other argues.

"Will be replaced."

"This is not your jurisdiction."

"What does that matter?" questions the owner of

the first voice, which is becoming more recognizable. "What's done is done. The pawns have been sacrificed to capture their king. The game is ours."

"No, the game is *yours*, and you're not even a player!" the other voice spurts out angrily. "I will tell the Master of your deeds, Steven." Oh, that's who the arrogant, annoying voice belongs to. That makes a lot of sense.

"You will do no such thing," Steven says, not an ounce of concern evident in his voice. Maybe it shows on his face, but I can't see him. "You shall stay here and be ready to fight."

"What?" the other voice demands, even more ticked off. "What do you mean fight? You have me sacrifice a legion of my soldiers to retrieve your little prize, and you have the gall to tell me to be ready to fight again?"

"Yes," Steven affirms. "I am summoning the boy."

"The blood-soaked demon? The one with a sword that glows whiter than any light?" What's with all the old magic and sorcery-type talk?

"Cutter," Steven says. "I will have him yet. The boy will join us, Lynch! He just doesn't know it yet." Actually, no I wont, but I'll tell you that myself, after I wake up.

"Why would you call him here?" Lynch demands.

"To either make him join me," Steven replies, "or bring an end to his miserable life," Let's see you try.

I wake up lying on a bed. I open my eyes and see

325

that I'm only wearing my boxers and necklace. First question, who took my clothes? Second, who cleaned me up? And third, where the heck am I?

Eh, does it really matter? I look around for a moment and establish nothing more than this is, in fact, a room. Shocker. I lay my head back on a surprisingly comfortable pillow and close my eyes. Almost instantly, images of piles of bodies bathed in blood force themselves in front of my eyes. It's all in perfect detail. I can see from where a sword opened one man's belly and took off another's head to how the piles of bodies redecorate the landscape to the oceans of blood pooled on the floor. It's like a video camera is slowly rotating, showing me everything. The camera ends on a lone person standing there, not a speck of his regular skin color visible beneath a dripping layer of too red blood covering his entire body. His eyes are filled with nothing but malice.

It's me. I'm looking at me.

My doppelganger smiles, his teeth and the whites of his eyes a startling contrast against the dark red that colors the rest of him.

"We did this," he says, making a grand gesture all around him with his arms raised, as if it was a golden kingdom to be treasured.

Instantly drawn back into reality—leaving that nightmare world behind—I spaz off the bed, gracelessly

326

landing more or less on all fours, and violently empty
the contents of my stomach onto the floor. Even when
I'm sure there's nothing left, it keeps coming. There
is barely enough time for me to suck in a breath of air
between retches. I'm sobbing. I can't stop. Am I going to
die from not being able to breathe while throwing up? It
would serve me right after what I just did.

Mercifully, my stomach stops its heaving. Still
sobbing, I scramble away from the puddle of puke in
something like a backwards crabwalk. My back hits
against a wall and I curl up into the fetal position, my
body shaking. I sit with my eyes open. I refuse to go
back to that dark place again! That's not me. I'm not
a monster. Am I? The image of my sneering, blood-
covered face flashes through my head for a split second.

I swear there's a hiss in my mind saying, *Don't worry.
You'll call for me in time.* I shudder and break out in an
even colder sweat.

Sam? I wince from pain and because I think my evil
twin is trying to talk to me again. Dac. It's only Dac.
There aren't any monsters in my head... just Dac and me.
But what if the monster really is me?

"What?" I say aloud, barely audible.

Are you going to be okay?

"I.." I start ready to reassure him, "I don't know."
Lying takes too much effort right now. I feel cold, and
I'm shaking, and nothing is right in the world. Actually

no, I don't feel cold. I would love to feel cold. Instead, I feel warm, as if I'm still wearing a thick coat of blood. Again my twin flashes in my mind.

Can people come in? Everyone has been waiting to see you. Fantastic. I'm the charity nutcase that everyone needs to take care of now. I don't want people to see me like this.

"Sure," I mumble weakly. Is my brain broken? I don't want anyone in here! Or maybe I do. I don't know.

"Just give him a minute," I hear Dac say, muffled by the closed door. "He's still pretty shaken." Even though I clearly heard him tell people to go away, I don't hear any movement. Great. They're going to wait me out. Can't they just leave me alone?

I spend what feels like far too long crying and try to reign in all my frustration and sadness. The odor of vomit wafting through the air keeps my stomach churning, never quite allowing me to get comfortable.

I sigh in resignation. At the very least, I want to be dressed when they come in to chain me up and take me to the loony bin. Don't think I'll go willingly either.

Where are my clothes? I ask Dac. My head hurts still, but it's not so bad to send this message as a passing thought.

They're still trying to get them clean. They're almost done, but everything was a little, ah... Blood stained... Got it.

He doesn't need to say more. I understand. That'll be my timer. When I get my clothes back, I'll see the others.

In the time it takes for my clothes to get clean, I manage to stop shaking and crying. There's a knock on the door before Dac wordlessly enters carrying my half ruined shirt and jeans, along with my reparable jacket. How my jacket manages to survive to some degree, but my shirt takes tons of abuse, I don't know. I stand up and take my clothing from him, first pulling on my ripped up jeans, then my one-sleeved shirt, and finally my jacket, slightly used. Finally dressed, I lean back against the wall and slide down so that I'm sitting there with my knees bent.

You ready for this? Dac asks. *Pretty much everyone in Hub Fourteen wants to talk to you.* Great.

"Ready as I'll ever be," I say to him, testing my voice out. It's raw and scratchy, but it's all I have.

I'll play doorman, Dac tells me as he crosses the room and goes back outside. I should stand up, shouldn't I. Nah, the floor is too comfortable. Seconds after Dac leaves, John, Rick, and Fred tentatively enter the room. John comes right over and pulls up a nice piece of wall next to mine. Rick and Fred stay standing. Not one of the three looks like they were involved in the fighting. That's good. They're still alive.

It's silent for a bit before John speaks up. "It was a lot safer on the rooftop." I can't help but let out a halfhearted puff of air that I hope passes as a chuckle.

"I got you a sword to use," I say. "There were just a few tiny little problems before I could get it back to you."

"Nah, it's not that bad," John argues, trying to sound like his joking self.

"How many did I kill?" I ask, not buying what he's selling.

"You should've seen everyone you protected," Rick interjects, changing the subject. Smooth.

"Yeah, we were in change of taking care of everyone that couldn't fight for themselves," Fred adds, gesturing to Rick and himself. "Those armored guys were about to break in, when they suddenly ran screaming. It was a miracle."

"That's nice," I say in a monotone.

John lays a hand on my shoulder. "You're going to be alright, man. Hang in there."

"Just give me a day and I'll bounce back," I say with a smile that doesn't quite reach my eyes. John looks at me, concerned, but chooses to let me believe my own lie. I guess lying isn't as hard as I thought it would be right now.

"I'll hold you to that," John says, using my shoulder to push himself to his feet. "It'll get better. Trust me." How does he know?

"We'll get someone to clean that up for you," Rick says, vaguely waving his hand toward the pile of vomit in the room.

"Thanks," I say as the three of them work their way to the door and let themselves out. I rest my head on my knees with a frustrated groan. This is going to be a lot harder than I thought. I don't want to act like everything's perfect right now. Jinn's dead, and I killed so many people that it'll haunt me until I die.

The door opens and closes again far too soon, and I hear four sets of footsteps in the room with me. Only when the footsteps stop right in front of me does somebody speak up.

"It smells like shit in here," a familiar voice says. And actually, it's vomit.

"What do you want, Arthur?" I say into my knees.

"To lose my sense of smell!" Arthur answers loudly. I hear the dull thud of someone elbowing him in the ribs, at which he grunts. I can't help but secretly let out a little smile at the thought of someone bossing him around. "And to tell you... thankyouforsavingmylife." He rushes through the last part so that it's not especially intelligible. I hear someone hit Arthur again.

"Say it clearly," a girl's voice criticizes. Rose.

"Alright!" Arthur bellows, "Now both of you stop hitting me. Thanks for saving my hide, kid. Happy?"

"Ecstatic," Rose replies smugly.

"Well?" Arthur says to me. "Aren't you going to look up at me?" Fine. Whatever. I raise my head to see Arthur

331

and Rose, both in partially-tattered clothes. I'd look longer if it weren't for the two people standing next to them. My eyes widen bigger than I knew they could go.

"What? It looks like you've seen a ghost," says Jinn, his voice raspier than usual, knowing full well I thought he was dead.

"Y-you're alive?" I ask, not believing it. Jinn isn't wearing a shirt, but his entire upper body, from waist to armpits, is wrapped with gauze.

"I sure hope so," Jinn says, moving his hands over the bandages as if to make sure there aren't any gaping holes in him.

"H-how? I saw your corpse. You're not a zombie, are you?" Seriously. That would be a good reason to be afraid.

"No, I'm not a zombie," Jinn laughs. "And I wasn't dead. There's a huge difference between totally dead and mostly dead." I blink at him.

"Don't try to make jokes," Mark says. "You're not that funny." My tunnel vision disappears as my eyes shift to Mark, who's standing next to Jinn. There's one startling feature that my eyes immediately move to.

"Mark," I say, trying to sound as calm as possible, "what happened to your arm?"

"Hmm? Oh," he says, looking down like he's just noticing it. His right arm is gone from about where a short-sleeve shirt would end down. His arm rather abruptly ends clean and angular where I'm assuming a sword took it off. "That. It's nothing."

"Nothing? Mark, you lost your arm!"

"I know," he says with a shrug. "I'm still alive, though, and I've still got my second favorite hand." He raises his left hand and wiggles his fingers. "Do you want to know the worst part?" he continues. "It still itches!" He futilely scratches at the air where his arm should be. "I could try scratching the stump, but it's still tender. There was only enough Blue Elixir to make sure the three of us didn't drop dead. Not enough to heal us back to one hundred percent."

Wait.

"Three of us?" I ask. Two makes sense to me. Jinn had one foot in the door and one out and Mark lost an arm so that makes sense too. Who's the third? Eli? I know he lost an eye, but he didn't seem to be at death's door.

"Yes, three," Jinn confirms. "Mark, you, and me." Hold on.

"Me?"

"Yes, you," Jinn says. "Apparently, you didn't end up much better than me." Um, how? Now that I'm thinking about it, my body decides it's a good time to let me feel everything.

I hurt. Everywhere. Excruciatingly so.

There are a few places that hurt worse than others,

but not by a whole lot. One of them is my arm, where I was cut.

I climb to my feet and shrug my jacket off so I can get a better look at myself. I don't need to roll my sleeve up, having cut it off earlier. Where I got cut is one heck of a nasty scar. It wraps itself halfway around my arm on the outside, leading me to believe that the knife bit down to the bone. That would explain a lot, actually. Next, I lift up my shirt to see where I was jabbed in the side with an electric staff. There's a scar there as well. It's as if I was stabbed by something pointy. I was hit by an electric staff, not something pointy.

"A few of their staffs had sharpened, poison tips," Mark Explains. "You were lucky enough to get hit by one of those." I'm not so sure lucky is the right word here. I continue investigating my body to find a new collection of scars and bruises that correspond to all my aches and pains. Purple's a lovely color on me. Bruises happen to get just the right shade.

"You and Jinn looked far worse than anyone else," Mark says.

"I'd say losing your forging arm puts you up in the running, too," Arthur interjects.

"It's fine," Mark says. "I'm really a lefty, so it doesn't matter." Mark's a lefty? How did I never notice this? I move to scratch my head and feel a massive, painful lump hidden by my hair.

"Ow," I say, rubbing it.

"Remember when you tried to head-butt a suit of armor?" Arthur reminds me.

"I didn't try to," I counter. Really, I didn't.

"So I found something out," Mark says abruptly, a different tone settling in his voice. "Kane discovered what's going on with the people down here." Ugh, do I really have to hear about Kane *now*? "Apparently, pretty much all of the Water Nation is under mind control."

"I know," I say, poking at a bruise on my arm. It gets really quiet all of a sudden. I look up and see that Mark is giving me a funny look, and the others are shifting their looks between the two of us. "What?"

"How do you know that?" Mark sounds confused.

"I saw it in their eyes. They are the same as Armando's while he's being controlled. I didn't know there were that many AI's out there."

"There aren't," Mark says. "Kane said they're using some sort of gas which they circulated through the air vents. The only reason this place is still normal is because it's set up on a different oxygen intake system than the rest of the Water Nation."

So that's how they did it.

"Samuel Cutter!" a booming voice echoes through the walls of this building, originating from the Hub's broadcasting system. That's one voice I really don't want to hear.

Without saying anything, I walk outside. Directly out front is a mob of Hub Runners, all of them looking up at the sky and listening. I get out of the building and look around, for some reason expecting there to be a giant video screen popping up on the walls.

"Samuel Cutter, can you hear me?" Steven. What does he want? "Perhaps I have your attention now. Samuel, I think it's time you and I talked again, wouldn't you say? It's been far too long. I know you may be thinking you might not wish to see me, but fear not. I have some incentive."

"You see, Samuel," he goes on, obviously enjoying the show, "Kane and I are having a little chat. We thought it would be pleasant if you could join us." Kane? I knew royals couldn't be trusted! Or maybe Steven really did take out our king. This is what he was talking about before! "Don't worry, he's perfectly safe and will continue to be so as long as you come accordingly. I plan to make a game out of it, so choose your players wisely. Meet me at the Water Tower. Your little friends will know the one and show you the way. I can't wait to see you again, Sammy."

Dammit.

Chapter Twenty-Five

All eyes immediately shift to me. Of course, all the Hub Runners know who I am, I've kind of made a bit of a show of myself. It's unsettling to have all these people looking at me. Why does it feel like they're about to start chanting, "Exterminate! Exterminate!" They must have misunderstood Steven's message and think we're on the same team or something. I reach into my pocket to grab my sword, just in case. Wait, where is it?

I grope around in my pocket as if it's the size of a living room. Nothing. Did they take it? I flick my eyes to the crowd of people staring at me, feeling naked. They all look guilty to me. Any one of them could have taken my sword.

I have your sword, Dac tells me. Then again, I've been wrong before. *It's still full size, so I'm not bringing it out there.* Some of the tension leaves my body, but I'm still uneasy. Dozens of people staring will do that to a person.

"What?" I say loudly to the mass of people. Silence. Nothing. I can't even hear any feet shuffling. This is probably bad. I stand still just as silently, straining my ears until I hear they start to buzz.

"He's with the Snatchers!" Oh no. "Get him!" Suddenly everyone is screaming, and the volume goes from mute to rock show in less than a second. I guess this is what it sounds like when an entire city is after your head. I don't like it. Nope. Not a bit. My heart sets to racing and all my new scars start throbbing again. There's that not fully healed thing Mark was telling me about. It seems like the number of angry eyes trained on me multiplies.

Sword. Sword. Please bring me my sword. I frantically think to Dac. All I know is that I would rather be armed when the fighting starts. Regardless, I don't know how well that'll work out. I'm still in a lot of pain from the battle just a minute ago. If I get swarmed by this many people, I think I'd last a good five seconds, ten tops. I tense, ready to try to fly away, worst case, but I don't think I could keep that up for long, either.

Well I'm screwed.

I can't even try to explain myself they're so loud. Someone grabs my shoulder and I jump, spinning around. My fists shoot up in front of me and I'm ready to fight if this is the beginning of it. Normally I wouldn't hesitate and would've already attacked, but right now if I throw the first punch, all it would do is hasten my demise.

"Easy, Wet Head," Rido says to me. I've only seen the guy twice but I'm able to recognize him. Maybe it has to do with the fact that he's the leader of Hub Fourteen and has had more than ample opportunity to order me killed. Like right now for example. "Don't worry. I'm not here to kill you... yet." Well that's reassuring. Sort of. Rido continues, "I'm going to do something quick and easy to prove you're with us."

I glance behind him and see the hulking mass that is Dac standing there. My sword is hidden behind his back, and he's looking totally suspicious. I didn't even know he could make a guilty face. I thought his face didn't really move.

Um, hold off on that sword for now, I tell him.

Good call.

Rido steps past me so that he's closer to the mob. He raises his hands and a hush comes over the crowd. Wow. That's... wow.

"Listen to me," Rido yells so that he can be heard, authority in his voice. That's a lot of noise coming out of such a little guy. He's probably five foot nothing! "Why do you now accuse our brother of treachery?" Brother?

They named you an honorary citizen of Hub Fourteen while you were passed out, Dac tells me. *Your name is officially Wet Head to them.*

"How many of your lives has he saved? How many of you would have been lost if not for him?" Rido's pointing at me and making grand gestures. From here it looks silly, but he's got a captivated audience. Hey, if it works, it works. "You want to test his loyalty? Fine, I shall test it for you." Wait wait wait wait wait. What? Rido turns toward me, a hard look in his eyes. "Wet Head," he shouts for all to hear, "if you're with the Snatchers, then cut me down!" He balls his fists and sticks out his arms, giving me a clean shot if I wanted to cut him open. "Draw your magic sword and use it to end me!" Everyone is silent.

I blink. "Um, what?"

"If you're against us, then kill me."

"I'm not going to kill you," I say, lazily pointing a finger at him subconsciously.

"Don't speak!" Rido proclaims. "Act!"

"That's what I'm doing," I argue. "Nothing."

A smirk comes across Rido's face as he lowers his arms. "There you have it!" Rido announces to the people of Hub Fourteen. He turns back to me. "Now, shall we go save a king? Eh, Wet Head?" He winks at me. The guy actually *winks* at me.

You little midget punk! You were putting on a show the whole time!

"About that," I say, still punting him across a football field in my head. "I have no idea where I'm going."

"Don't worry about that," Rido laughs. Oh yeah, go ahead and laugh. Laugh while you still can before I use you to score a field goal. "I'll drive you. How long do you need to prepare?"

Dac walks up and hands me my sword. I twist it around a bit so that it fits right in my hand, accidentally making the blade dance in small circles.

"Ready," I say. Rido stares at the sword, eyes wide, realizing that I didn't even have it on me during his dramatic little performance.

"Then I guess that makes me the hold-up," Rido says, subtly coughing into a closed fist, regaining his composure. "Gather your forces and meet me by the Council House in an hour." With that, Rido disappears into the crowd of people that may or may not still want to kill me.

I decide my best move is to not move right now. I simply stand there, sword in hand, staring at the crowd still gathered before me. After a short, but still far too long, awkward silence the mob begins to disperse. I actually feel myself relax, my shoulders lowering as the people shuffle away in all directions.

What is this place!? Mood Swing City!?

I think that went pretty well, Dac says, stepping up behind me.

"As far as still being alive goes, I completely agree," I say out loud.

"Should we go find the others?" Dac asks.

"That'd probably be a good idea," I say, still somewhat in a daze as we go to search for everybody.

It doesn't take us long to find everybody and tell them to armor up. Well, really Dac finds them while I just kind of trail along, not sure where everybody is.

When we're told to armor up, do we actually get armor? No. How about possibly collecting more Blue Elixir? That would be helpful, right? We're out. Do we make sure that everybody actually has a sword? Well, yes. That one we actually do.

Jinn, Mark, Dac, Arthur, Rose, Gabriel, Nathan, Sarah, John, Rick, Fred, and I are all waiting outside of the abandoned theater—the Council House—a few minutes before Rido told us to be here. Personally, I'm pretty amazed that not only am I on time for something, but I'm early. Everyone looks pretty nervous. It hasn't been that long since our last "big fight" with the New Power, but here we are again, ready to have our collective ass handed to us on I think the same day. I tried to talk John, Rick, and Fred out of fighting, but they'd have none of it, saying something like they wanted to be a part of it and I can't leave them behind this time, or something like that. My eyes slide over them as I sit down against the wall of the amphitheater and I notice they look relatively calm. We all do.

Dac is standing off by himself, shut down for the moment. He told me as soon as we got here that he was going to power off for a bit so that his batteries could partially recharge. I hope he has enough juice in there for this.

Jinn and Mark are talking with Arthur and Rose. The Royals are clumped together, looking the most anxious out of all of us. It makes sense, they're actually related to Kane. Who knows what Steven has been doing to him all this time? Gabriel looks sick to his stomach, Sarah is pacing and talking, trying to keep herself occupied, and Nathan is staring at me. He hasn't stopped doing that since we got here. If I cared enough, I might actually go over and ask him what his problem is. I can tell he really wants to come over and talk to me about something, but his dad and sister keep him stuck in place. He'll just have to wait.

I close my eyes and try to sleep for a bit. I'm tired, hurt, sick about how many people I've killed, and I'm cranky. Unfortunately for me, it doesn't come. I sit here with my eyes closed, trying to relax, but it doesn't work out so well. I guess I'm a little anxious. And my arm still hurts. And a lot of other things run rampant in my mind. Today is just not my day.

While I'm in the middle of debating asking someone to hit me in the head to put me to sleep, I hear footsteps, followed by, "Is this everybody? Eleven of you?"

"Twelve," I say to Rido, standing up. I didn't think it was that hard to see me. "How many are you bringing?"

"Thirty of my best," Rido says like a proud father. "Eli wanted to come, but I told him that he's too injured to be here."

"And I told you that you could shove it. Respectfully, of course." Another voice interjects. I look in the direction the voice came from and see Eli standing on a one-story rooftop, a sword at his hip, and fresh (actual) bandages wrapped around his head. He lowers himself down to the ground and somehow makes it look graceful where I would've made it look horrible and face-planted. "I told you I would be coming, like it or not," he says firmly, taking long strides towards Rido.

Rido closes his eyes and sighs, a hand pinching the bridge of his nose, "And I told you that you're too valuable. I can't have you dying here."

"I have no plans of dying," Eli counters as he reaches the group.

"For the hundredth time, go home," Rido begs.

"Not happening," Eli says. "I won't be sitting this one out. It's payback time."

Rido looks at each of us in turn, looking for support. We don't say a word.

"Fine!" Rido says, caving in, "But if you die, you'll be in big trouble."

"Understood, sir," Eli says with a smile that makes

the cut on his face look haunting. Instantly he stops smiling and winces. Clearly, smiling is too painful right now.

"Are we ready to go?" Rido asks, sounding impatient and irritated, probably mostly because of Eli.

I open my mouth, but Gabriel speaks first. "Yes." I was going to say that! Fine, whatever... I'll let him say yes. He did kind of conquer the planet and all. Rido looks at me, my mouth still partially open. I snap my jaw closed and let it be.

"So where are we going?" I ask.

"Follow me," Rido says with a wave of his arm, starting to walk. "We have a few boats and chasers ready."

Time to reactivate, buddy, I tell Dac. The body almost instantly whirls to life and Dac starts following along. I ask him, *How much power do you have?*

More than enough to get through this, he assures me. *I'll power down again on the boat to get a slightly longer charge.* Sounds like a plan to me. We follow Rido through town to the edge of the Hub, where a dozen boats are already parked halfway into the wall. Like Rido said, there are roughly thirty people milling about, waiting for us.

"Alright, everybody," Rido calls out. "It's show time!" All the Hub Runners move to one of the boats or another. I'm guessing they were already instructed where to go. The twelve of us stand here, awkwardly waiting for directions. "As for you guys," Rido says, turning towards us, "just find a boat that has room in it." Rido heads towards one boat that looks slightly larger than the others, but not by a whole lot. While the others in our group start to disperse, Rose comes over and hugs me out of the blue.

"Make it out of there, okay?" she says before kissing me. Life-threatening situations get me kisses? Who would've thought?

My brain turns to mush as I say, "You, too."

That was pretty pathetic, Dac says, climbing into a boat with Mark.

Hey, who's the one that just got kissed?

Touché.

After Rose heads off, I notice Nathan walking straight towards me. Oh boy, what does he want?

"Sam," he says when he gets reasonably close, "I need to talk to you about something."

"Yeah, what?" I ask, trying to use my kindest tone possible.

"It's about your swor–" he begins to say before he's cut off.

"Wet Head," Rido hollers to me. "You're with me! Come on." Saved by the height-impaired leader of Hub Fourteen.

"Sorry," I say to Nathan. "We'll talk after this is all

said and done." I start to walk away before my brain kicks in. I turn around and, walking backwards, add, "And don't worry. We'll get your brother back!" They're siblings. Maybe Nathan is having a panic attack. But why did it sound like he wanted to talk about my sword then? How could my sword be significant right now? Oh yeah, he actually knows what the colors mean. I guess he never saw that mine is white until whenever that last fight was.

I've learned that I have no idea how long I pass out for when I get seriously injured. It's sad that it has happened enough for me to actually say that I can't ever be sure. Could be an hour, could be a day, could be two weeks. Oh, I'm still a little ticked about that one. That wasn't sleeping, *that* was a mini-coma! Thanks a lot Jinn.

I step into Rido's boat and am surprised by what I see. "Britney?" That's not even the best part. "Gus?" Why the heck is Britney's little brother here? I notice in the back of my mind that this boat is pretty much standing room only. The only actual good looking chairs are the two occupied seats up front.

"Hi, Sam," Britney says pleasantly.

"I make big boom!" Gus yells ecstatically. Why am I suddenly terrified of the eight-year-old?

"What are you guys doing here?" I ask.

"Well he's here to shoot his cannon," Britney says, mussing Gus's hair, "and I'm here to take care of him.

Conner's not much for fighting, so he stayed home."

"By cannon, do you mean the one he wants to make that can destroy an entire Hub?" Seriously, it's a very important question. If this kid is in charge of that much firepower, I refuse to go where he's shooting.

"No," Britney says, unconvincingly. "This one's a prototype." My eyes bulge out of my head. I don't want him shooting near me!

Rido approaches us. "Wet Head, I'd like to introduce you to our pilot, Ms. Devany Brooks."

A woman sitting in one of the boat's two seats turns around to look at me. "Nice to meet you," she says. I notice she's wearing goggles. Why is she wearing those? Isn't it already dark enough down here? Maybe they're just for esthetic purposes?

She begins to talk to Rido. "My best bet is that they'll have ships floating around, defending the tower, ready to attack us as soon as we get close. Half of our ships are armed and prepared for combat. This one is the most heavily armored."

"Great," I say unenthusiastically, totally excited by the fact that we're going to be shot at during all this. Why wasn't I told about this before? I never would've taken the job of dashing, witless hero if I knew how many people would want me dead for it. I already had enough enemies before, but now there's even more. *Way* more.

"And this is our co-pilot, Mr. Rodger Knocks." Rido go on to say.

"Good to see you kid," Rodger says. I nod my head at him. Rido looks from one of us to the other and shrugs.

Rido picks up a radio microphone from the front cabin, pushes a button on the side, and brings it to his mouth. "All ships launch. It's time to assault the Water Tower."

Chapter Twenty-Six

"Have you ever been in a dogfight before?" Rido asks me, holding on to a handle attached to the roof of this thing. We have been traveling for a while, but not terribly long. Britney is playing with Gus, trying to make sure he doesn't shoot off the cannon just quite yet.

"Actually, yes," I say, supporting myself against the wall because I can't find a handle to hold on to.

"So you know how messy they can get?"

"All too well," I respond.

Rido grunts. Kneeling down, he flips open a lockbox I didn't notice before. He pulls out a neon yellow thing, and throws it at me. "Put this on," he says while it's midair. I catch it clumsily, but I don't drop it! I unfold the bundle and end up holding it by the sleeves. It's a shirt.

"Is this some sort of fashion statement?" I ask, turning it around to inspect the neon yellowness. There's some sort of texture on here similar to the outside of the boats, but that's about it. Not sure I've ever seen anyone wearing a shirt like this.

"No," Rido says, not amused. "It's a jump shirt."

Because that totally helps me understand.

"And what, exactly, is a jump shirt?" I ask the obvious question.

"Oh, right. You're not from around here, are you?" Rido recalls.

"Not quite," I say.

"Alright then, a jump shirt allows you to pass through the walls of the Hubs and buildings without the help of a ship. I'll admit that it hurts, but it'll get you through. Also, it'll propel you through the water, but you can't really turn. It's a straight line kind of deal." I foresee pain in my immediate future. Why couldn't I foresee a nice, soft, comfy bed?

"What about getting through the walls of the boat? Isn't that a bit of a problem?" I ask. Seriously, even if this thing lets me through whatever special glass coats pretty much everything here, the boat itself looks like it's made of solid metal.

"No," Rido says. "We use a specially-sealed and pressurized exit. A minute amount of water comes in, of course, but it'll drain out as soon as the door shuts. The system is only used in emergencies." That's interesting. So using this thing is not recommended, not safe, and not fun. I don't think. "Oh, and there's nothing for you to breathe with, so you'll have to hold your breath." Even better.

Today is not going to be a good day, Dac observes.

Couldn't have said it better myself.

Are you really going to jump out of the ship? he asks, somehow believing that I'm not quite that stupid and reckless. *And I thought we were friends.*

Not if I don't have to, I admit. I really, really, really don't want to have to use this shirt, but I pull it on anyway, replacing my jacket over it and tossing my trashed one sleeve shirt aside. I'm trying to convince myself that everything will be okay when our pilot speaks up.

"Sir, we're almost there. Scanners show that they have sixteen crafts present," Devany reports.

"All probably armed and prepared for combat," Rido speculates, scratching the scruff on his chin. "Contact the others. Tell them we're going to be coming in hot." Devany nods and grabs the radio microphone.

"Attention all units, prepare for combat. Enemy has sixteen ships waiting. Repeat, prepare for combat." She continues giving Rido's commands while he himself flips the lockbox closed with his foot.

"Aren't you guys going to put one on?" I ask, gesturing to my new, gaudy yellow shirt.

"No need," Rido says. "We'll be staying with the ship. You're the only one who's going to be departing. That guy over the loud speaker called for you specifically.

It'd be a shame to keep him waiting, right?" Real shame all right. I don't know what exactly Steven has in mind, but I'm pretty sure at least one person isn't going to be walking away.

"If you're staying here," I ask, "who's going to lead all your troops that'll be landing?" Please don't say that I am. I don't want to handle that kind of responsibility.

"Eli can handle that. He *is* in charge of our defense forces, isn't he?" Rido cocks a knowing eyebrow at me. It is my fault that Eli is in that position, although I'm pretty sure he wanted it.

"Battle formations," Devany finishes before I can even get a shrug in. Through the transparent portions of the boat, I see our other ships start to get closer, making some kind of formation that I can't really see. All I know is that we're probably ready for a fight.

"Ready, Gussy?" Britney asks her brother.

"BOOM!" he yells excitedly before pushing a button on a console in front of him. His cannon and chair move straight out through the ship, so now he's in the open ocean. A sort of bubble encapsulates him, but leaves the business end of the cannon exposed. I vaguely see Gus move some sort of joystick on his control panel before the entire bubble rotates the ship in the direction he wants. Now that's cool.

I look out at the ships around us and see John and Fred enthusiastically waving at me from the ship to our left. I raise my hand and barely move it. They look like they're trying to yell something to me, but I can't make it out. They don't look particularly scared or I would think there's a cannonball headed straight for us. They actually look excited, making grand gestures with their arms that in no way can pass as a form of communication. Unable to understand, I decide they're talking about a pizza. I pantomime something back to them that looks like a gorilla. I bounce from one foot to the other, flailing my arms about with my cheeks inflated. That's like a gorilla, right?

What are you doing? Dac asks me. I instantly freeze my spaz-monkey dance and turn around. Of course, I see Dac and Jinn staring at me from another ship, looking completely confused. Their gunner, who's stationed on one side of their boat, is looking at me strangely, too.

Um, attacking a city as King Kong? It's a stretch.

Right. Sure. I see Dac relay what I said to Jinn and he simply shakes his head. I think he's probably used to my weirdness by now. It's probably good that I stopped dancing because I'm starting to hurt more than usual. Stupid injuries.

"You may want to quit goofing off," Rido says, his voice getting that same hard edge he used when he put on his little burn-the-Surface-dweller performance. He's like a statue, staring straight ahead. I turn and look in the same direction, and see a pretty good reason to stop joking around. Not too far away, maybe a couple miles, rests a tower taller than most I've ever seen on the Surface. It's a squared-off shape with windows scattered about it. I can't tell much more about the tower from this distance, other than that the top forms a pyramid. The tower seems unmolested by the water surrounding it. It's not like the water isn't touching it, but it seems more like the water is incapable of damaging the apparently metal building. It's not encased in a Hub or anything. This tower stands out on its own in the ocean, like a monument to resistance and being different.

Even though we're on the bottom of the ocean, the tower is lit up as bright as day. Most of the Water Nation has been well lit, but this place is especially so. I wonder what's so special about it that it deserves the extra attention?

Another thing about the Water Tower is that it seems like the New Power are fans of it too. Just as Devany said she saw on the scanner, there are sixteen boats armed for combat, guns already mounted on their sides, and bottoms, and tops, circling the tower like sharks waiting for their prey. Just perfect.

"What do we do?" I ask, feeling useless standing here. At least the gorilla dance was a distraction. If we can see them, they can probably see us. But the enemy ships continue to circle the Tower, so maybe they haven't noticed us. I swallow and try not to think about how achy my body feels. My little dance at least showed me that I'm hurt. Many parts of me hurt too much to function normally. I trying flexing my fingers and find that they suddenly don't even want to make a fist anymore.

I sigh as I twist my neck from side to side, trying to relax. It doesn't help. Everything hurts, and there's nothing I can do from in here.

I guess it's only fair. I can only cheat death so many times before something catches up to me.

Doesn't mean I'm going to stop running though. Mister big scary cape can come back another day.

I roll my ankle and cringe. Damn, that hurts. This isn't exactly inspiring any confidence. Oh well, fortune favors the absurdly idiotic, right?

I don't think that's how it goes, but I'll give it to you, Dac says. *In your case, you do seem to get a little extra dose of luck.*

"What're we waiting for?" I ask Rido as much as myself. Really, I try to come up with a list of reasons we can keep waiting. I mean, seriously, what if somebody left their oven on? Shouldn't we go back and check that? Or I think I need to use the bathroom. Yeah, that's it. Let's take ten, then we'll come back.

No?

Rido leans over and gently puts a hand on Devany's shoulder. "Attack," he says calmly before righting himself. With a nod, Devany pushes the controls forward and the boat lurches ahead so that I have to work to catch my balance. Through the glass, I see that whatever formation our ships were in is broken as they spread out. It looks like a pretty random maneuver, but maybe it's a plan that I'm not in on.

Our ship abruptly recoils, and I see a trail of bubbles swiftly carve their way through the water. I can't make out what it is, but I'm fairly sure it's a large metal ball of death leading the trail. I'm happy it's on our side.

Meanwhile, the circling ships abruptly shoot out toward us, using their momentum as a slingshot. "Open coms," Rido says as the enemy ships' cannons light up. Did ours do that?

Lances of light explode from their cannons, racing toward us. "Evasive maneuvers! Open fire!" Rido screams seconds before our ship careens to the side and down. Rido takes a firm hold of the seat in front of him and manages to remain standing while Britney and I are flung to the floor. I land hard on my shoulder and side. I want to scream, but no sound comes out. Being beat up sucks. Britney tries to climb to her feet but before she can get up, the ship tilts and she's sent tumbling into the wall. I roll across the floor, flopping gracelessly on the cold metal before my back slams into the wall.

Rido has managed to scramble into a chair and is busy buckling himself in. Just as he gets the last of his buckles secured, the ship turns even further so that the rest of my body slaps against the side of the boat.

"Right the ship!" Rido orders, grabbing onto the belts crossed in front of his body.

"I'm trying! I'm trying!" Devany yells back without looking over her shoulder.

Britney is in a kind of push-up position, with one foot on the wall (current acting floor) and one on the actual floor (current acting wall), looking disheveled. That's probably a good idea. I twist my head and notice that I'm pressed right up against a window. Thankfully it didn't break when I body-slammed it.

I glance out the window and see one of our ships not far away. In the blink of an eye, a brilliant flash of light collides with it. Our boat rocks, the pressure inside changing for a second as the ship I was just looking at explodes into wreckage, and flashes of red shoot out from where it used to be. The water is painfully illuminated by the remains of the shot. A painful lump of terror settles in my stomach.

"Sir, we just lost Personal Transport Two," Britney reports. I can hear Rido swear under his breath as I squeeze my eyes closed as hard as possible and turn away from the window. I have to swallow back a bit of vomit before it reaches my mouth. With my eyes closed, I can't help but hear the buzzing sounds of more missiles whizzing by. If I could crawl into a corner and hide, I would. Damnit why can't I do anything!?

I tumble back over and hit yet another surface, with a whimper and a bounce. I open my eyes and see that I'm back on the actual floor. Britney's standing and already flinging herself into an open chair. "Strap in!" Rido orders. Don't have to tell me twice.

I push myself to my feet despite my protesting body, as another dampened explosion rings out. I fall into the closest chair and frantically grasp at the straps and buckles. The buckle looks like some that I've seen on the Surface, so I actually know what I'm doing as I pull a heavy strap over each shoulder and connect the clasp above my stomach.

"Hang on!" Rodger yells back to us a second before the ship goes into a barrel roll. I involuntarily scream as I get to know what dirty laundry in a washing machine feels like. Britney and Rido are screaming, too, so my masculinity isn't further damaged. It's a close call with Rodger excitedly hollering, "YEEEEEEEEE-HAWWWW!"

Why are you so freaked out? Dac asks as we go into our second roll. *You've done this a thousand times in the sky.*

That's when I was in control! I somehow manage to respond to him as I scream my head off and try to control my bladder. I can't decide if this would be world's best or worst rollercoaster. Just with less people trying to kill me.

Light from the windows pours into the cabin, illuminating everything inside. Normally, I have no problem with more light to see by, but knowing where it's coming from makes it terrifying as all hell.

When we finally stop spinning, I check outside the window again. Boats race around each other, but there are not enough distinguishing features to tell ours from theirs. Rapid fire weaponry and cannons are being shot back and forth, missing their intended targets more often than not. The fight looks similar to a lethal fireworks display. Okay, maybe not quite, but it's the only thing I can pull to mind at the moment. I think that's pretty good, all things considered.

Our own ship rocks with recoil as the eight-year-old keeps shooting. Who thought it was a good idea to let the kid use the cannon!?

Sam! Dac shouts into my head. *Get more forces to cover us!* Two ships zip right outside the window I'm looking through. They're so close that our ship reacts to their wake. Moments later, a third ship with a rear-mounted cannon passes by. A handful of heartbeats later, a bolt of light head back in the opposite direction. The sound of a dulled explosion rings out behind us, and our ship is momentarily thrust forward at higher speed.

Sam! Dac shouts again.

"Rido," I say, trying to stand up but held in place by my harness. Ow. I hope I didn't just stupidly give myself a bruise. "We have to protect them."

"Sir, those are our two remaining transport ships," Devany reports.

"Order attack squad seven as a personal guard," Rido barks without hesitation. Devany relays Rido's orders to the other ships, and three peel away from their combats, heading directly after the three ships that just passed us. They form together so that the two transport ships have a guard on nearly all sides.

Enemy ships try to dive in and shoot at our guys, but the guards fight them off, launching a barrage of missiles to counter. Bright cracks of light pierce through the blackness of the sea, burning my retinas, as one light missile collides with another, neutralizing both. Fast enough to be called a controlled crash, two transport ships park themselves in the side of the tunnel leading to the tower. The ships stop halfway through, as usual, and the guards pull around in a wide arc and return to the fight. I can't see anything else as we turn further, and the window is no longer facing that direction.

Apparently the fast landing hurt the others, but at least we've landed, Dac tells me. He pauses for a few seconds, then abruptly says, *Oh, that's not good.*

What? What's not good? Besides most of today, I mean.

New Power. Lots of them. Go figure. We're in the middle of attacking their base, aren't we?

We bank left, and I lay back in my chair, leaning with the turn. I look ahead through the front facing window, peering around the pilots' chairs. Beams of light and balls of light fly around—or is it swim around, since we're underwater?—, colliding with each other and destroying ships in spectacular explosions. Is this what it looked like when I thought it was a good idea to play bumper cars with Sky Bikes? I must be bat-shit crazy.

Eh, that's what makes life fun, right?

It's also what almost gets me killed a lot.

You win some, you lose some? I don't know about that. This seems more like you lose some, you lose more. Maybe after I lose more, I'll finally win some.

Right in front of us, two ships collide head on. Even through the water, I can hear the booming crunch of metal against metal as the ships become more compact. For some reason or another, I expect them to explode or catch fire, but neither happens. I guess catching fire underwater is a little far fetched, isn't it?

We pull up hard and fast, just missing the wreckage beneath us.

The radio crackles to life and a partially broken-up voice says, "Sir, Billy is en route. Be here soon." Billy? As in the giant squid Billy?

Forget the fire thing, I'd prefer to see the squid do some fighting. Fire and I are having a bit of a disagreement these days anyway. Stupid fire. Sam Sam no like hot hot.

"Are we able to drop remaining foot soldiers?" Rido asks. I don't know if he's asking one of our pilots or if he's asking everyone through the radio.

"It's too hot," the radio crackles again with a different voice. "They're going to have to use jump shirts." For some reason, my heart starts beating even faster, hammering away in my chest. I'm actually scared it might break through my ribs and explode.

After a moment of thought, Rido replies, "Launch for all floors of the tower. We don't know where our forces inside are. As much as we need to retrieve the King from the Snatchers, we also have to protect our own." He pauses for a beat before continuing, "We'll launch first. Follow suit after ours lands." He turns his gaze toward me and I get another one of my "this is not going to be fun" feelings.

"Now, wait just a mi–"

"Prepare for launch," Rido says, not letting me finish, undoing his buckle and pushing himself to his feet.

"Why me?" I mumble to myself as I undo my harness.

"Keep us steady," Rido says. "We're only going to have one shot at this." That's not very inspiring. "You're not going to have any way to breathe, so you need to hold your breath," he reminds me. He pushes aside my jacket and starts poking at the gaudy yellow jump shirt I have on underneath. That's only slightly creepy.

"Okay," I say. Hold my breath. It can't be that hard. I've done it plenty of times. I glance out the window and see how far away the tower is. Just how far is that? Oh boy.

"You'll want to keep your arms to your sides," Rido advises. The ship shakes just then and Devany mumbles an apology. "You'll be moving fast through the water," he goes on. Then he pauses for a few seconds, looking at me. "Oh, and one more thing. Good luck."

He goes and buckles himself back into his chair. Um.

A glass wall drops down in between me and where everyone else is. Double um.

"Deep breath," Rido says, looking at me expectantly.

"N-now?"

"Yes, now. The longer we delay, the more dangerous it gets." Great. Nothing like a time limit to calm the nerves.

I loudly suck in a breath of air, ribs stinging.

"Launch," Rido commands. The ship opens behind me, and I'm ripped from the boat, out into the ocean. As soon as I hit the water, I shoot off. If I wasn't used to the feeling of flying with Dac, I think I would scream. That wouldn't end well in a place where I can't get another breath of air. My arms are pinned to my sides by the pressure of the water. The sound of rushing water dominates my ears, but I can still hear—more clearly than before—the sounds of cannons firing and the deafening explosions when targets are hit. There is so much light, I quickly lose sight of the tower. Glowing bullets whiz by my face, and a few bubbles come out of my mouth. Crap. Not good.

I'm sure all my hair would be standing on end, if it could, as more missiles pass by all around me. Ships dive and wind every which way in an intricate sort of dance around each other. Holy crap.

My lungs burn as I speed ever closer to the tower. How the heck am I going to get in there? I'm just going to crash into that thing and make like a bug. Squished! It's not that I don't trust Rido, but I really don't trust him. I guess it's too late now, though. Goodbye cruel world!

Shut up! You'll be fine, Dac reassures me.
How do you know that? I ask back frantically.
I don't. I'm trying to be optimistic.
Optimism isn't going to help me right now!
You never know.

I look over to the side and see a ship traveling right next to me. Maybe Rido thought it would be a good idea to get somebody to guard me, like he did for the other transport ships. The ship's gunner appear, swiveling over the top and aiming right at me. Oh shit. Oh shit. Oh shit. *Oh shit! Oh shit! Oh Shit! Oh Shit!*

The muzzle of its cannon is so bright it hurts, not even closing my eyes and turning my head would help.

Is there anything you're supposed to say before you go? Other than "goodbye," I mean? I won't even get a chance to say that! I won't even get to yell defiantly at them. This sucks.

Well, I can try. I furiously howl a torrent of bubbles at the cannon as it fires. A second after the shot fires, a ship speeds in between the blast and me. The ship instantly explodes, shrapnel flying around me. My heart skips a beat... or five. If I had any air left in my lungs to scream, I would. I tumble out of control, being pushed by the shockwave created by the ship's destruction. I'm going to be sick.

I'm ready to explode as I continue to race toward the tower, my body furious at me. The edges of my vision darken as I finally see the windows of the tower. From the looks of it, I'm hurtling towards the second floor from the top, and our guys are still two floors lower than this. There are quite a few people waiting on this floor, standing in a formation where one is clearly ahead of the others who are back a bit and clumped together. All of them except for the lead guy are wearing New Power armor. And from what I can tell, I'm headed right towards the lead guy.

Twenty bucks says I can hit him, I think to Dac as the tower gets ever closer, vision darkening, lungs protesting.

You're on, he responds, seconds before my imminent

squashing.

I slam straight into the wall! But... I'm still alive. How is this possible? The moment my head hits the wall, instead of cracking like an egg, I just feel tremendous pressure as I keep moving through it. It's like I took a million vacuum cleaners, dialed them up to super-overdrive times twelve, and stuck them everywhere on my skin, all the while a boulder is trying to turn me into a diamond. This sensation is felt on every inch of me as I pass through the wall, which is much thicker than I would have thought, without slowing down at all.

I gasp for air the second my mouth gets inside of the building, even before my torso has made it all the way through the wall. My hair feels air, but is dripping wet, my body feels like my ribs are going to cave in and my arms become toothpicks, and my legs are still in the ocean. Weird.

I'm probably only inside the wall for a matter of seconds, but it feels much longer as I squeeze through, reenacting my birth. Without losing any speed, I fly through the air headlong right into the guy in the lead. I make impact with him and hear a collection of startled gasps as we both go tumbling across the floor.

Ow. Oof. Ouch. Mommy.

Wait, if I hit the other wall, am I going to be thrown back outside? Not good! I sprawl my limbs in a desperate attempt to slow down.

Lucky for me, between flying straight into a person and awkwardly bouncing and rolling on the ground, I slow down and stop before reaching the opposite wall. I push myself up to my hands and knees and look behind me. The other guy doesn't look like he tumbled much, more like he just fell back and hit the ground. That isn't nearly as cool as I was hoping it would be.

He also starts crawling back to his feet, surrounded by his cronies trying to help him up. All they seem to be doing, however, is making him mad. He shakes off those trying to assist him, angrily flinging his arms out to the side.

"Get off me! Get off!" He shoves one of his lackeys so roughly, the person falls straight onto his back. The man stands up, finally, forcing his way up, not like it's natural, but more like he's muscling through it. How the heck do you make standing up look that awkward? He glares daggers at me, which is an oddly comforting thing. Why is it comforting that somebody hates me!?

"'A dangerous nuisance who's a chronic pain in the ass and refuses to die,'" he says like he's quoting someone else. "You must be Sam Cutter. Steven warned me about you."

Only now do I get a clear enough look at him to realize that he's familiar. I've seen him before. Lynch.

Chapter Twenty-Seven

"Well, well, well, *boy*," Lynch sneers at me. Seriously? I thought we were over the whole *boy* thing. "Have you come to die?"

"Have you ever considered a more original threat?" I answer, jaded. I mean, seriously! *Kill me this way, kill me that way...* it's all I ever seem to hear anymore!

"Why bother?" he responds, unsheathing his sword. "The result will be the same." He grins.

"You on the floor?" I reply as I draw my sword out of my pocket, never taking my eyes off Lynch. I hold my clenched hand to my side and dramatically elongate my sword slowly. Its white light grows in intensity as it gets bigger. Hey, a little flair can go a long way with people who don't know what this thing is!

More than a few gasps escape from the gathered crowd of soldiers.

Told you so.

Lynch's eyes immediately shift from my own to the

glowing couple feet of Sky Iron in my hand. The white light my sword casts brightens the room. Hmm. I guess this floor could use a few new light bulbs. I'll be sure to tell Kane right after we save his sorry butt.

I guess I owe you twenty bucks, Dac comments.

Oh yes, you do. But I will accept the payment of you getting up here right now!

I'm working on it, he says.

"Ah yes, the Flying Demon," Lynch speculates. As wrong as that is, it's actually not a bad nickname. Sure the thought of what I did to earn it makes me want to heave, which would be really unsociable in front of, oh, I don't know, more than a dozen New Power soldiers, but it's still not a bad nickname.

"Um, just call me 'boy' instead," Yeah, that'll work. Somehow, "boy" doesn't make me nearly as sick.

Seriously? Dac says.

I know!

"I shall put it on your tombstone!" Lynch says, bringing his sword up.

"How considerate," I say, tensing myself for a fight. "A New Power who is willing to buy me a tombstone. Will you even read a sad poem at my funeral?"

"It would be my honor."

"So, how're we going to do this?" I ask, stalling for time. "Just you and me, or am I going to have to whoop all of you?" Now even though I gave you two choices,

Lynch, you're only allowed to pick the first one.

"Oh, I do believe it would be much simpler to kill you if we all worked together. Think of it as a going away party." Crap.

With my free hand, I push my dripping wet hair out of my eyes. I know I don't normally react well to those staff's shocks, but at the moment I'm hurt and soaking wet. I'd say one hit and I'm done. *Hurry up!* I scream at Dac.

"Well, Cutter?" Lynch baits, inviting me to make the first move. I stay quiet for a moment to buy more time. I can hear the hum of the New Powers' staffs louder than the distant fighting in the building, louder than the constant explosions just outside.

Through a window behind Lynch, I see the small outline of a rapidly-approaching giant squid. I suppress a smile.

Unable to stall any longer, I decide to scream. "AAAAAAAAAAH!" It's a battle cry intended to scare my enemies, not at all because I'm scared. Some of the New Power noticeably tense up at my manliness. Oh yeah, take *that*!

My life feels like it goes into slow motion as I charge toward the group of people who would prefer me gone. I know I should be paying attention to all of them, but I don't. My head's spinning, and I'm excited just to be on two feet right now. Instead of trying to work out some crazy intense plan, I shut down and let my instincts take control. Instincts I'm not even sure I have.

Right off the bat, instead of trying to cut Lynch's head off, I duck. By duck, I mean that I essentially fall to my toes and fingertips. I sweep my leg around, taking Lynch off his feet before shooting up and head-butting one of the fully armored goons in the chin. I'm pretty sure I just dented my skull, but the goon is stunned. Still moving, I bring my sword around and cleave through another goon, sending him sprawling on top of the recovering Lynch with a scream. That takes care of Lynch for another little bit.

Another soldier brings his staff around, trying to get me. I block it, pushing away the electric tip with my forearm. My bones feel like they want to snap, but I manage to run the guy through with my sword. He spits out blood, falling back. I look over my shoulder, following the gore splatter, and see another New Power soldier jabbing the sparking end of his staff at me. I let my legs give out beneath me and tilt my head so I'm looking right above me. Two soldiers opposite each other, lunching at where I used to be standing, collide with each other, sending a visible wave of electricity running through each other's armor. I catch myself on my elbow, and half that arm immediately goes numb, as the shock-twins fall to the ground, bodies convulsing.

I try to get back to my feet but slip on the puddle

beneath me. I hit the floor hard. Stupid water. Why couldn't the gaudy shirt come with a dryer? I try to roll out of the wetness, but end up running straight into somebody's legs. My sword arm pinned beneath me, I waste no time rolling back away to free it so I can hack into one of the legs. The owner of the leg screams and leans over to clutch at the bleeding armor. I grab onto his shoulder, pulling him down as I lift myself up. I slip over his back, my wet body squeaking over his metallic armor, before he hits the ground. More soldiers trip over their immobilized comrade as they try to get to me.

For a split second, my eyes shift and I see a stairwell leading up. I'm closer to it than before, but I don't quite think I could make it if I ran for it. I grunt as I push a New Power soldier out of the way, cutting down his back. I grab the (temporarily?) paralyzed body and throw the heavy load at the incoming horde.

"Cutter!" someone howls from beside me. I turn in time to see Lynch coming at me, sword raised and ready to take my head as a trophy. My eyes go wide as I can't help but let a terrified expression come across my face while I raise my sword up. I barely manage to push his blade aside as he brings it around to decapitate me. His sword skims me, leaving a red line across my neck. My free hand flies to the cut as I prepare to parry yet another of Lynch's blows.

Ugh! I really don't have time for this! I still have a

stupid king to save. Seriously, how does someone who's been alive for hundreds of years get captured this easily? In all fairness, Steven did nab me off the street when I came out of Arthur's, but that's different! I'm not the freaking king of an entire nation.

Da, da, da, da, da, da! Dac sounds in my head, like a trumpet announcing an attacking army. I know what that means. I duck to the side, covering my head as a mountain of metal pile drives Lynch, carrying him along as he bulldozes over another few soldiers on the way. There's a loud crunch of someone's bones breaking thanks to Dac.

"Stop killing them all, you glory hog!" Arthur yells as he lumbers past me, swinging his massive scythe. He actually manages to cut one guy clean in half and gets partway through another. Ouch. He lets go of the scythe, letting it carry its embedded victim across the room as he draws an unusual-looking sword which is broader at the tip than at its base. It looks weird, but as he slaps a soldier upside the head with the flat of the blade, I realize that I really don't care. It works and actually looks kinda cool.

"Why don't you listen to your own advice?!" Jinn yells at Arthur as he trips one of the soldiers with his sword before running him through with it. That has to hurt.

"Hurry! This way!" I hear a chorus of New Power

voices yelling as our enemies gather reinforcement.

"Go!" Arthur yells. "We have this floor covered. Go get those idiots upstairs." Arthur's words of wisdom. "Hurry up before I have to kick your ass, too!" He adds as he cuts down yet another of the soldiers.

"Uh, right," I stutter as I make a break for the stairs.

"I'm coming with you!" Jinn shouts, kicking over yet another of the soldiers before running after me. "Why are you dripping wet?"

"I decided to stop at a water park on the way. What do you think!?" Seriously, man. That's a story for another time. Another time being any time but now!

We mount the stairs and take off. I almost slip and fall a few times because of all the water. I feel the squishing beneath my feet as I take one step after another, pounding my way up he stairs. With my brain functioning a little better, I notice that Jinn is breathing really heavily. It's not just the I'm-tired-and-out-of-breath huffing. It's more like the Oh-God-I'm-going-to-drop-dead-any-second-if-I-have-to-keep-going type of huffing. How do I know this? I'm on the verge of it myself.

Watch out for yourself, Dac reminds me.

"Right," I say aloud between my own labored breaths. "You ready for this?" I ask Jinn.

"Born ready," Jinn confirms.

We crest the top of the stairs a moment later, and see

two people waiting for us. The roof is all glass, giving me a clear view outside, where boats are still diving around each other, now joined by a giant squid. Go Billy! An explosion overhead illuminates the four of us and the room, casting an intense glow and causing harsh, sinister shadows.

Steven and Kane stand calmly, despite the chaos just on the other side of the glass. They have probably witnessed the entire water battle from here. Steven smirks like his normal arrogant self, the shadows actually making him look a little scary. Is that even possible? He lets out a hum as if he is judging the time it took us to get here. Kane is standing there, dark and brooding, the shadows affecting him the most, making him look downright malevolent and evil.

Um, why does he look like he's here willingly?

Chapter Twenty-Eight

There's another huge explosion, further extending the shadows claws and bathing us in light. There's little to no furniture up here, but apparently plenty of support beams to cast the shadows. It almost seems like this floor is a tourist trap, a way to look out at the Water Nation. I'm a little busy staring down some bad guys at the moment or I would actually take the time to enjoy the view. Wait, Did I just say bad *guys?* Plural? When did I start thinking of Kane as a bad guy?

Probably about the same time he decided to look like he wants to kill you.

Ah, that's right.

"W-Wait, what's going on here?" I say to Steven and Kane. "You two don't look like you're trying to kill each other." I would love a little clarification right now because I am seriously confused!

Steven sighs, shaking his head and pressing his fingers to his temples. "Honestly Samuel," he says,

"I'm disappointed in you. You take all this time to get here and you don't even realize the seriousness of the situation." Why do I feel insulted? "Honestly, I arrange such a grand entrance for you, and you let it go to waste. You even got yourself injured!" He moves his hand around in lazy circles, aimed in my general direction, as he speaks. I reach up to my neck and feel that it's all nice and sticky with blood. "And why are you wet?" he asks.

That one I can actually explain... Wait a minute! I don't owe you an explanation!

"The blood's to make me look pretty," I say, flicking a few drops of it off my hand.

I think your comebacks are getting worse, Dac advises.

Are not!

Are too.

Are not!

Are too. I want to stick my mental tongue out at him. Is that possible? You'd think I would've figured that one out by now.

"Charming," Steven says, keeping up the pleasantries. "You simply get more and more eloquent with each interaction we have." Again, I feel insulted.

"Whatever," My grace and tact are boundless. And not to say anything of my word choice. Flawless. "Come on, Kane. Let's go." He doesn't move. "Come on, we came all this way to save you. Can't you at least be a team player?" Or at least get me a towel to dry off.

"Why did you come here?" Kane says, his face still in shadows, not looking at us.

"Um, didn't I just say that we came here to rescue you?"

"Please, your Majesty," Jinn pleads. "We have to go. Many good men are giving their lives as we stand here talking."

"You seem to misunderstand which are the good men though," Kane says matter-of-factly. At that second, Billy lets out a loud squid-ish roar. I didn't even know squids made noise. Trust me though, it's plenty menacing. "You come here and kill the brave men and women fighting for the cause." With these words, Kane finally meets our stares.

Something's wrong. His eyes are off. Inside the cloudy color they naturally have from living in the Water Nation, it's like there's a swirling mass of orange dust, moving around in three dimensions. It might be one of the coolest things I've ever seen. Also maybe one of the creepiest.

"Oh, that's not right," I say for more than one reason.

"Your Majesty?" Jinn says, confused.

"Can't you see?" Steven says, walking closer to Kane and putting his hand on his shoulder possessively. "Kane here has finally seen the light. He knows that we can lead the world into a new and glorious age. He has realized that the kings have failed the world for far too long."

"It is true," Kane says, his voice clear yet lifeless. "My brothers and I have failed. It is time we pass the torch, or accept advice from those who know better."

"You see?" Steven says, triumphant.

Jinn is silent, shocked. I let the silence go on for a second before I carve through the tension laden air.

"Well, that's a load of crap." I say, tactfully of course. "Is this some bad mind control joke? Trust me, I'll fight the guy! I don't have any problem with it. Actually, I'd love to kick his ass. I'd just like to whoop you more."

"Is that so?" Steven says. "I was hoping you would join us. The Flying Demon is *so* appealing, cause of untold death and destruction. You would be the perfect tool for us." He's basically salivating over the thought of having me as his puppet. Sorry, but I don't look good with strings attached to all my parts.

"See, that right there is what's wrong with you."

"Hmm?" he says. I roll my eyes. If you would stop drooling and listen to me, you would've heard! "What was that?"

"You're problem. It's pretty easy to see what it is," I laugh. I grip my sword tighter. "You piss me off!" I lunge forward, whipping my sword around. Finally, this guy's going to get it! But...he doesn't look worried at all as I get closer and closer. Actually, he's smiling. What the?

As I bring my sword in for the blow, I'm met with steel. Kane. The stupid, mind controlled jerk actually blocked my attack! His sword isn't anything special, just a normal steel sword. You would think he'd have Sky Iron. Guess not.

"What are you doing?" I ask him, pushing harder against his sword.

"Protecting my master," he says without emotion.

"What a joke!" I burst out, shoving his sword out of the way. While his arm's wide, I ram my shoulder into his stomach, forcing the wind out of him. With a grunt, Kane stumbles back a few steps and attempts to remain standing. I raise my sword to run him through, but he knocks it aside with his blade.

"Sam!" Jinn yells behind me. I turn and see Steven preparing to slice me in half. Oh crap.

CLING! Just before Steven can get to me, Jinn steps in the way, blocking his attack. "You're not allowed to kill the king!" Jinn tells me. Oh yeah, I forgot about that. Trying to stay alive and all that.

"Then *you* fight him!" I say, pushing Kane back. "Because if I'm the one responsible for him, I'm going to accidentally kill him!"

"Stabbing him with a sword nine times isn't an accident!"

"Same difference! Go low!"

Jinn and I both set our respective opponents off

balance and spin past each other. I go high, raising my sword passing out the outside of the spin as Jinn ducks and passes beneath me, his sword extended out as well, swiveling on his feet. The white and blue lights from our weapons swirl around each other, never quite touching, sending out a color the shade of a light blue sky. I slash into Steven, leaving a bloody mark from shoulder to shoulder, just beneath his collarbone. I hear a reaction from Kane as Jinn strikes him. It can't be that bad, though, since he's being careful not to kill the oaf.

"Y-You cut me," Steven says, patting down his chest.

"I'm about to do a whole lot more than that!" I assure him as I bring my sword back around, looking to turn that cut into a backwards seven. At least it would make sense when he looks in a mirror. That's assuming it doesn't crack when he looks at it.

SO not the time for insults.

There's always time for insults!

Steven brings his sword up to meet mine, using it to guide my blade away from his body. Was he always this good at fighting? I press forward, taking another step, and a jolt of pain travels through my leg when I put weight on it. It's probably even planning to make my leg its vacation resort. At least I know I can attribute Steven being as good as he is to my injury. There's no way this guy actually has any talent.

With both our swords pushed to the side, I bring

my left fist around for a punch. There's still the weird mix of no feeling and the pins and needles from before in that arm. My left hook smashes into his face, sending a painful tingling down my arm. I'm pretty sure I feel a crack beneath my splitting knuckles as Steven's eyes roll into the back of his head. Did I really hit him that hard?

"Sam, jump!" Jinn yells. I do so with no hesitation, tucking knees to chest to get as high off the ground as I can go. I actually get some pretty good air as a sword meant to take off my legs passes below me.

I land and stumble away a few steps to make sure he can't take another pass at me. Kane's on the ground, blood oozing out of an injury on his leg. Jinn's standing just behind Kane's feet, looking almost as bad as I feel. He's doubled over, holding his side with one hand, and the other dangling at his side not doing anything very important. He then moves said useless hand, apparently still in working condition, and presses it down on top of the one on his side, wincing as he does so. He lost his sword at some point. It'd probably be smart to get that back.

"You okay?" I ask him, dodging out of the way of another swipe from the crawling Kane.

"Not really," he says with a grunt. "I don't think it'll kill me, though." Kane tries to push himself to his feet, but I kick his injured leg as soon as there's pressure on it, sending him sprawling back to the ground. Between

Kane's wails of anger and pain, I hear a bottle being unstoppered. How did I hear that? I look over at Steven, who's still on the floor, in time to see him drain a vial of some unnaturally bright red liquid. The vial looks suspiciously like the ones Blue Elixir is kept in. As Steven swallows the liquid down, something potentially really bad occurs to me.

"Um, Jinn?" I say, my eyes glued to Steven. I shift my sword around in my hand, getting a better grip. Jinn moves around in the corner of my vision as I ask him, "What does Red Elixir do?" I notice Jinn's head spin at lightning speed to look at Steven. His eyes open wide.

"Are you sure it was red?" Jinn asks sharply. "It wasn't orange, was it?"

"I'm pretty sure it was red," I say, still watching as Steven starts to move more. His suit's a mess, complete with holes and bloodstains, some of which are mine.

Steven tosses the vial aside and it flies far, crashing into one of the glass walls. The vial is instantly obliterated, shattering into a million pieces. But the real problem is the wall. It's cracked. Now there's a dent and a crack in the glass, which, by the way, is the only thing between us and instant death! That's not normal! I was thrown heels over head against one of those things and nothing happened to it!

"Cutter!" he roars, his voice not sounding human. He sounds more like a monster. Freaky. He punches the ground beneath him as if to stand up. The floor shatters beneath his fist, leaving a hole all the way though.

"Hey, watch it!" I hear Arthur yell up through the hole. "You almost killed one of them. Aim better next time!" Steven punches the ground again with his other fist, creating another hole. "There you go!" Arthur calls approvingly. Look at that. I guess somebody got squished down there. Or at least clonked on the head.

"Jinn," I say, trembling a little, "I think I know what Red Elixir does." Steven actually howls as he stands up, dragging his fists back up through the floor. That's not natural!

"RUN!" Jinn screams in a panic.

"Already on it!" I yell back, sprinting in the opposite direction. I scream like a little girl, which is understandable under the circumstances. While the sound of my feet slapping the floor and thin layer of water sounds perfectly normal—especially considering the running for my life part—Steven's footsteps sound like vats of molten metal falling to the floor in the factories. I don't like that sound normally. I like it even less when it's chasing me!

WAAAAAAA! What do I do? What do I do? What do I do!? My feet and brain are racing in a panic.

Now there's an idea. Probably a bad idea, but an idea nonetheless.

"Hey, ugly!" I shriek at Steven.

Stop having all your insults start with ugly! Not now!

"You're so poorly dressed, you make children cry!"

Other than the fact that he might like making kids cry, that's not a bad one.

Judging by the howl of rage Steven lets loose, I'd say he doesn't like it.

"Cutter!" Steven growls. "I swear I'm going to rip you apart. I've offered far too many times. The hand of good faith shall no longer be extended to you."

"Like I care!" I stick my tongue out at him over my shoulder. Me, childish? Never.

Luckily, the Red Elixir didn't speed Steven up at all. It just made him a ridiculously strong meathead with anger management problems. Well, the anger management problems might have already been a problem to begin with. I turn my head back to the front and see that I'm about to run headlong into the wall. I drop into a skidding turn, peddling across with both my hands and feet. Steven sends a straight punch to where my head was two seconds ago, but hits the wall instead. It doesn't seem to bother him as his fist goes straight *through* the wall, ending up in the water. That can't be good.

Steven screams as his now broken hand hits the water. He's stuck in the wall past his elbow and only his hand is barely in the water. Good to know. Red Elixir makes you stupid strong, not stupid durable. That just means my plan may work better than expected. Contrary to sane thinking, I shrink my sword down and shove it into my pocket.

As Steven pulls his hand back into the building, water starts rushing in through the hole. Well, Water Tower is really going to earn the name now. I pull a full u-turn and jump onto Steven's back.

Please don't kill me before I can even try this.

I plant my feet firmly on his back and kick my boots onto full throttle. Without letting go of Steven, I force my boots against his back. If I have any luck at all today, they'll work like the jetpacks do.

As Steven screams, the even louder sound of an intercom system comes to life with a squeal with a *ping-ping-pong-ping.* "Attention, everybody in the Water Tower." It's Rido. How did he get access to the loud speaker? "It appears that a giant hole is about to appear in the roof of the building. To all Hub Runners and people from the other nations, may I suggest running as fast as humanly possible. To all Snatchers, please stay put. Thank you." There's a brief pause, and then, "Oh, and Sam, stop with the piggyback ride." The intercom shuts off with an annoying squeal of feedback.

And it's not a piggyback ride! This is a serious battle maneuver!... it just happens to look like a piggyback ride from hell.

I hold on for dear life while Steven thrashes about

trying to grab onto me or knock me loose. I open my squeezed closed eyes and see something rather disturbing. Centered on top of the building, just on the other side of the glass is a way too excited Gus aiming his way too lethal looking cannon right at us. Oh boy.

"Jinn! Grab the idiot and *RUN*!" I refuse to let go of my idiot.

There's a grunt from him, and then I hear him say, "Sorry, your majesty." A second later there is a crack followed by the thud of a body falling to the floor. I thought we weren't supposed to kill him! A moment later Jinn rushes past us with an unconscious Kane slung over his shoulders, splashing through the pooling water as he goes. "Time to go! Everybody out!" he yells as he heads down the stairs. Hold on a second. I know I told him to, but did he just leave me here? That jerk!

The next thing I know, I go flying. Not how I like to. It's more like there was a giant explosion right next to my head and the shockwave sent me for a trip.

I smash into the ground, cracking a few ribs as I tumble across the floor, choking on the growing layer of water on the floor. I can't inhale, so instead I keep blowing out bubbles. A new torrent of water rushes in, slamming me against the wall and keeping me pinned there.

"Gus, you stupid, bomb-happy maniac!" The fact that he's only eight years old is completely beside the point.

How do I get this shirt to work? Go! Activate! Save me! Super fishy powers unite! Anything?

I struggle to my feet, the water level rapidly rising. I run a hand down my face to wipe off the water, and see Steven-Kong manage to right himself. Physically, he doesn't look any different, but he's definitely stronger, more powerful. His soaked suit sticks to his body awkwardly and looks ten times heavier than normal. He's breathing heavily, as if he's been seriously injured. Did my boots actually manage to hurt him? Did the cannonball directly hit him? Or is this something to do with the Red Elixir?

"Cutter!" Steven growls. Who, me? Water's cascading down the stairs, keeping the level regulated on this floor. But even over the deafening sound of rushing water, I hear him yell, "I will tear you limb from limb!" He pauses to suck in a few loud, deep, labored breaths. "You've made a mockery of my master and even worse, you've made a fool of me."

"Death before dishonor and all that," I say. "I know it's out of order, but I would be glad to help you with the 'death' part."

Steven, in all his twiggy super-strength, charges at me.

This is an even worse idea!

Doesn't matter, I say without thinking. *Is everyone almost out of the building?*

Of course it matters! It's going to look really cool! And we're working on it. We're running down the stairs as we speak. There's a lot of water coming this way.

There's even more up here!

I step forward and to the side diagonally, dodging down and away from one of Steven's wild punches. I try to scramble through the water on all fours, but it's much harder to move and I end up tripping and flipping over onto my back. The water begins to pile up on one side of me before I jump up seconds before Steven stomps down, sending his foot right through the floor, causing him to fall to one knee. Seizing the opportunity, I wind up and kick him in the head as hard as I can. His head whips to the side, blood flying. He spits out a bloody tooth before lifting himself out of his hole in the ground. Oh no, you don't! I ball up my fist and smash it into his jaw, hitting the same place I kicked him.

Steven lurches to the side, set off balance. I don't let him get far as I take my other fist and drive it into his stomach. I can hear the wind rush out of him as he doubles over. He flings his arm out in a desperate attempt to push me away from him. He connects and I go flying through the air. I pass through the waterfall created by the cannonball's hole, and go bouncing across the floor like a skipping stone, grunting every time I hit the ground.

"Oooooow," I moan as I push myself up to my hands

and knees. My body feels like it's ready to fall apart at the seams. I cough up blood before I manage to get myself to my feet. "AH!" I gasp, clutching my ribs and half falling back down. I let out a moan in agony. At least one of my ribs is cracked. Maybe broken. Definitely broken. I can't stand up straight. It hurts too much. Even though I can't see Steven, who is perfectly hidden behind the waterfall, I can hear him perfectly well because he's making such a racket. Judging by his moans, he's in worse shape than I am. If that's true, I've got nothing to worry about. Okay, I have a lot to worry about, but I can still win. "Let's go!" I plunge forward with my best scream, still holding my side, kicking up water as I go.

I charge through the waterfall to see Steven doubled over, huffing in pain. He looks up at me, eyes wide, surprised that I'm still alive. Doesn't he know that I'm resilient to death as long as I can be a pain in somebody's ass? Right before I get to him, I leap forward, putting as much force and weight into it as I can. The sore and exhausted muscles in my legs scream at me with the exertion and the demand to keep going on, despite pushing myself way too far.

With everything I have left and then some, I slam my shoulder into Steven.

Chapter Twenty-Nine

With the force of the impact, Steven and I both go flying. Even though the water somewhat cushions our fall, it still hurts like hell. Steven goes straight down and hits the ground first. There's a splash from the layer of water on the floor, followed by a skull-cracking thud. I flip over him, basically doing a handstand, before landing on my back. Water splatters all over the room as I flop onto the shallow pool covering the floor. My clothing shifts around me loosely in the water. Neither Steven nor I stir. It hurts too much to move. Lying here and breathing sounds like a good plan to me.

Stupid! Get up!

But the floor is so comfortable. The water slaps my face as I enjoy the simple pleasure of taking in air. I have to spit some water out of my mouth as I go, creating a tiny fountain above me. My chest heaves up and down and up and down, as I try to suck in enough oxygen to calm all my complaining muscles. I would take a drink of some of this water to help my throat, but Britney told me not to drink it.

Although it feels like forever passes, it's not long before I hear some movement behind me. What's going on? Steven starts making more noises beyond panting. I hear grumbles and moans and curses coming from above my head. A shadow comes to rest over my body and I see Steven standing there, looming over my head. But for some reason, he doesn't look like he wants to kill me, or take over my mind, or torture me, or anything even remotely like that for once.

"Consider yourself lucky, Samuel," he says right before coughing up a bunch of blood. He barely even bothers to slightly turn his head, so I'm sprayed with *some* of his blood. "Next time we meet, I do not plan on letting you go so easily." Like you really have a choice right now. I follow him with my eyes as he walks over to a part of the floor that he didn't destroy, partially dragging the leg he sent through the floor.

It's cold. This water's like ice, and I'm lying in it. I start to shake involuntarily as Steven takes out some sort of breathing apparatus and stumbles back over to where the water is rushing in from outside. While he limps, he moves his hand around on his chest in a distinct pattern, generally only using his fingertips. I'll bet he has one of these people-torpedoing shirts on, too. Stupid jump shirt.

He turns over his should back to look at me. "This is where we part ways, but fear not. I am sure we shall meet again before long." He puts that weird device into his mouth and bites down. Two pieces of tubing, perhaps two inches long each, immediately unfurl horizontally on either side. He steps into the relentless down pouring water. As soon as he touches the water he shoots up, out into the open ocean eventually going past what I can see. On his way out he avoids all the ships still buzzing around as well as Billy even though he has no control. Is it luck or just really good timing?

Hey Dac, can you somehow tell Rido that I need him to blow another hole in the building, then give me something to bounce off of?

Your ideas are getting worse and worse as you go.

Believe me, I know. I just don't think I can make it down the stairs right now.

Fine. I'm on it.

Oh this is going to hurt. This is so going to hurt. Why did I even come up with this idea? I can hardly even move right now, how am I going to aim right?

I close my eyes and breathe in and out, trying to gather all my wits for this. Why is this water so cold dammit! There's no feeling left in the parts of my body the water is covering. After I don't know how long, spending the time cursing the water and trying to relax, I hear back from Dac.

Alright, they're circling around to shoot another cannonball at you. The building is already sealed off down here to keep the water contained and it's rising fast.

"Kane! Kane, where are you?" What was that? Why is somebody else here!? I would jerk my head around, but I can't move it. "Kane!" the voice calls again. Footsteps come up the stairs, and finally followed by a tired-looking Nathan.

"Are you kidding me!?" I shout. Seriously? I'm so done with idiot kings! "What the hell are you doing here? You should've left with everyone else!"

"Y-You? Why are you still here?" Nathan asks, confused.

"Answer my question first! Are you stupid or something? The whole place is going to be full of water any second now, dumbass!" My voice sounds scratchy while I yell at him, and partially cracks at one point.

"I need to get Kane first," Nathan argues. "Is he up here?"

"No, Jinn took him and left a while ago. He probably ran right past you to get out of here."

"H-He did? That body he was carrying was Kane?" Nathan sounds genuinely astonished.

"How do you not recognize your own brother?"

"He was slung over Jinn's shoulder with his clothes pulled over his head. How was I supposed to recognize him?" What were Kane's clothes doing pulled over his head? Never mind... I don't want to know.

Sam, I know you can't move much and there's an idiot king there, but they're about to fire, Dac tells me. Damn, out of time.

"Nathan, lie down and hold on tight to me. I know it sounds weird, but do it!" I'm probably not very inspirational, seeing as the only parts of me that can move right now are basically my eyes and mouth. Details. Nathan looks out through the glass and sees a ship there, cannon probably already pointed at us. He moves instantly, dropping to the floor and grabbing tightly onto me.

In the same instant, a huge impact rocks the building, or at least feels like it does. A torrent of water crashes over me and I shoot off just as suddenly as before thanks to the shirt. I don't even have time to suck in a proper breath before we hit the open ocean. Surrounded on all sides by water again, I can again hear the muted yet amplified, waterlogged sounds of the ending battle ringing out around me.

The extra weight of Nathan is evident, making this almost as awkward as when I was carrying John while trying to fly. I would scream if I had any air left. I use all the energy I have left for probably the entire year to keep us going relatively straight.

Up ahead of us is Billy, who's floating around. Um, what's he going to do, and why am I more scared for my life now than I was just a second ago?

As we race towards Billy, he reaches out with one of his long tentacles. What's he doing? Wait! Go back! Let me drown! I'm scared! Billy wraps the end of one of his long tentacles around us. It's impossible for me to properly describe the slimy, horrible feeling of being squeezed by the huge appendage, sucker cups gripping onto me included. It's the weirdest thing I've ever experienced. If one thing never happens to me again in my life, it we be being manhandled by a giant squid. Never again. Never!

Billy spins us around the long way, letting me release the almost nonexistent amount of bubbles I have instead of screaming for my life. Stupid water. Billy takes us for a nearly full-circle squid-ride, then lets go of us, tossing us towards a nearby tunnel! The water around my jeans suddenly gets warm in two spots. Ew, Nathan.

I doubt there are many people in this world that can say they've been thrown by a giant squid before. It's probably for the best.

As we race toward the tunnel after being flung by Billy, I can't help but think about going splat. I know I already lived through this once, but it still scares the hell out of me! I don't like flying into walls! It makes me feel like a bug on a windshield. Splatto-Sam featuring Splatto-Nathan. Noooooo!

I start to lose consciousness as we run into

the tunnel wall. The feeling of being squished into nothingness and vacuum cleaners comes over the parts of me as we pass through the wall and fall to the floor, not losing any speed. Nathan and I separate after we tumble across the floor, rolling and bouncing randomly. My already injured ribs launch a formal protest as they smack against the floor again and again. I try to suck in a breath, but can only silently scream while more ribs snap under the pressure of the impact. Maybe they're only bruised, but seriously! Ow!

When I stop moving, I can suck in a painful breath, wheezing. Oh how am I still alive? I'm not a cat, am I? Even if I am, that's only nine lives. How many have I used up already?

Nathan coughs and slowly pushes himself up to his knees while I lie here on my stomach. As much as I would really love to at least roll onto my back, I can't move. Nothing. It all hurts too much to do anything.

"Is your sword white?" Nathan asks me through a few deep breaths after a few tense moments of sucking in air that's more amazing than any air I've ever had before. Nothing else. Even though he was just as scared as me a second ago, his voice is hard and serious now.

"What?" I barely manage to whisper between painful wheezes of air. I feel like I'm going to pass out any second now. I can't keep going. It's just too much right now.

"Sam! Sam!" I hear a chorus of familiar voices yell along with the sound of several sets of pounding footsteps coming closer, but I almost don't notice it as Nathan repeats what he said.

"Is your sword white? Does your Sky Iron sword glow white? Tell me." His voice keeps getting harder and harder.

"Yeah," I manage to say before sucking in another breath. I hear Nathan swallow a lump in his throat as my vision darkens. Wait, he actually knows what all the colors mean. "Why?" I wheeze, "What does it mean?" I'd love to know, but right now, sleep. Before I pass out, I hear Nathan tell me what it means. That alone is enough to make my heart stop. There's no way it can be true… And yet, it's the last thing I remember before being swallowed up by blackness.

"It means you're probably the single most important man in all of creation."

End of Book Two

James has long been in love with the stories told in Science Fiction and Fantasy. A self proclaimed nerd, he proudly lines his room with the books that he loves. James generally choses to write instead of paying attention during class, where he seems to get most of his writing done. Water Tower was written during his senior year of high school. James cannot wait to get started on telling even more stories, but for some reason, can't find the time to do so unless he stops sleeping all together.

CPSIA information can be obtained at www.ICGtesting.com
Printed in the USA
LVOW12s1043250914

405836LV00001B/1/P